From now on she would forget despised little Caroline and truly become forward, desirable Cleo, she told herself militantly.

Then she would trample all over Rob's deepest feelings and humble his pride, just as he had destroyed her hopes and mocked her dreams without a qualm. And wasn't he doing so still? Losing him a second time might hurt her far more than his rejection and stony silence after their wedding ever had.

She was too angry to examine her feelings. Nothing could have survived the cruelty of that treacherous kiss on their wedding day, she reassured herself. No, she was going to take revenge for herself and all the unfortunate females taken in by a gentleman's easy smile and pretend affection, no more and no less.

Elizabeth Beacon started daydreaming about handsome and brooding heroes while she was still at school and should have been paying attention. After being distracted by them during a short career in the civil service, and whilst teaching, temping and managing a garden centre, she has finally given up and written about some of those heroes and their feisty heroines, and hopes her readers will enjoy meeting them as much as she did.

Elizabeth lives in the West Country, with an eccentric rescue dog who could easily be half Springer Spaniel and half hearthrug. When not immersed in every historical romance she can lay her hands on, or looking for the perfect setting for her next book, she can be found enjoying other people's gardens, or walking through the beautiful countryside around her home, musing about a new hero.

AN INNOCENT COURTESAN
is Elizabeth Beacon's début novel.

AN INNOCENT
COURTESAN

Elizabeth Beacon

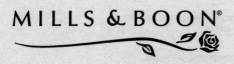

First published in Great Britain 2007
Harlequin Mills & Boon Limited,
Eton House, 18-24 Paradise Road, Richmond, Surrey TW9 1SR

© Elizabeth Beacon 2007

ISBN: 978 0 263 85178 6

Set in Times Roman 10½ on 12¾ pt.
04-0607-84858

Printed and bound in Spain
by Litografia Rosés S.A., Barcelona

AN INNOCENT
COURTESAN

To my late father, John, who never gave up on his dreams, and to his beloved Annie—who still believes in their daughter more than she does herself.

Prologue

'Confound it, the wench looks like a puffball in that appalling gown!' a particularly ancient wedding guest told her companion in a voice that echoed around the suddenly silent church. 'What's that? Nonsense, nobody can hear me,' she bawled on in tones Orator Hunt would have envied. 'The Besfords are up to their eyes in debt and Warden holds their mortgages, so we all know why he's marryin' her. It's a very low connection, though; I hope Rob don't expect me to receive little Miss Moneybags if she has the impudence to come calling in Twickenham.'

The harassed companion staged an artistic faint, but it was too late for Caroline Warden's lovely bubble of happiness. She, at least, had not known the bridegroom was only here because Henry Warden had given him no choice, and she shuddered to think how he had contrived to force Rob Besford into soliciting her hand.

A whisper of nervous laughter ran through the congregation and the vicar frowned his disapproval, but Rob Besford continued to stare at a weeping figure on a nearby tomb as if he was as deaf as his aged relative. Come to think of it, he resembled one of the marble classical statues she had once seen decorating the hall and gardens of a large country house. He looked just as unfeeling, if rather better dressed for an English January in the scarlet-and-gold dress uniform that annoyingly refused to clash with his chestnut locks.

The wild idea of running back down the aisle and into the grey winter streets was tempting, but Caro could not seem to make her feet carry her any further than the altar rail. Properly trained in ladylike behaviour, terrified of her father's disapproval, she had no choice but to step forward and give herself to her stony-faced bridegroom, whether he wanted her or not.

'We need to talk before the guests arrive, madam,' her new husband announced when they finally arrived at her father's house.

'Surely it's a little late for that now?' she argued flatly, but green fire blazed in his gaze as if she had taunted him mercilessly.

Even through the gauzy veil he had refused to remove in order to kiss the bride, Caro's light brown eyes stung with the effort of meeting his furious glare, but she was determined he would not know it. She signalled the hovering butler to open the doors and swept regally into her father's book room, her ridiculous train following with an irritated twitch. She felt like the injured party here, not the *Dis*honourable Robert Besford, who had known the truth all along—how dare he treat her as if she was beneath contempt?

'See that we are not disturbed,' her bridegroom rapped out as abruptly as if he was on the battlefield, and slammed the heavy door in the fascinated man's face.

'Before God, why could you not pick another fool for your father to buy you, madam?' Rob demanded before the echoes had died away, grabbing her arms as if he wanted to shake her, and then dropping them just as quickly in case he could not stop.

'I suppose no other was so easily bought,' she observed coolly.

'Oh, no, madam, not easily at all,' he stated in a voice so frigidly cold his previous fury faded into insignificance. 'I cost very dear indeed, but I will pay back every last penny to that damned vulture you call a father before I honour today's lies. There is but one vow I am happy to make you, *wife,* and that is to breed sons on a whore from the Haymarket before I seek your bed at your father's bidding.'

'I would have respected your opinions more if they had been expressed before you wed me solely to gain your mortgages,' Caro told him defiantly. 'If you imagine that I wanted to wed *you,* then you are an even bigger clodpole than I thought, Colonel.'

Even as she crossed her fingers behind her back she knew that reckless lie would infuriate him even more, but suddenly she didn't care. Fury made a fine barrier against the misery that would engulf her if she let it go, and the very idea of breaking down in front of him made her shudder.

'And you must admit, only a clodpole would let my father roll him up so completely,' she added with an airy indifference that she was rather proud of.

'Better to be a buffoon than a scheming harpy—you wanted my father's title so badly you would have ridden into hell for it, wouldn't you, my unlovely Caroline?

'Don't bother playing the innocent,' he went on. 'Warden named his price for not foreclosing on those mortgages you profess to despise, madam. "I wants my grandson to wear scarlet and ermine one day," he told me, as if my brother's shoes were already vacant. Well, I can make sure he lacks his precious heir, and I pray God you never have the satisfaction of calling yourself "Viscountess" either.'

'Why call myself your anything?' she asked defiantly, for he was not the only one who could lash out in pain. 'Since you obviously never intend us to have a real marriage, I might well set up a cicisbeo.'

'Expect me to acknowledge your bastards and you will very soon discover your error, madam. Try it and you will acquire a title you better deserve—that of whore, for I shall never bed you and don't care who knows it.'

At last he ripped the suffocating veil away from her face to properly survey her flushed face. He sliced a hard stare at her disastrous wedding finery, her plump countenance and fluffed-up curls and shook his head emphatically. He brought his face so close to inspect her manifest lack of charms that she could finally smell the brandy fumes on his breath, and wondered numbly just how much Dutch courage it had taken to get him to the altar.

'You will never get your money's worth out of me, wife,' he enunciated with perfect clarity. 'I refuse to share a room with a title-hungry she-wolf, let alone a bed.'

'As you seem to be sharing a room with me at the moment, you are a fraud, Colonel. Luckily I would rather be torn apart by hounds than spend a single night in your arms, so we will both be deliriously happy once today is over.'

'Liar!' he challenged, and something dark and feral blazed from his green eyes as she finally realised what an idiot she had been to see him alone.

It was too late to be wary once he seized her in a rough embrace and brutally plundered the soft mouth she gasped open to protest. She wondered in a shocked daze if the cognac on his breath had inebriated her too, for heady fire was scorching wherever she felt the sure touch of his exploring hands on her shaking body.

Any attempt at rational thought vanished like mist in a July sun as he ruthlessly dizzied her reeling senses—such a world of cynical experience in his skilful, sinful kisses. He plunged his tongue inside her mouth and traitorous warmth jagged through her like sheet lightening, until suddenly she was fighting them both.

Frightened by the intensity of it, she tried to pull away, but he just used her retreat to entrap her between a silk panelled wall and his mighty body. With his muscular frame so intimately locked against hers, she had no defence against his ruthless, practised seduction.

Reeling from the onslaught of a raw masculine lust so emphatic that she knew her wildest fantasies had been pallid shadows, shame ran neck and neck with desire. Then he shifted her between the unyielding wall and his dominant male body, lifting her on to her toes so that one of her legs must wrap round his narrow flanks for balance, and still she tried to keep a small part of herself sane while her body went out of control. He was not merciful enough to allow her that kindly delusion for long. Looking as if driven by equal parts of passion and fury, he ripped the laces of her frilled bodice and then her chemise aside, brushing a shamelessly proud nipple with knowing fingers as he did so.

Heat jarred through her in a flash of bewildering fire—she hadn't known such wanton feelings existed, let alone dreamt that he could arouse them in her with humiliating ease. The very idea of any other man looking where he was gazing so hungrily might fill her with revulsion, but under the heat and arousal ran dark desolation. She was less than nothing to him; all the time he was seducing and demanding and teasing like a lover, in his heart he despised her. If she had any sense at all, she would rip herself out of his arms and run out of the room as fast as her shaking legs could carry her.

Instead she stood mesmerised by furious, hungry emerald eyes. She knew her own must be reddened by the rush of humiliated tears that she could no longer hold back. He held her gaze as a fox might a terrified rabbit's, and his merciless, knowing touch drew her back into a dark world where desire and hatred ran neck and neck. At last he surprised a shamed moan out of her and ruthlessly repeated that bold caress, his fingers as gentle as his eyes were hard.

It only took the thrilling suggestion of his mouth dipping down to echo his fingers' caress and 'yes' gasped from her lips and shattered her pride, but could not have stayed unsaid if her life depended on it.

He took a pace back, his eyes contemptuous as he dwelt on the ridiculous clusters of ringlets that emphasised the plumpness of her round face. His taunting smile ruthlessly tallied her tearstained eyes, and the full and aching mouth that even now longed for his kisses, down to the bared breast still begging shamelessly for a lover's touch.

Cheeks scarlet with humiliation, she grabbed the wreckage of her ridiculous gown, covered herself hastily and shifted under Rob's frigid scrutiny, wishing for enough sophistication to boldly blaze hatred back at him even now.

'Somehow I don't think you will be happy in your lonely bed, do you, Caroline?' he said in a soft, deadly voice that hurt far more than her father's harshly expressed contempt for his only child ever had.

How weary she was of being the butt of masculine fury, she realised with an invigorating flare of white-hot anger.

'Not yet, but I shall be when you grovel at my feet and beg

to be there with me, and, before God, how little compassion I shall have on you then!'

'I want nothing of yours.'

'Good, for I shall be happy if I never see you again.'

'Somehow I don't think you will be, wife.'

Then he gave a mocking bow, turned on his heel and left as lightly as if the whole sorry fiasco had been a farce arranged for his entertainment.

Caro stood as still as an ice sculpture while the over-decorated gilt clock ticked away the chilly minutes. Luckily she was beyond the comfort of tears at last, considering she could not leave this room unseen. Pride would not let her appear in public red-eyed and humiliated and she ruthlessly controlled the tremors that threatened to topple into hysteria. One day he would pay for this—she would remind him of every hard word, every telling gesture and, most of all, that hateful, betraying, false kiss!

Mrs Caroline Besford raised her chin, willed back the tears that threatened despite her fierce resolutions, and tried to put the blushing bride back together. For once she blessed the frills and furbelows her father always insisted on adding to her gowns, and managed to pin enough of this one back together to hide the devastation her husband had so coldly wrought. Then she put on a determined smile that forbade any false expressions of sympathy and pinched her cheeks to get some colour back into them.

Opening the door in the face of an eager audience she would have gone a long way to avoid, she eyed those wedding guests rude enough to gather in the hallway to overhear what they could with as much haughty contempt as she could muster. From somewhere she then found the strength to breeze through a wedding breakfast without a groom, and carried it off with such aplomb that even Rob's ancient aunt wondered loudly if the cit's daughter might not have possibilities after all.

Chapter One

Rob Besford shot the sardonic devil looking back out of his mirror an impatient look. There was no trace of the eager fool who had gone off to fight the good fight in his hard gaze now. Perhaps he should thank his wife for destroying his remaining illusions. His dark brows drew together in a straight line and he shook his head in brisk denial, before impatiently reducing his wayward chestnut locks to stern military order.

During the last two months he had honed his muscular frame to the peak of fitness at Jackson's Boxing Saloon, and refined his wits by putting his brother James's venture into trade successfully back on course, yet his thoughts still dwelt upon his abandoned wife far too often.

If Gentleman Jackson had sometimes seen raw fury in his client's eyes that made him glad not to face him in a public ring, he had tactfully kept his feelings to himself. There was a new hardness in the Colonel's famous green gaze and his sensual mouth was often set in a stern line that warned friends and enemies alike not to trespass on forbidden ground.

He had managed to ignore the youthful widows and matrons of the *ton* who made it clear more than their sympathy was on offer so far, but he knew odds were being offered in the clubs as to which one would snag him first. How on earth could he conduct any liaison with discretion, when half of London was anticipating it with such unholy glee?

The answer was that good taste forbade it while Caroline was living under his father's roof, so somehow he must persuade her to set up her own establishment while they tried to dissolve their fiasco of a marriage. If only his bride had been different, he could have hoped that some besotted fool would run off with her, so that he could sue the idiot for criminal conversation with his wife and perhaps gain his freedom. Unfortunately, only a complete lunatic would cling to such a forlorn hope when he was married to the former Miss Warden.

Well, tonight he intended to forget he was for one glorious evening, and the devil could fly away with tomorrow. He took the starched neckcloth his batman was holding out and deftly folded it, then tied it in the style he had made his own. Carefully shrugging himself into the dark blue superfine coat newly arrived from Weston's masterly hand, he thought wryly of times in Spain when a clean shirt would have been considered the height of sartorial splendour. Accepting his immaculate top hat and cane from his batman, he finally sallied forth to celebrate his new prosperity, and hopefully forget Robert the married man for a few short hours.

One or two bottles of fine claret later and he was well on the way to that happy oblivion. He stopped to count the strikes of a nearby clock with the determination of a man who had drunk more than he decently ought to, but not enough to examine his gold half-hunter in the uncertain light under the nearest lamppost. Although a good turn up with an enterprising thief might relieve his pent-up feelings, even three-parts drunk he knew the news that he had been brawling in the street would distress his father, and the Earl of Foxwell had enough to bear.

Midnight tolled out, and the intermittent moonlight was tense with an unhealthy mix of frost, fog and danger. As oblivious to such hazards as Rob himself, Captain Charles Afforde, RN, known to his friends as Rowley, detached himself from the clutch of drunken beaux and fell back to eye Rob dubiously.

'Y'do know serenading La Watson with you glowering like a thundercloud will only get us sent away with a flea in our ear?' Rowley demanded owlishly.

'As you do that she's Will's woman until one of them decides otherwise, I suppose?' he replied.

'Might *know* La Watson chose Wrovillton,' Rowley finally admitted, 'but don't mean I want to know it, if ya see what I mean?'

'You have got it bad, old man. Never mind, you'll soon be off to sea again and you might manage to pull a mermaid out of the Atlantic this time.'

'Mermaid in the hand, worth two in the bush,' his old friend averred, mixing his metaphors with the conviction of the very drunk.

Then Rowley noticed the others had forged unsteadily on, and sped after them in case virtue was contagious. Rob removed his fashionable top hat, ran a hand through his hair and suddenly the frosty air felt glorious on his face after all.

Either dirty, indifferent London was suddenly wafted by the fragrant airs of Olympus, or that last bottle was taking effect at last. All he needed now was a charming and clever wench to make him forget his wife, and his evening would be perfect. He conducted a mental review of London's courtesans and drew a blank. None of the fashionable impures currently angling for a new protector had the bearing of a goddess and the looks of Helen of Troy—so Will had swept the board again with Aleysha, the lucky dog.

Rob was bidding a regretful goodbye to his paragon of very little virtue when an urchin girl shot round a corner as if the hounds of hell were on her tail, and flew straight at him. With so much momentum behind even so slender a form, there was no chance of avoiding a collision. She slammed into him with such force that they almost fell into a nearby hedge as he absorbed the full impact of her flying body.

Not so drunk that he was going to let some dip from the stews pick his pocket, Rob hung on to his captive as they lurched and nearly fell on to the pavement in a tangle of limbs. Somehow he contrived to keep them both upright and relatively unsullied, although his magnificent new hat would never be the same again, he decided ruefully, as he watched it roll into the gutter without much regret.

He was rich enough to buy them by the dozen now, he remembered hazily, more concerned with the female resting in his arms than the finest headgear Bond Street could offer him. If he had failed to keep his balance, and they had landed in a tangle on London's less than pristine streets, he might just have lain there as dazed as a callow youth in a twilit summer meadow upon being given a murmured 'yes,' instead of an indignant 'no!' by his sweetheart.

Soft and sweet against his powerful body, the wench was temptation incarnate and he could not have said why for half the new fortune he shared. They had the night and a grubby, intermittent sort of moonlight, and in her arms he might at least forget his wife for a while.

'Dashing about like one of Congreve's rockets could lead you to fall in with all sorts of rogues, sweetheart,' he murmured, and nearly fumbled his grip when she began to struggle as if she had just woken from some sort of swoon. 'Maybe you're not quite so sweet after all, then, my little dove,' he said cynically and saw her eyes flash fire even in the muted light of the street lamps.

He could have sworn she was about to rant and rage at him and even heard the shush of breath she gathered in for the purpose, but instead she let it out on a long sigh and went on wriggling silently in his arms. Their sensuous combat set his pulse racing and, even as desire raged through him in a hot tide, he retained just enough sense to wonder why. What light there was showed him her clear profile and finely cut features, but finding a sane reason why he was potently attracted to this woman rather than all those others who had thrown themselves at him since his marriage was beyond his current capacity for thought.

Giving up on such insoluble problems for now, he decided to enjoy the assault on his senses without questioning his instant arousal. She smelled wonderful, of course—as if she had doused herself in wine and roses just so a man could get drunk on the scent of her. Far better than civet or ambergris he decided dazedly, and wondered if his gift from the gods had been a lady before she took to whoring.

There was something vaguely familiar about her fragrance and, sober, he might have questioned his odd notion of knowing his delightful captive almost by instinct. Drunk, he concluded that wine and propinquity were to blame for her potent effect on his senses and gently but ruthlessly subdued her struggles. Whether she had started life in a hovel or a palace, no lady ran the streets at midnight.

Realising that she was not going to free herself easily, the wench finally went still, but even in this fitful light he could see a flush of anger on her high cheekbones that warned him she was just regrouping. Muttering some far from ladylike curses under her breath, she tried a sharp twist to break his grip, but he countered by pulling her even closer. She held herself stiffly unmoving in his arms, and he would be a fool to think he had won the bout when he could almost feel the resistance coursing through her veins. She was very good at this game, he decided, almost too good, if that was possible.

'Let me go, you great dolt,' she demanded in a throaty undertone that completed his enchantment.

'When the stars fall out of the sky,' he muttered into the absurd topknot she presented him with, apparently in the hope of avoiding more intimate contact.

For some reason Rob found the wild mass of curls tickling his chin unexpectedly erotic, and wondered dazedly what he would find irresistible about a woman of the night next.

'Wrong answer,' she muttered darkly and he came sharply back to earth when she kicked him on the shin with as much force as she could muster, considering he had her clasped so close to his hard body.

'Wrong weapon,' he countered.

He had been running an exploring hand further down her delightfully formed spine and hid a wolfish grin in the darkness. Shod in slippers as she was, her foot had bounced ineffectually off his muscular legs and she had very likely hurt herself more than she had him.

Enjoying his exploration enormously, he heard a gasp that was not quite shock and not altogether encouragement, and moved that hand a little lower to encounter a delightfully pert *derrière* under the rather flimsy cloak and clinging dark gown.

Added to the sensation of her ragged breathing against his powerful chest, her responsiveness turned him eager as a boy.

'You could easily turn into an icicle, dressed for high summer as you seem to be, sweetness.'

'Keep your opinions and your hands to yourself, you great poltroon,' she said between her teeth and he had to move quickly to make sure her slender fingers were trapped between their bodies as he felt her ball them into fists.

The gesture would have been much more convincing if he had not felt the fine tremors that were running through her, and he would have applauded, if he could spare his hands for the task.

She was playing him so skilfully—giving just the right amount of opposition to make him more eager for her eventual capitulation, but not too much to make him think the game was not worth the candle. And yet there was an element of enchantment to this odd encounter that told him she was more than just a lightskirt luring in a rich quarry. She had a unique quality about her he could not pin down, a peculiar sort of innocence that told him she had not done this very often. There was the dark promise of unruly passion running under every move they made together.

Used to keeping all his senses on the alert in the Peninsula, when lives depended on him staying one step ahead of the enemy, Rob had always prided himself on keeping a strict curb on his more unruly emotions, as befitted a good officer. He remembered the scene in his father-in-law's bookroom on his wedding day with bitter chagrin, and now his passions were threatening to spiral out of control once again. Hastily he buried the memory of his wife's fiery and untutored responses as his chance-met ladybird wriggled restively against him, and demolished the last of his scruples without trying.

Something about this frosty March night felt different,

and not even a poet could claim the smell of a few thousand fires, too many human beings and their chattels crammed into vast, smelly London, were likely to carry a man away with enchantment. Yet if the others were still laughing and joking he had stopped listening. If they had abandoned him to his fate, he was simply grateful.

'Little wildcat!' he chided unsteadily, and the catch in his breath had little to do with alcohol and a great deal to do with his burning need for a wench he had never even seen properly. 'Give me one good reason why I should let you go.'

He felt her gather breath to storm at him, to pretend black was white, but instead she let it go in a long hiss and glared furiously at him.

'A gentleman does not need a reason to obey a lady,' she finally spat the words at him and he couldn't help but chuckle at her ridiculous assumption of gentility.

'A lady would never run the streets at this hour of the night.'

Her burning glare intrigued him, because he could feel the response of her body and the catch in her breath, and both belied the militant set of her luscious mouth.

'Silence is golden,' he murmured, then bent his head to persuade her to drop her nonsensical pose of outraged virtue, before both he and the night faded away.

He brushed his mouth across her full top lip and back along the generous softness of her lower one. He adored her mouth as his tongue darted out to run along the gap and linger there like a bee drunk on nectar. He coaxed at that tantalising pout, even as he found himself guilty of treating a lightskirt as if she was the most precious and innocent creature he had ever kissed. Then his hand came up to explore what he could not distinctly see in the murky light, and this time she didn't even wriggle, let alone kick him.

Surely this midnight madness was not just affecting him? He brushed a caressing finger along the silky skin over a high cheekbone, on to the unexpected intimacy of a delicately made ear, crying out to be kissed and explored if he ever managed to spare the attention from her responsive mouth. He feathered his caress back along her jaw, and reached the unfamiliar wonder of her lush lips locked against the entreaty of his—as if they relied on one another for air to breathe. A sliver of magic made him woo her, while need drove him mercilessly on, urging him to take her to their mutual satisfaction.

Impatient with supplication at last, he joined his hands under the wild mass of curls at the nape of her slender neck and drew her even closer. Now his kiss was dominant, and his heartbeat hammered victory as he felt her respond with all the passion he had sensed in her wild nature at long last. He plunged his tongue into the sweet depths of her mouth, past pearly little teeth. And glory be! She was sending hers questing tentatively towards his, finally letting it tangle and dance with his.

Suddenly she felt as if she belonged in his arms. A more ridiculous notion he had yet to hear than cynical Rob Besford being held in thrall by a lightskirt. Doubt jarred through the smoky passion he had lit so effectively in them both. In protest he lowered his hands down her back to pull her even more securely into his embrace.

Through a haze of alcohol and passion he ordered himself to remember what she was, and take her in pursuit of their mutual pleasure. With that, some of the wonder froze on the cold night air and even as he held on to her as if the gods might steal her back if he let her go, he bitterly regretted the loss. He felt a shiver run through her, but try as he might to recreate their exclusive bubble of warmth and magic, it was fading as the world made everyday creatures of them once again.

'Come on, Rob, share and share alike,' one of his cronies demanded and the puzzle of novelty, familiarity and fire finally cleared his fuddled mind.

'No, you can go and catch your own songbirds,' he protested at last, surprised by the unsteadiness of his own voice as he came back to the reality of a damp and chilly night.

'No chance of Tubs doing that when he's drunk as Davy's sow,' pronounced one swaying blade sagely.

'Well, so am I, but I still caught her, didn't I? Told you the army would always prevail with the ladies.'

'A devilish hard head more like,' Lord Wrovillton cut in tersely.

What right Will had to disapprove, when he was keeping La Watson in luxury, quite escaped Rob. He met his friend and former comrade's stern look with a challenge that could have spelt trouble, if they had not spent half their lives soldiering through India and then Spain and France together.

'What I have, I hold, my friends,' he replied defiantly.

He could read Will's silent message that he should know better than to fall from grace so publicly and didn't care for caution from such an unlikely quarter.

'The rest of you can serenade the fair Aleysha until cockcrow as far as I'm concerned—I'm for bed with my pretty little nightingale.'

Rob looked down at his prize as she struggled anew in his arms, before seeming to despair of ever breaking free. She hadn't liked his frankness, if the stubborn set of her delicious mouth was anything to go by, but what else did she expect him to call such a willing little doxy? Still, maybe she needed a little more reassurance before she sang all night in his arms, he decided, and tried to summon up the practised seduction that had won him such success among the beauties of Madrid and Paris.

Startled when his captive sank sharp little teeth into his hand and thrust her knee towards a strategic part of his anatomy, mighty Colonel Besford freed her to protect himself from this slender female whose head just about reached his chin if she stood on tiptoe.

Feeling inexplicably as if something very precious was being torn away from him, he watched her back away and tried to be cynical about those few heady moments of magic amidst the shop-soiled shadows of a London night.

Then she turned at last and ran the last hundred yards or so to Aleysha Watson's front door, just as the pack let out a view halloo and thundered after her. He had to admire her turn of speed as she pelted breathlessly up the steps and hammered a tattoo on the shining brass knocker in time to a desperate heart-beat. No reply—the fair Aleysha probably thought it was one of her legion of disappointed suitors howling at the gates.

His ladybird turned to watch her pursuers close in, looking wildly about her for some weapon to protect herself with, even as Rob tried to reason out her true status and motives through a haze of claret and frustrated need. She found nothing, of course, and crouched low, probably in an effort to make herself as small a target as possible against the grasping hands that must look as if they were reaching out of a nightmare, if the white terror on her face was any indication.

'No!' he bellowed, seeing her stark fear even as he struggled with a base urge to chase after her himself and haul her back into his arms. 'Leave her!' This time his voice was lower but still harsh, and she flinched visibly. 'You only have to look at her to see that she's terrified half to death,' he added, as the drunken bucks hesitated and lost momentum.

Unconvinced by his friend's sudden conversion into protector of the innocent, or that there was any of that commodity present to be defended, Rowley Afforde wobbled to a halt and protested.

'We ain't animals, man; she'll take us to her friends if we make it worth her while. All very well for you to be sanctimonious when you're wed, but what about the rest of us? Although Will don't count, as he's got the cosiest armful in England to cuddle up to him at night.'

Lord Wrovillton looked thunderous and Rob gave a bitter laugh. A picture of his stout and overdressed little wife the last time he had set eyes on her swam before his eyes. A younger, more idealistic Rob tried to persuade casehardened Colonel Besford that the wild charmer yonder was nothing like the grasping harpy he had married, but experience argued she was as mercenary as the rest of her sex and he would be an idiot to dream otherwise. Yet could he contemplate forcing himself on an unwilling female, or seeing his friends do so, just because he was married to a greedy harpy and bitter as gall about it?

'Only remember what I'm wed to, Rowley, and let her be.'

Even through the gloom he saw the pale oval of the wench's face as she lifted it from shielding hands. Now she looked as stark white as an alabaster statue as she rocked back on her hard seat, for all the world as if she had just received a mortal blow, and even Rowley faltered to a stop.

Another gallant who had kept morosely silent up until now plumped down on the steps of a nearby house, beginning a song so bawdy it might even have made an infantryman blush. Two or three of the others soon joined in, and before long they were making so much noise the whole street began to stir and Miss Watson's front door opened abruptly in response to the cacophony.

Chapter Two

The brightest comet to light up the demimonde for many a day stood at the top of the steps for one long moment as if surveying her kingdom. As tall and dignified as an offended queen, Miss Aleysha Watson held a small but businesslike pistol in one white hand and a steaming jug of hot water in the other. Tonight she was dressed rather demurely for a fashionable convenient, yet her extraordinary beauty shone brighter than ever in the lamplight. Even Rob silently conceded that she knew how to set a stage, and a barrage of calls and whistles broke out from the revellers at the sight of their latest goddess as she waited regally for the noise to subside.

'I have not the slightest desire to hear your feeble explanations for this childish disturbance, so luckily you are spared the effort of taxing your addled brains,' she announced. 'If you have any sense left, you will go home and put your heads under the pump. Tomorrow I may listen to your apologies, but pray do not place any money on receiving my forgiveness or that of my neighbours after such an unfortunate lapse of good taste, *gentlemen*.'

She flashed a final, contemptuous look around the group

and her eyes lingered for one impassive moment on her lover before she turned to sweep into the house like offended royalty. As she did so, her gaze caught the girl's frightened white face in the swing of the lamplight, and Rob thought he saw the courtesan start at the sight of such a dishevelled apparition on her immaculate doorstep. If so, she recovered magnificently and beckoned the girl to follow her inside, then made her stately exit with an extra acolyte in train as the door closed sharply behind them.

His anger at the girl's escape could not quite overcome the beguiling memory of her warm curves soft against his hard body. For a while the heady mix heated his blood and he spent several minutes wondering whether to storm the citadel and retrieve his lightskirt, then reluctantly gave up the scheme. La Watson did not look to be in any mood to listen to his pleas or promises, and maybe this was not the time and place to negotiate for a new mistress after all.

His smile was cynical as he decided that deference to his friend's property and a certain ingrained respect for women he could not always manage to overcome prevented a night sortie. So he turned to leave with his friends and tried to ignore the feeling that he was losing something precious.

Trying to rationalise his irrational fixation on a street urchin, he concluded that until now he had been so angry with his wife that eschewing her sex had not proved a hardship. The girl had effectively cured him of that happy state, as well as leaving him aching with frustrated desire. He ordered himself to stop acting like a moonling over a demi-rep, and retreated to fight another day.

It was only when they fetched up at Rowley's lodging that Rob realised seeking one of the girl's sisterhood to slake this craving she had left him with held no attraction whatsoever. Cursing the very gods he had so recently thanked for their unexpected gift, he fought down a feral desire to howl at the moon. He would just have to drown the memory of the little strumpet hot and sweet in his arms in Rowley's cognac. Morning would bring a return to his usual cynical clarity of thought all too soon, along with the sore head he richly deserved.

Inside the neat house in St James's, the creature her more respectable neighbours stigmatised as 'that woman' issued a series of concise orders to her household, waved her unexpected guest into a warm and welcoming sitting room and shut the door behind them with a decided snap. The famous courtesan was dark, Junoesque and impeccably turned out even at this time of night—and Mrs Caroline Besford was small, fair and newly slender and felt as if she had just been dragged through a hedge backwards. She knew she lacked her old schoolfriend's classical beauty, and just now her own more gamine features were pinched with shock and exhaustion.

'Did those drunken idiots do you harm?' Miss Watson asked abruptly.

Caro thought of her furtive escape from the great house in Berkeley Square and her choking fear as she ran alone through the midnight streets, not sure if she feared pursuit or whatever horrors lay in the shadows most. At last she had overcome her own diffidence and society's notions of propriety to break out of an intolerable situation, only to run straight into the powerful arms of her husband and make it all so much worse. Given the debate held over her person, and the appalling risks she had run by tacitly accepting her husband's inebriated attentions for the second time, she wondered if she wasn't entitled to that fit of the vapours she had been denying herself for so long after all.

'He kissed me as if he meant it, Alice, then pawed at me as though he owned me and refused to let me go like the great drunken fool he seems to have become! So, no, he didn't actually harm me and I have learned to live with his contempt.'

'I really don't see why you should have to, after two months of marriage.'

'Ah, but we are not married.'

Miss Watson raised one beautifully shaped dark brow, and Caro refused to let her eyes fall before the challenge in her friend's famous ultramarine gaze.

'Not really,' Caro added, as if that explained everything.

Both eyebrows rose at that statement.

'He hates me,' Caro informed her friend flatly.

'On the contrary, it sounds to me as if he wants you rather badly.'

'Hah! He just wants an obliging female to warm his bed.'

'More by good luck than good judgement you have no idea what you are talking about. In running the streets in the little hours, you were in danger of finding out in the worst possible way just what that entails,' Alice told her severely.

Caro shuddered as she finally let herself think about what had almost happened to her. She despised herself for wanting to stay in Robert Besford's arms as much as the contrary brute had suddenly wanted her there. That uncomfortable piece of self-knowledge seemed worse than her escape down the backstairs, a terrifying journey through the dark streets with fear tugging at her every step *and* being waylaid by a pack of drunken idiots who mistook her for a streetwalker. All of it paled to nothing at her fear that she was still as besotted with her husband as ever. No! That was impossible, she reassured herself. She hated him as roundly as he hated her. How could it be otherwise after all he had said and done to her on their wedding day, and his cold silence ever since?

Yet she had thought she had reached sanctuary for a few mad seconds when she flew into his arms. How the polite world would laugh if it ever found out that Rob Besford had propositioned his own wife! But they would go on to sneer at her for getting into such a ridiculous situation. By their rules she would be condemned rather than him, although he had been so castaway that he could not tell a hawk from a handsaw—or his wife from a ladybird. Still, she had seen enough of both him and the *ton* to last her a lifetime, she reminded herself, and what she did not hear could not hurt her. The prospect of never seeing her husband again cheered her so wonderfully that she sank wearily into a comfortable chair by the fire and tried not to cry.

'For Heaven's sake, stop ripping up at me, Alice. I have worn a hair shirt ever since my wedding day and I need no more reproaches to render me suitably humbled.'

The temper died out of Alice's extraordinary deep blue eyes as she took in her friend's pale face and the pinched fatigue evident there.

'I'm sorry, love,' she apologised. 'Tell me why you came here tonight.'

'It is well known amongst the *ton* that Colonel the Honourable Robert Besford refuses to approach his unfortunate wife without wild horses intervening,' Caro announced majestically, sitting bolt upright in her chair in a fine parody of her former chaperon.

Her friend's quizzical smile, and the warm laughter in her indigo eyes, invited her to see the funny side of her predicament, but Caro stifled a chuckle because she was half-afraid it might turn into hysteria after all.

'Even if the facts seem to prove quite otherwise?' Alice asked gently.

'How do you mean?'

'I saw you in his arms, love, and you were so wrapped up in one another even I thought you were a…a woman of the night.'

'You were watching?' Caro was horrified at the idea.

Her friend nodded, and the flush that burned high on her cheeks made her look more like a lovelorn débutante than a sophisticated courtesan. So Alice had been anxiously on the watch for her tardy lover!

'But whatever are the Besfords about, to let you run the streets at such a godforsaken hour?' Alice asked hastily, as eager to change the subject as Caro was not to linger on that ridiculous interlude in the lamplight.

'The Countess was the only member of the family at Foxwell House since my husband refused to darken its doors—but she has left for a visit to the country. As I was finally alone, I thought I'd escape this mockery of a marriage.'

Alice blinked, then smiled. 'Well, and who can blame you? You cannot stay here, though, love. Even your rackety husband would never countenance you living under the same roof as a woman of my stamp.'

'How would he know?' Caro's question was contemptuous. 'He held me in his arms and kissed me just now, and didn't know me from Adam.'

After she had humbled herself in those very arms on their wedding day, she found that sin harder to forgive than all the others put together for some odd reason.

Now he had pushed himself back into the centre of her world again, and then gone blithely off into the night with his drunken friends as if nothing untoward had occurred. No doubt he would soon be importuning some other silly female with his heady kisses and drunken promises, but she dared not consider where that might lead, or she really would end up sobbing her heart out to Alice.

'Well, he would be even more of a fool than he appears if he thought you an Adam, but you must admit it's little wonder he did not know you from Eve. You have lost a great deal of weight since I last saw you, and it shows off your fine features, as well as displaying your curves to great advantage,' Alice told her encouragingly.

'Does it?' Caro asked indifferently.

She had her way to find in a world where plainness would be much safer than attracting attention, and was busy mulling over her limited employment prospects when she looked up and saw the speculative gleam in her friend's famous dark blue eyes that had always spelled trouble when they were at school.

'What now?' she asked apprehensively.

'Remember that play Miss Thibett made us learn for tying the tabbies' bedchamber doors together?'

'Which one? There were so many I have lost count.'

The headmistress of their school in Bath had designed that particular punishment especially to keep her most enterprising pupils occupied long enough to learn a play and perform part of it in front of their peers instead of making mischief.

'*All's Well That Ends Well,* Caro, you must remember it. The one where that stuffy Count Rousillon rejects poor Helena after he's been forced to marry her against his will.'

Seeing all too many parallels to her own situation, Caro shot out of her comfortable seat by the fire as if she had been stung.

'I never want to see him again, let alone sneak into his bed one dark night! Will you help me get to Bath, Alice? I dare say I can get a job at one of the schools there if Miss Thibett will only give me a reference, and I promise I will pay you back as soon as I am able.'

'No. For one thing, it's the first place they will look for you; for another, I have something far better in mind for you than becoming a stuffy schoolmarm, forced to waste away for lack of appreciation.'

'I dare say I had better start walking to Bath then. I would be even more of an idiot than I was tonight to listen to whatever harebrained scheme you have thought up,' Caro said with a wry smile.

'Stop being so feeble. Do you want to punish that stupid husband of yours or not?'

Caro thought of the dire predicament she had found herself in tonight, the many insults she had endured, and the shrinking, shamed creature her inconvenient marriage had almost turned her into.

'Of course I do!' she replied emphatically.

'Good, then for heaven's sake sit down before you fall over, and we can decide how best to go about it.'

A picture of Rob Besford, his eyes blazing with passion and hope instead of fury and contempt, made a seductive, impossible picture in Caro's weary mind. How mercilessly she would trample *his* desires and dreams when he abased himself before her and begged for her favours! Then she remembered her wedding day with a shudder, and almost succumbed to hysterical laughter at the very idea of the proud Colonel beseeching her for anything other than a hasty dissolution of their marriage.

'Rob would hardly take a step out of his way if I lay dying,' she vowed, and sank wearily into the chair by the fireside and held out her hands for much-needed warmth, because suddenly she could not seem to stop shivering.

'He would have taken a great many tonight,' her friend argued in an attempt to comfort her.

'Yes, because he thought I was Haymarket ware and he wanted a woman.'

'No, he must have wanted you for yourself. Believe me, your husband is far too high in the instep to pick up a light-skirt in the street. His last amour was reputed to be a Russian princess in Paris for the peace, and before her there was a noble Spanish beauty with an ancient husband and a burning passion for your undeserving Colonel.'

'Then obviously tonight he had so much wine that he forgot his usual fastidiousness. Even I know that what a man says and does in his cups has little bearing on his sober thoughts and desires,' Caro replied stoutly, trying to push the contrast between such exotic beauties as Alice described and her plain and workaday self to the back of her mind.

'No, he wanted *you,* not some kerbstone hack picked up by chance.'

'He was drunk, so he wanted what he stumbled upon so conveniently. Propinquity made him want a woman stupid enough to throw herself at him twice, even after he had rejected and reviled me the first time,' Caro insisted.

'Say what you will, it was you he wanted and no one else.'

'No, if he does not end up in some other woman's arms tonight, then next time he will find a more convenient female to offer his so-called protection.'

'It's true that he must be ruing tonight's meeting for leaving him so unsatisfied, but he will be back for more, make no mistake about it. I read as much in his face, and you can trust me to know when a gentleman is in thrall to a lady, if for nothing else. He wants you, Mrs Besford, and I suspect no other woman will do, whatever you say to the contrary. So maybe it *is* time you joined my unholy sisterhood after all, love.'

'And since when have you been subject to these windmills in the head, Alice dear?'

'From the day I was born, according to my noble relatives—who sincerely wish I never had been—but never mind me. Sleep on the idea, love, and if you still feel you cannot go through with a fitting revenge, tomorrow we shall cast about for something suitably dull for you to do with the rest of your life.'

Caro let herself feel the dragging weariness of too many sleepless nights, and looked down at her dishevelled person with horror. What a wild woman she must look, she realised at last, so perhaps it was no wonder Rob had not known her after all.

'I don't see how you expect me to sleep now you have thrown that outrageous scheme into the pot, Alice dear.'

'Well, if ever anyone's life needed rearranging it was yours, love. I never realised respectable marriage could be so confoundedly complicated—I am quite glad to have been spared it after all.'

'Oh Ali, I have missed you so,' Caro declared with a slightly wobbly smile and they exchanged affectionate hugs, before seeking their beds at long last.

The fact that she was bone-weary and it was the middle of the night did not seem to have much bearing on her racing mind, Caro decided crossly, as she lay back in the extremely comfortable bed Alice had allotted her some time later. She stared up at the airy canopy as if it might provide some distraction from the ridiculous treadmill her thoughts were set on, but saw only shadows. As soon as she closed her eyes, a picture of Rob Besford would appear, smiling where once he had been stern; wanting where previously he had looked at her with such disgust she had wanted to fade into the silk panels of her father's sitting room.

Tonight his green eyes had been fiery and urgent even in the lamplit shadows. She remembered his ardour with a long shiver that belied the warm brick at her feet and the banked fire in the grate. Alice's suggestion was outrageous. Rob was part of a past she intended to bury as effectively as if Caroline Besford had actually died tonight. Yet somehow she was seriously considering Alice's preposterous scheme, despite all her reservations.

She told herself that he need never know who she was, but she would know. Remembering heady moments when she was utterly desired by her husband, only to walk away and leave him frustrated for a change, might help her blot his contemptuous rejection from her memory in the empty years to come, and hadn't she promised herself retribution on their wedding day?

She smiled reminiscently as she recalled the fine tremor that had shaken the Colonel's mighty frame as he curbed his own desire for a lightskirt tonight. Horrified to catch herself on the verge of those ridiculous daydreams yet again, she reminded herself sternly of how he had forced a Caro she had never known existed into the open, and promptly destroyed her without mercy. The softer emotions might never have a place between Rob Besford and his wife, but, thanks to him, darker passions might be loosed after all.

Yes, she would know, and revenge would be as sweet as if the story had been published from the rooftops. A mix of fury, foreboding and a small niggle of conscience stalked her, but her mind was already made up for mischief. She burrowed into the downy pillows, fighting the memory of a lover's kiss on her still-tingling mouth, and she finally fell asleep on a sigh.

Rising at a scandalously late hour the next morning, Caro was bustled into a wrap of cream satin and old lace even as she tried to regain the fine bravado of last night. In the unforgiving light of day she had severe doubts about Alice's wild scheme, and only had to contemplate the idea of meeting Rob dressed as a courtesan to quail cravenly. She reminded herself sternly that he would be hard pressed to describe her if his life depended on it, and was still wondering how she could fool her husband that she was anything other than plain as a pikestaff, when the hairdresser was finally admitted and the game was well and truly on.

A couple of hours later her artfully tousled curls were tinted a perfectly natural-looking auburn, instead of her usual shade somewhere between blonde and brown. The little man had left with many an exclamation over his own genius, and a rather risqué female was staring out of the mirror at Caro with a host of unanswerable questions in her tawny eyes.

Maybe a gentleman at odds with the world might seek comfort with such a female, she decided at last, and was so taken up with the notion that she let herself be extracted from her night-gown and bundled into a mere wisp of a shift and some daring silk pantalettes. She finally emerged from a daydream where her husband was importuning her on his knees for her acceptance of his ardent and improper advances, when her easy-fitting stays were banished and a new set put in a painful appearance.

'I am *not* wearing these monstrosities,' she protested, but was ignored as the maid pulled the dreadful things ever tighter at a nod from Alice. 'I dare say I shall spend all day fainting on the sofa if you force me to keep the wretched things on,' she warned.

'Look at the effect they have on your figure and remember you are not dressing for a débutantes' ball now,' Alice said with a mischievous smile.

Caro looked down and realised what her friend meant. In the past her bosom had been all but hidden by the embellishments her father insisted the dressmaker add to any available space on her gowns. Now her breasts rose lush and rounded and her waist looked impossibly small in contrast. It made her feel decidedly wicked to be flaunting herself so brazenly, but after a few token protests she gave in. After all, if she was to hoodwink Rob into believing she was no better than she ought to be, there was little point in spoiling the ship for a ha'porth o' tar!

The dangerous notion of deceiving her hawkish husband sent her thoughts into a spin and, during a brief luncheon, she wondered if she would ever eat properly again as the iron grip of her new stays restricted a stomach already full of butterflies. Telling herself not to be so feeble, she imagined walking into the elegant drawing room of one of the haughty society hostesses in this new guise, and a wicked smile lit up her amber eyes. A rather wayward creature seemed to be emerging from Caro Warden's unattractive chrysalis after all. Lud, if this *outré* creature dared to saunter into one of their afternoons of scandal and speculation, it would cause a flutter in the noble dovecotes fit to lift the roof clean off!

'The dressmaker, ma'am,' announced one of the large footmen from last night and the whole whirligig spun relentlessly on once more.

Alice briskly reeled off a vast list of requirements. There were to be satin gowns in a rainbow of colours for the evening and silk afternoon gowns for entertaining 'ahem, ze visitors,' as Madame Mirelle termed the lovers her magnifique gowns would surely draw irresistibly. At last the prodding and pinning was over, and Alice and Madame were locked in debate over fabric samples and cut. As both seemed deaf to the sound of her voice, Caro finally gave up protesting at such an orgy of spending, belted the frivolous wrap as tightly as she could and crept downstairs.

Only yesterday she had been plain little Mrs Besford, married solely for her money and easily ignored by all and sundry—today she was being rendered unacceptable for entirely different reasons! She caught sight of herself in a gilt-framed mirror and a mischievous smile tilted the lush mouth of the hussy staring back at her. Caro gave a shiver that was half excitement, half dread.

The butterflies were performing extravagant flights of fancy in her stomach again, and she almost ran to retrieve her old clothes before they were given to the ragman, but ordered herself not to be such a coward. At last she found a fine pianoforte in Alice's drawing room, went through a few scales and exercises to get her fingers supple, then began to play. Books and music had long provided her with an escape from the less-than-pleasant realities of her life, and Herr Mozart's magnificent cadences did not fail her this time.

Since Will was so besotted with the lovely Aleysha Watson, Rob felt he owed it to his friend to take the beautiful courtesan's wrath on his own head for last night's shenanigans. He assured himself that his presence in this quiet corner of Mayfair, where his friend housed his inamorata, had nothing to do with his own late-night encounter with a demi-rep. She had been an air-dream, a brief moment of madness and drunken folly, and he would not ask to see her again and risk becoming more disillusioned than he already was.

Left to cool his heels in Miss Watson's hall by a footman who evidently shared La Belle Aleysha's jaundiced view of him, he was drawn upstairs by piano playing of unusual skill and passion until he found himself trespassing on an irresistible tableau. One glance at the enchanting figure seated behind the fine pianoforte and his new-made resolutions flew out of the window along with his wits and his hangover. She was, he decided with the detachment of shock, an irresistible assault on his best and basest feelings. Of course, gentlemen only lusted after the muslin company, so this could not be a *coup de foudre,* even if it felt like one.

Last night's dishevelled amateur mermaid had turned into a fascinating houri, dressed, if you could call it that, in a clinging wrap her vigorous playing had caused to gape deliciously. One red-gold ringlet had taken advantage of its freedom to snake round her throat and lovingly shadow the rich curve of her bosom. He desperately wanted to feel the bloom of her flawless skin under his exploring fingers again, to trail kisses down the valley between her lush breasts and onward to…

He wrenched his eyes back to her face, just as she caught her full lower lip with pearly white teeth, still completely absorbed in her music and as unaware of him as if he was standing in another county. Cynic though he considered himself to be, he acquitted her of artifice, so complete was her accord with the music her slender fingers were producing. Yet she looked so unconsciously sensual, so innocently seductive, that he gave up trying to control his heated senses and allowed his hypnotised gaze to absorb every delicious detail.

From the top of her artfully disarranged curls to the tips of her rosy toes she was pure, or impure, temptation, and his last shred of resistance surrendered without a fight to her heady spell as a faint drift of that familiar perfume snared his willing senses. Carrying her to her bedchamber and keeping her so well occupied she wouldn't need her discarded slippers for a week suddenly seemed like an excellent plan. He had not burned for a woman so urgently since he was a spotty youth, but somehow she had demolished barriers within him that he had never dreamt could be breached so effortlessly, and he couldn't summon the nous to dislike her for it.

She was both pure mystery and extreme temptation, an enigma of a young woman ready to sell herself to the highest bidder. Trying to reconcile the passions she revealed in her playing with her louche lifestyle would only torture him if he let it. So he gave himself up to both music and player and listened in something of a daze—until she made a mistake at last and crashed her hands down on the keys in disgust.

Chapter Three

◦━━━━━━━◦

As the spell of Herr Mozart's music faded and she came back to earth with a thud, Caro finally realised she was not alone. She shrank from the idea of anyone seeing her in such a shocking state of undress, and then started violently as she forced her eyes to focus on the intruder at last. Fate had conspired against her again, she decided, and her heart beat hard and heavy as she met her husband's burning look. Now he would march her back to Berkeley Square in disgrace, and if he had despised her before, what in heaven's name would he think now?

She shuddered, felt sick and steeled herself to defy him, before she finally managed to read the emotion making his eyes glow so brilliantly green. Her husband had not recognised her at all—he merely wanted her! Her heart jolted uncomfortably again as his gaze swept intently over her figure, now so openly on display, and fire wanted to ignite everywhere his eyes lingered so explicitly. Somehow she willed her body into submission and eyed him coolly, forcing herself to see the facts and not the fantasy lover a naïve part of her clung to so stubbornly.

Until she looked up and saw him hotly eyeing her artfully displayed body, and not knowing her—when she would have known him deaf, dumb and blindfolded—she had been having doubts about this outrageous scheme again. Now she forgot them, and hoped he had missed the flash of revelation in her golden-brown eyes as she finally embraced her new self. Colonel Besford had begun to burn, she decided triumphantly, and his wife would be the last person to try to put out the blaze; indeed, she sincerely hoped it consumed him!

Blissfully unaware that she had anything on her mind but extracting the maximum price for her favours from a besotted suitor, Rob saw only the cat-like smile of satisfaction that lifted his inamorata's sultry temptation of a mouth. Then she lowered her eyes to the music as if she was a pattern of modesty—and how she could pretend that in her flimsy provocation of a robe and with her hair an artful temptation of disarray about her shoulders was beyond him.

'Your eyes are like honey, so tell me—will your lips still taste of it too? And I wonder if you will sting me, or kiss me back when I sample them again?' he said softly.

He watched intently as those lips parted on a soft 'oh' of protest, or complicity. Such innocent-seeming eyes she had, while the rest of her roused him to such a state of driving need he just had to seduce every delicious inch of her far-from-innocent body very soon, or run mad.

'The former, of course.'

Her voice was low and husky and completed his enchantment. Rob was not to know the sound of it nearly gave Caro a fit of nervous giggles, because it was so different from her normal soft tones. Where she was finding all these unexpected quirks in her once-upright character was beyond her, but they certainly added spice to the game. If the intensity in her husband's eyes was anything to go by, then it was well and truly on—whatever it turned out to be. Excitement dissipated her lingering scruples, as she felt more alive under his hot gaze than she had been in her entire life.

'Don't you want to find out what I taste of, my dear?'

Seduction and deceit, Caro decided with a shiver, remembering his betraying kisses on their wedding day. Today his wicked grin invited her to share his sensual enjoyment of their scandalous circumstances. Not that lightskirts could be accused of impropriety, she reflected, being improper by their very existence. Yet she needed to remember that he was dangerous, and so was the hope that had stubbornly reignited at the sight of him. She had to douse it somehow.

'No, and as you refuse to respect my solitude,' she replied coldly, 'I shall leave you to *your* privacy, sir.'

A quick flash of colour stung his tanned cheeks at having his manners corrected by a Cyprian, but his smile was sardonic as he blocked her escape.

'First let us take the gloves off, my lovely. I want you enough to let you name your price. You might as well stop baiting the hook now—your fish is well and truly landed.'

Her smile was mocking; after all, he could afford to purchase the attentions of the most exclusive courtesan in the land with his new-found fortune burning a hole in his pocket.

'It is quite beyond your means, I assure you, sir,' she told him with a bland smile she sincerely hoped would make him question his ability to charm the birds out of the trees.

'You do not know what they are, so why not name your price, my dear?' he demanded imperiously, and for all his false endearments he sounded as if he was in charge of his brigade again, and dealing with a recalcitrant recruit.

'No, thank you, I am already spoken for.'

Which was true enough, given the promises she had made him before God and man. While the spectacle of Colonel Besford, propositioning his own wife under the roof of an exclusive courtesan suddenly struck her as exquisitely funny, he evidently did not see the humour of being brought low by a harlot. She gave him a challenging look, and held his green eyes as if the heat latent in them meant nothing to her.

'Whatever he has offered, I will top it. Jewels, money, a carriage and pair.'

If she let him, he would use their locked gazes to reinforce the attraction singing between them, almost as if he would bore a way into her soul. Refusing to look away first, she managed to ape his usual cynicism.

'Only a pair? And I had *such* a fancy for a team.'

'Then you shall have two, one for weekdays and another for best.'

'No, thank you,' she said contrarily, 'I prefer to ride.'

'Oh, so do I, my lovely. So do I,' he replied outrageously.

She blushed uncontrollably, ashamed of herself for even vaguely guessing at a meaning instinct told her was disgraceful. As mischief faded from her golden-brown eyes, she wondered if she met something gentler than mere desire in his emerald gaze for a fleeting moment. If so, he recovered soon enough.

'Tell me who acts for you. I will have my lawyer call on him and arrange matters as you please.'

'I doubt if he could ever do that.'

Which was something close to the truth, for once.

'You might be surprised by my resources; I am a very wealthy man all of a sudden.'

'Are you, sir? How, pray, would I know that?' she managed to say indifferently, despite a burning desire to box his ears.

'Your pardon, madam,' he drawled. 'Colonel Robert Besford, currently of the Duke of York's staff, and entirely at your service.'

He bowed with exquisite grace and Caro decided critically that he was overdoing it. 'Very pretty, sir,' she said, examining her newly buffed fingernails with spurious concentration.

'If you have heard my pockets are to let, I can reassure you on that score. Nowadays, I could buy an abbey if I happened to want one.'

Their ships had come in at last, had they? So her father was less omnipotent than he believed and they had found a way past his well-placed hurdles after all. Which explained last night's debauch, she supposed, but what a pity their venture had not succeeded a few weeks earlier and saved her the humiliation of becoming Rob Besford's unwanted wife.

'Indeed, Colonel?' she said with a brief, insincere smile, 'Then you are to be congratulated, but, like you, I have another interest; so I must wish you good day.'

'Last night you were as hot for me as I am for you, sweet liar.'

She managed to look as if she was making a great effort to recall events so remote she had all but forgotten them.

'Oh, so that was you, was it? Then I am doubly glad to refuse you, sir.'

'And I am not even to know why?'

'Because I like to have an element of choice in my dealings with gentlemen of your stamp,' she told him huskily—how true that was! 'And your friends spoke of a wife, I believe?'

'If females of *your* stamp went about rejecting other women's husbands, you would soon be in the basket. So pray don't try throwing that red herring at me again, my dear—we both know you have no interest in my morals whatsoever.'

'I have no interest in the rest of you either, Colonel Besford.

As I told you, I have another offer—so I can afford to be fastidious, can I not?'

She gave him the bland, arch smile she had seen the beauties of the *ton* use to such effect, and saw genuine frustration shadow his face at her lie. His air of suppressed power gave him an edge over many other gentlemen reliant on mere good looks. With so many natural advantages, she doubted he often experienced rejection, so the novelty would do him good.

'And the name of my successful rival?'

He sounded as if he had accepted her rebuff, but she managed to maintain a faintly amused expression. Her own duplicity both scandalised and elated her, and trying out her new freedoms was heady.

'I have a certain code, sir, although you obviously think otherwise.'

'Yes, I have heard there is honour among thieves.'

At least she already knew that ice-cold look very well; after all, he normally saved it for his wife.

'Are you usually successful with such methods, sir?' she asked with an air of detached interest. 'Dear me, all the ladies that rumour credits you with seducing must be forbearing creatures indeed, if so. I am surprised you survived the bedchamber, let alone the battlefield, Colonel.'

'You are impudent, madam.'

She was not sure if the spark in his extraordinary eyes was born of amusement at her effrontery, or baffled fury.

'Good, then we are equal,' she replied pertly and realised too late that the emerald fire in his gaze was a mix of lust and triumph, not angry defeat after all.

He had come dangerously close while she was lost in silly speculation about his emotions and now he nipped her neatly in his arms, imprisoning her against his muscular strength before she had a chance to dart away. Fool to let him get so close after last night! Or was it what she had secretly wanted all along? In which case, she was worse than a fool and should be confined to an asylum for her own safety.

'We are now,' he murmured.

The fiery, forbidden luxury of him against her, the faint smell of lemon water and clean male, and the heady sound of his quickened breath almost sent her senses out of control yet again. It was too soon after last night, and her barricades had not been rebuilt strongly enough after all. She reminded herself that he was just a wolf in search of a tender prey, but why on earth had she stayed here arguing with him in such a ridiculous state of undress in the first place if that was all he was?

She resolutely fought the wild bolts of feeling that insisted on shooting through her body as the sensitive and overexposed fullness of her breasts was brought up against his mighty torso, despite every order her besieged brain sent out to be all icy indifference and self-control. Ever since they first met, she had been fighting a primitive voice that told her to do anything, say anything, risk everything to be his. Now her body was conspiring with her baser self to achieve that end. Male against female, his hard masculine frame was wrapped about her soft curves as if as intimate a contact as possible was the stuff of life itself. To her he was temptation almost beyond reason, but exactly what was she to him?

Unable to pretend she was indifferent to him or his touch, her cool determination to be avenged was floundering in the face of this extraordinary new intimacy. Rebuilding her barriers seemed impossible while she was locked in his arms, and very aware of his protective strength and dishonourable intentions. She tried reminding herself that he thought her capable of selling herself to any man with sufficient means to pay her price, but her eager senses refused to listen.

His mouth came nearer, until at last it was so close that she could feel his breath on her mouth as his lips formed the words. He was so nearly kissing her that it felt more seductive than if he had plunged straight into her mouth and greedily taken her senses by storm.

'Well, are you interested yet?' he whispered.

'No!' she croaked, furious that she could not force the sound out more robustly.

'Liar,' he murmured against her lips, then kissed her with such gentleness that he undermined any frail defences she might marshal in one brilliant manoeuvre.

His mouth was warm and teasing, and he refused it more than a few seconds' contact anywhere. Sweeping light kisses over her closed eyelids; he worked his way down the tip of her nose, and back to each corner of her mouth. She moaned and he pulled back to look down at her. Her long eyelashes swept up unresistingly, as if he had taken command of her smallest reflexes, she thought dazedly. His eyes were blazing a true green with triumph and desire that even she could sense was on the verge of raging out of control, yet still she trusted in the extraordinary will power he was apparently master of.

'I was only trying to be interesting,' he said provocatively, then swiftly took her mouth again before she could spark back at him.

Awed by such a heady mix of dark seduction and iron restraint, she forgot sad Caroline Warden, and forsaken Mrs Besford, as the wanton creature she became in his arms melted under his kisses. Oblivious to where she was and how outrageously she was dressed, or undressed, she welcomed her state of dishabille as his questing, teasing fingers crept downwards and his mouth opened on hers. He darted his tongue into her mouth, then paused for a moment as she gasped at the lightning bolt of hot need that tore through her. He lifted his head mere inches, to look down at her with triumph and blatant desire heating his eyes and telling her it was mutual without words.

'Now, aren't you going to tell me that I'm going too fast for you?' he asked, in a voice she was fiercely glad to hear was as unsteady as the wild beating of her silly heart.

She colluded in her own downfall by squirming closer to him and refusing to fight the heated demands of her suddenly wilful body. Why not let her own husband teach her the secrets of the marriage bed, which even Alice refused to discuss? It was the word 'marriage' that grew to unease at last, and broke through the enchantment. It sniped at her, even as his fingers explored her waiting curves and went on to finally reach the objective that threatened to draw her inexorably into his web, as he pulled aside her gossamer shift to caress her breasts and make her gasp with extravagant pleasure.

Even the memory of what that same caress had done to her on her wedding day could not stop the current of heavy warmth that suddenly flooded through her and threatened to render her boneless. Then his knowing thumb grazed a sensitised nipple and fire shot through the core of her, and she almost lost control of her wavering legs. He lowered his head in the wake of his incendiary touch and his tongue's sweet, provoking rhythm sent shivers of longing down her spine to the very core of her. He skilfully fed the blaze within her with warm, teasing promise.

Magic she had never dared dream of seemed to spark through her everywhere he touched her. Yet the heavy memory of their farcical wedding day now marched in step with her body's sensual demands to surrender right here and now, and the devil fly away with the consequences. Even as he kissed and caressed her with exquisite fire, and she wondered if a woman could melt from sheer physical pleasure, she recalled the pain of trusting him with herself and being bitterly disillusioned.

She opened her eyes and looked down at his curling dark chestnut hair with dazed wonderment. He took such whole-hearted pleasure in her, and the feel of his powerful shoulders under her questing fingers was a seduction all on its own. She was so tempted, so hot, and so full of unknown, dragging demand to let him pleasure them both, right here and now, that it was nearly irresistible.

Today his mouth seemed to offer forbidden paradise, but the first time he kissed her it had been a devil's goad, she reminded herself. This enchantment was unique to her, but commonplace to him, and how could he not know her? A picture of him, hard-eyed and condemning on their wedding day, came into her mind, and she found the strength to push away from him at long last after all.

He stood and watched her through heat-hazed eyes, as if he had been drugged by the very potency of his passion for her, and tried to pull her back into his arms. She dodged away, putting the width of the piano between them, and hastily covering as much of herself as her garb allowed. She suddenly felt cold, as well as wretchedly exposed to his burning gaze. Part of her might want to be wrenched back into his arms, as unquestioning of the passion that had sprung to precocious life between them last night as he seemed to be. She reminded herself sternly that silly little Mrs Besford was no more, and tried to get her rebel senses back under control.

The little witch was panting as if they had run a mile together and Rob wondered for one baffled moment if they had, because he felt as if he had been winded by their latest passage of arms. Then the loss of his siren's tender mouth and glorious body, snatched away moments before they would have achieved a breathtaking completion, stung bitterly and the savage grind of unsatisfied desire well nigh unmanned him.

'Upping the ante?' he rasped bitterly, hating to find his self-control inferior to that of this lovely, mercenary harlot nearly as much as he longed to consign his scruples to the devil.

The very force of his own need shocked him. Yet there was something elemental about this obsession he was developing for her that almost made him wish he had never laid eyes on the little witch. In the past he had prided himself on choosing his lovers with discernment and keeping them as friends once the liaison was over.

He could not imagine parting from her with anything but frustration and the utmost reluctance. Witch indeed, he thought darkly, and fought a merciless drive of frustrated need that was far too close to pain. He was still enough of a man of the world to know she wanted him, but she was playing a dangerous game if she thought it was safe to tease more out of him than she already had.

'Think what you like, I told you, no,' Caro replied at last.

Childish dreams of a gentle hero who would rescue her from her drab life and love her, spark at her, and laugh with her for the rest of their days finally faded for good. The man her silly heart had marked out for the role wanted to offer her a luxurious, convenient corner of his life and never know more about her than her supposed profession told him.

'That was no refusal,' he said coldly.

'Well, you would not accept my word, would you, Colonel?'

'Why? I want you and I think you return the favour.'

'Maybe I do, but take what you think is yours now, Colonel, and you will never see me again.'

'I don't fear your disappearance, Circe, for I think you want me as passionately as I do you,' he said with a hot look. 'You are hesitant about this whole business and I will not have you throw that fact back at me in a week or a month's time. Come to me because you want me as badly as I need you, or not at all.'

She opened her mouth to offer some disclaimer that she would ever go to him, but he had bridged the gap between them and gently touched her lips together before she could speak. She gasped and watched him with wondering eyes as need flamed through her at the very touch of his fingertips.

'If we are to meet again, don't you think we both ought to introduce ourselves?' he asked softly.

A shadow of her own name would do, she decided, hastily casting about for a suitable name for a lightskirt. He would not notice any similarity to his forgotten wife's name, for he had obviously blotted her from his life very effectively indeed. Her mother's maiden name would serve very well for the same reason—she could afford to give the broadest of clues and not fear him picking them up when he chose not to know anything about his own wife.

'I am Cleo Tournier, Colonel,' she said huskily, crossing her fingers behind her back as she lied through her teeth.

He smiled that wicked smile that had made her knees tremble from the moment she had laid eyes on him before saying, '*Au revoir,* then, Cleo,' and suddenly she did not want him to go after all. 'See that you do not forget me,' he added. Probably the most unnecessary command he had ever issued, she decided crossly.

She frowned, but he seemed encouraged rather than cast

into the doldrums, so she tried imitating Alice's haughty look as she had confronted her admirers last night instead. She must have failed miserably, because then he had the effrontery to laugh at her.

'I say *au revoir* because I will be back, as certain as the sun sets in the west, my Cleo.'

His Cleo? They would soon see about that. She offered him a cool *adieu,* as if his lustful interest in her was merely amusing. Instead of being properly disheartened, he impudently snatched one last teasing kiss as she stood, lips parted and all undefended, then left her standing there with nothing to say to his insufferably arrogant parting shot.

'Never mind! Soon, my sweet, very soon,' he promised, then left the room as coolly as if he had just paid a polite morning call, rather than failed to seduce a potential mistress.

The moment she heard him run lightly down the stairs, she dashed to the window, noting the assured swing in his long stride as he walked down the street with a preoccupied frown pleating her brow. If the swagger in his step was anything to go by, he didn't believe she was indifferent to him any more than she did herself. She was still wondering whether she was glad to see the vital, compelling man she had first thought herself in love with return from the icy wastes he seemed to have inhabited since their marriage, when he finally turned the corner and was lost to her sight.

Wanton longing racked her for the ardent lover he had suddenly become, but, like the wise child taught to fear the fire, she flinched from the very thought of the frigid aristocrat she had encountered on their wedding day and abandoned her window gazing. Anyone who saw her would think she was lovelorn, and nothing could be further from the truth, she assured herself militantly. A man who could promise so much, then leave his inamorata without even a backward glance was not worth wasting another moment's heartache on after all.

Chapter Four

'Whatever have you been up to, Mrs Besford?'

'Alice! Lord, how you made me jump.'

'Good, for I am not used to witnessing scandalous displays of depravity in my own drawing room, and I shall succumb to a fit of the vapours if you don't explain yourself immediately.'

Caro's hand went to her mouth in horror.

'You didn't really see us?'

'Oh, but I did, and you were communicating so effectively that I left you to it. You did not…let him, you know? Did you?' Alice ground to a halt and Caro was amazed to see her worldly-wise friend blush.

'What, Alice dear? Let him know I was his ugly, common dab of a wife? Or think I am no better than I should be?'

'I meant that I hope you did not let him take you right here, where anyone might walk in and catch you.'

This time it was Caro's turn to flush. Such a scandalous tableau would have shocked even Lord Wrovillton, if he had strolled in to find his best friend so intimately occupied in his lover's drawing room. The image shook *her* to the soles of her suddenly freezing feet, so goodness knows what it would have done to his lordship in the heat of the moment.

'No, er…no—that is, not quite. I called a halt.'

'Robert Besford must have been delighted,' Alice said with satisfied glee. 'You are halfway to punishing him for his sins already.'

'I doubt it, and he should be out searching for me, Alice, not bidding for a mistress. Does he care so little even for appearance that he won't make the effort to find out if I have returned to my father's house?'

'If I know anything about men, they made a night of it and Will's man has done a sterling job of repairing the damage. If your Colonel has so much as set foot in Foxwell House or his lodgings this morning, then I am the Queen of Sheba.'

Although his superfine coat would pass muster anywhere, Rob's pantaloons *had* seemed overlarge and he had shifted his feet a couple of times, as if his Hessians pinched. He had been wearing evening breeches, stockings and shoes last night, so the offending items must be his friend's, along with a fresh neckcloth and a sober, if rather tight, waistcoat to replace the exotic one she had glimpsed even in the uncertain lamplight the night before.

'Then why come here before he went to his own rooms?'

'To plead Will's case, I suppose. I made no secret of the fact that I was furious with him last night, and they have been friends since Eton. Maybe he was going to own that it was all his fault before you diverted him.'

'Lord Wrovillton is a grown man and he could have stayed at home. Or remained here with you.'

'Robert Besford has been going to the devil ever since he came back from France, and Will is too loyal a friend to just sit back and watch him do so.'

'Has he? Even before I let Papa bullock me into marrying him?'

'Long before that. According to Will, your Colonel's brother's illness has had a profound effect upon Rob. I can understand his feelings, right up to the point when he took them out on you. Lord Littleworth always was the best of the Besfords after all.'

Incredibly Alice blushed again and Caro looked at her suspiciously.

'Do you mean to tell me that James Besford was one of your lovers?' she queried in an awed voice.

'Well, you must admit that your brother-in-law *is* devilishly attractive, Caro, and excellent company besides. Why refuse him when most so-called gentlemen are his very opposite? It was over before he was wed, of course, and we parted friends.'

'Yes, he makes a good friend.'

'I know.' Alice sighed. 'Poor James.'

'Aye, and poor Jane—they were kind to me when almost everyone else laughed at Papa's ridiculous pretensions, and in return I have made their family a laughing stock with the alliance Papa forced on them.'

'They are bright enough to work out the whys of it all for themselves, and I am quite sure James will try to find you, even if his brother won't stir himself.'

'Then I must get word to him that I am safe, or maybe I had better go back. Jane is due to consult Sir Richard Croft tomorrow, so I dare say she is at Foxwell House by now. I thought I could not face them, but I was a coward.'

'Nonsense! You are brave as a lion to marry that idiot in the first place, and you are not going back now. It's high time Robert Besford learned to be sensible again, so write a note to reassure the Littleworths of your continuing existence and I will get it delivered.'

'Pursuing a courtesan while his wife is missing and his family are all on end does not fit any definition of sensible I ever came across, Alice.'

'It makes more sense than anything else he has done lately—but never mind that now, we have work to do,' her friend declared militantly and bore her guest inexorably back upstairs to be fitted with some very frivolous bonnets by the exclusive milliner Alice had somehow lured from Bond Street.

The spring that meeting Cleo again had put in his step was beginning to leave Rob's long stride by the time he reached his destination. He had spent the walk to Berkeley Square wondering how he would rearrange his life to suit everyone and a brief smile quirked his lips at such a laughable notion. It could not be done, of course, so he would just have to make the best of things for once. In the meantime there was Cleo, and her fiery presence in his life would soften the blows his pride must suffer while he tried to obtain a legal separation from his wife.

Foxwell House was in a state of chaos when he got there, Lord and Lady Littleworth having arrived from the country in good time for the staff to summon the courage to reveal that 'Mrs Robert' added invisibility to her small pool of talents.

'I hope you are happy now you have finally driven poor Caro away,' his sister-in-law said sternly when he knocked on the door of the Littleworths' suite.

Apparently James was resting after the journey, which left him to confront his Viscountess, who was as furious as a kitten with her fur rubbed the wrong way.

'I stupidly refused to believe you were so callous as to abandon poor Caro,' she continued, 'until I got Aunt Samphire's letter telling us you had not been near your wife since the wedding day, and now the poor girl has run away. Heaven knows what you said and did to make her behave so irrationally, but if you can live with the idea of a vulnerable young woman facing the world alone, I certainly cannot. I suggest you start searching for her immediately, unless you expect James to do it for you, of course,' she ended scornfully.

Rob had always considered Jane the ideal society wife for his discerning brother, with the added surprise that James was as much in love with her as she was with him. Today her golden beauty made her look like an avenging angel, given the stern expression on her usually gentle face.

'You must not get so agitated, Janey, and you really should sit down,' he said, waiting for her usual sunny smile in vain as she stayed determinedly upright. 'Why so many allowances for my wife and none for myself, love? She used you quite shamelessly to scrape an acquaintance with the family, so surely you cannot still intend to be thick as thieves with her?'

'Rubbish, she did no such thing,' Lady Littleworth said, stubbornly refusing to be led to the nearest sofa.

'I beg to differ.'

'Then you are a fool. Caroline's father has ridden rough-shod over her all her life. Her wishes would mean nothing to him when it came to marrying her off. It strikes me that you have just taken over bullying her where he left off, and I never thought I should have to say such an unkind thing to someone I think of as a brother.'

'No, love, of course you did not,' he said gently, and then flinched as she turned a contemptuous look on him.

'I told the servants Caro left a note to say she was going to visit a sick friend in the country, but I don't know that they believed me. I do know that Caroline is alone and vulnerable. Luckily I am not such a noddy I cannot tell an innocent girl from a harpy, although the evidence suggests that you are not so discerning. I have no wish to see James become fagged to death from sorting out a mess entirely of your making, Colonel. Kindly find your wife and come to some sort of agreement with her, if you cannot honour the solemn promises you made her before God.'

With that, the Viscountess swept out of her boudoir, and the silence she left behind was so profound that Rob could hear her skirts whisper before she shut the door of her bed-chamber with a decided snap.

He could hardly attend Gentleman Jackson's Boxing Saloon when the whole world might soon know his wife was missing, but a bout of fisticuffs might have done him the world of good, he decided grimly. If this juicy piece of scandal leaked out, he might as well set himself up as a sideshow at a fair for all the privacy he would have left to guard. Then he contemplated the humiliation it would heap on his wife if he set a strumpet above her, and wondered if he didn't deserve to be the butt of the gossips.

Rob often found himself fantasising about lovely, de-sirable Cleo, even while he searched fruitlessly for his missing wife. He found no trace of her and marvelled at her ability to disappear so completely. Beginning to suspect that Caroline had depths he had never bothered to plumb, he also discovered he could hardly remember what she looked like. Perhaps it served him right that he always seemed to find Cleo 'from home', and yet he passionately hoped she had not forgotten him altogether, because he might just as well try to wipe the sun from the sky as destroy the memory of his amateur temptress.

It would take a drink from the waters of the River Styx to make Caro forget Rob Besford. A warm shiver shook her every time she imagined his response to the dark arts of attracting a gentleman's improper attentions that she was learning from her stern mentor. She doubted she could cope with more of his attention than she already had, and found her thoughts wandering back to that encounter in Alice's drawing room whenever she contemplated exchanging long and languorous glances with her stern husband.

Except, of course, that for Cleo his gaze would be hot and wanting, his hunger as explicit in his emerald green eyes as his hatred of Caroline had once been. Anyway, she had other concerns beside Robert Besford, she reminded herself impatiently. Unfortunately whenever she thought about his passionate wooing of a potential mistress, she could not quite remember what they were.

On the way to Drury Lane Theatre a week after her escape from Foxwell House, she was torn between terror and a curious excitement that she dared not examine too closely. How Colonel Besford would burn with humiliation if he suspected his wife of flaunting herself in front of the *ton* in such a scandalous fashion! She was still angry enough with him to find that notion extremely satisfying, even if he was unlikely to credit his dull little wife with such a wild adventure.

'At the theatre I can regulate who is admitted to my box and who must be kept out.' Alice had reassured her earlier in the day. 'With James and Frederick looming over the entrance like a pair of prizefighters, and Will present to put down the pretensions of the unruly, you will be safe enough, love, I promise you.'

Lord Wrovillton had looked curiously at his lover's protégée, as if wondering why she was being groomed as a high-class courtesan, but at the same time kept isolated from her would-be keepers. She had shifted uncomfortably under the scrutiny of his acute grey eyes and offered him a bland, defensive smile. He seemed to forget the matter soon enough and tonight Alice was in such looks he only had eyes for her, but Caro was slightly uncomfortable in his company all the same.

Despite Alice's reassurance, Caro felt giddy at the very thought of so many assessing eyes centring on her, even from a distance.

'Courage,' she ordered herself sternly, and glanced down at her immaculate and very improperly turned-out person.

She only just managed to resist the urge to hitch up the low-cut bodice of her outrageous gown, and tried to remember Alice's strict instruction not to fiddle with perfection. She would never be perfect, despite the attentions of the best dressmakers, hairdressers and perfumiers in London. And perfectly *what*, in any case?

If she had ever been a conventional débutante, then nobody would dream of calling her one now, and she had no place among the young matrons overawed by their own sophistication. She was not even the high-class courtesan signalled by the discreet touches of glamour not permitted the most daring young wife.

You are not flesh, nor fowl, nor good red herring,' she silently told herself, a wry smile tilting her carefully reddened lips.

'Are you worried, love? We could always turn round and go back home,' Alice offered anxiously.

'And waste all this?' Caro said, waving the fan that was apparently almost a lethal weapon in the seduction business at her own scandalously clad person.

'They're just clothes, Car—Cleo.'

Casting a furtive look at her lover, Alice gave Caro a quick look of apology and went breezily on in the hope her slip would go unnoticed. 'I imagine what some of the quizzes would look like without theirs whenever they deign to notice my existence—it puts them in their place quite wonderfully.'

'I can quite see how it would,' Caro admitted with a smile.

'And you will quite put me off my supper if you go on putting such unappetising pictures in my head, love,' his lordship added with a wry grimace.

Caro sent Lord Wrovillton a furtive glance, but his expression betrayed nothing. Deciding that he could not have heard Alice's slip after all and that she was still safe, she took a deep breath and nodded silent encouragement to herself, then took his other arm and they stepped into the box as planned. A myriad of speculative eyes instantly seemed to converge on her, as if she was a novel item on tonight's playbill.

'A packed house tonight, is it not?' Alice observed in the world-weary voice she often used to conceal her feelings from a hard world.

'Then let us hope Keane is worthy of their rapt attention then, for I never heard such a gathering of magpies,' Lord Wrovillton replied with a knowing glance at the crowd straining to see the latest addition to the demi-monde.

Catching the glint of laughing tenderness in his eyes when he looked at Alice, Caro was not surprised that her friend could easily ignore the scrutiny of tonight's audience, but how she longed for a similar state of oblivion! She disposed herself elegantly on her gilt chair, then surveyed the crowd rather less brazenly than they were inspecting her. Would he be here? Or were all Alice's plans to come to nothing after all? While she sincerely hoped Robert Besford was at a stand on the wife-hunting front, would even he have the effrontery to seek out a potential mistress at such a time?

She wafted her delicate painted fan as if ennui might overcome her any moment, and slowly let her eyes explore the company under her darkened eyelashes. Hot glances slid over her from so-called gentlemen, who let their eyes linger boldly on her face and her cunningly displayed curves in a fashion quite new in her experience. For a moment she wanted to shrink from them, to slide her chair back further into the back of the box and hide, but she had spent too much time cowering in corners already. Forcing herself to continue her languid examination of the theatre and its avid audience, she had to fight a desire to giggle. Hysteria, she wondered?

Oddly enough, elation underlay the fright that was making her heart pit-pat in quick, light beats. She was safe enough, as Alice had said, and since few had bothered to look at Caroline Warden twice other than to criticise her, she would surely not be recognised? There was even a certain rueful amusement to be found in spotting one or two of the gentlemen who had been trapped into dancing with Miss Warden the Wallflower, fumbling with their quizzing glasses to get a closer look at a new star among the Cyprians. Her eyes met Alice's and she rolled them at her as one of the would-be beaux nearly fell out of his box in his eagerness to inspect her well-displayed charms, then smiled reassuringly as she recognised the worry in her friend's ultramarine gaze.

It was suddenly no effort at all to assume the faint air of amusement that apparently added to the allure of a high-class courtesan. Most people were here to see and be seen after all, so she was not so very unusual. Then the crowds faded as she singled out Rob's broad shoulders, set off by a scarlet coat and regimentals tonight, instead of the quietly immaculate civilian dress her colonel seemed to prefer, and she realised why Alice had looked so concerned.

With a huge effort of will, she let her gaze slide over him as if he was a stranger and carried on her study of the rest of the company, who might have been standing on their heads or dancing a jig round a maypole for all she cared. Catching a glimpse of her friend's worried face once more, she managed to summon up another smile. After all those hours of lessons, the endless tedium of standing while gowns were tweaked and twitched and perfected and, most of all, the memory of his contempt, she was certainly not going to turn cat in pan and run away just at the sight of her own husband.

'And who is this fabulous creature, fairest Aleysha?' a deep voice spoke from behind them, and she nearly leapt out of her seat in shock.

Although she had encountered him only twice, she would have known the voice of her husband's groomsman, Captain Charles Afforde, anywhere after that disastrous wedding breakfast. He had a reputation for dash and brilliance in his successful career as a frigate captain, so if she passed this test, maybe the toughest one of all was not beyond her. She turned her head, raised one slender brow in languid surprise and called up all her acting abilities.

His expression conveyed an open admiration he would never have dared show a lady so brazenly, but no hint of recognition. Indeed, the laughter that never seemed far from his bluest of blue eyes blazed out of them now, along with rather less platonic emotions. His good looks, barely suppressed merriment over the follies of the world and the hot desire in his azure eyes added up to a potent mix, so perhaps it was just as well she was already well and truly in thrall to a very different rogue.

'Rowley, you are *such* a liar,' her friend informed him. 'You have obviously transferred that superlative to my friend, so I shall not introduce you to her out of pique.'

'It was either that or have Will run me through, Queen of my Heart,' the Captain declared, with one hand over that fickle organ and a soulful look in Alice's direction.

'I doubt I would trouble myself with such a Captain Hackum, but pray introduce him to your friend, my dear, if only to put a stop to his nauseating posturing.'

'Very well then, but, Cleo, I must warn you that this gentleman never meant anything seriously in his life. So Captain Charles Afforde may meet Miss Cleo Tournier, if he promises to behave himself.'

'As if I ever do anything else,' declared the Captain, with such a saintly expression on his tanned face that he might have sat for an altarpiece.

Caro was hard put not to laugh, especially as she had witnessed him misbehaving very thoroughly only a few days ago. She held out an elegantly gloved hand with the air of a woman accustomed to admiration from the opposite sex, and felt rather proud of herself.

He kissed it at some length, giving her a soulful look and quirking one eyebrow in comical question now and again as he saluted each finger in turn. He was undoubtedly a rake, but he would break a woman's heart with such lightness and humour that she might remember the glow and not the pain. Luckily hers was as well armed as his famous frigate, so she could enjoy his improper attentions without taking them in the least bit seriously. The novelty of being courted by Rob's friend and rival was too heady for her to give him the cold shoulder, and anyway, she did not want to. Caroline Warden had experienced so little freedom under her father's roof that she did not see why Cleo could not enjoy the liberty she had once longed for—with a little interest added on for Rob's bad behaviour.

'Captain,' she acknowledged, laughter at his antics lighting her eyes, even as her expression remained serene.

If his keen gaze on her subtly painted face detected nothing familiar about her from her dreadful wedding day, surely he would not remember her voice under the husky tones that now overlaid it?

'Fair Cleo, I am like old Roman Antony, struck dumb by the beauty of your namesake,' he said dramatically, but his dancing blue eyes invited her to laugh with him.

'Not noticeably, Captain.'

She raised her fan lazily, but he snatched it away.

'My task, beautiful Cleo,' he said, wafting it and letting his eyes drift over her cunningly displayed person in a way he would never dream of doing if he had the slightest idea of who she really was.

She could not control her blush at the bold expression of outright desire on his handsome face. As he then fanned all the harder her heightened colour must be visible, even through the exquisite maquillage she had hoped would disguise her as surely as a mask.

'It would never do for the tabbies to connect respectable Mrs Besford with that *dreadful* Cleo Tournier, so we will apply paint in the right places,' Alice had told her, 'and Robert Besford will be knocked all to pieces when he sees you again.' Seeing the sceptical expression on her friend's face, she went on even more emphatically. 'Truly he will be your slave, love, then all you need do is reel him in and, voilà, a model husband.'

So her curling lashes were now blackened and her eyes had been outlined with kohl until Caro had a job to recognise herself. Even to her they looked huge and exotic and rather knowing. Alice had applied only a hint of colour to her cheeks and lips, the better to heighten the impact of Caro's amber gaze. Which was all well and good, but Alice had not seen the 'he' in question when he had made his contempt for his plain wife so brutally clear. If he ever discovered who she really was, he would only hate her all the more and her stomach lurched at the very thought of it.

For one agonising moment panic ruled her, but she refused to play the coward. She would see this farce through to the bitter end and pay him back a tithe of the agony he had caused her, then she would become a schoolmistress after all. She refused to consider the uncomfortable idea that ringing down the curtain and walking away from this masquerade might cost her far more than it would him. She told herself firmly that she would enjoy her holiday from reality—then settle down to the narrow life she had mapped out when she ran from Foxwell House. There would be plenty of time to count the cost as she dwindled into a properly mousy schoolteacher, with no hint of scandal to besmirch her imaginary background.

The mere sight of the beautiful lightskirt installed in his friend's box instantly enraged Rob. How many similar jaunts had there been while he was otherwise engaged in the thankless task of searching for his wife?

Jealousy roared through him in a primitive surge. He had known Rowley Afforde since they were repellent brats in their cradles, but now he wanted to tear the damned petticoat merchant limb from limb. He regretfully dismissed the idea of hauling his former friend outside by the collar of his dress uniform and indulging in an undignified bout of fisticuffs. For one thing, Rowley was nigh as powerfully built as he was himself, and for another their falling out over a lightskirt would provide better entertainment for the company than the farce they were blithely ignoring on the stage.

Cleo was at least dressed this time, he noted, but that aquamarine satin abomination ought to be consigned to a dark closet and kept for occasions when only he could see her in it. The wretched thing could easily cause a riot if she bent forward. Admittedly it was cut only a little lower than the gowns of the young matrons who so carefully ignored her, but the way it was draped made a man gasp every time she moved, in case he might catch a glimpse of more. They would not, of course. What point was there in employing the best dressmaker in London if not to enhance the mystery?

The sea-green colour, the shining mother-of-pearl comb in her tumbling auburn curls in the shape of a shell, all reminded him of the mermaid her draperies hinted at, and he fought back the thought that it was all too appropriate to her profession. He fought a rearguard action against the maddening effect a few yards of satin could have on an otherwise sane man across a crowded theatre, and lost.

She ought to be swathed in black bombazine from head to toe whenever she went out, he decided savagely, and, if he had anything to do with it, she soon would be. There would be no more advertising her fallen status, or flaunting of her delightful body for every fool to gape at, once she was safely under his protection. Protection it would certainly have to be, in every sense of the word, for she obviously needed to be saved from the consequences of her own recklessness. In the wrong place, which was everywhere except in his bedchamber, she could bring down far more trouble on herself in that flimsy wisp of satin than either she or her more worldly friend could handle.

His eyes continued to move over her exquisite figure, despite stern orders from the logical part of his brain to avert them and stop acting like a mooncalf. Imagining the rise and fall of her breath and the effect it would have on her firm young breasts when he was close enough to observe them properly, was a refined form of torture. He moved on, eventually, up to her slender neck, artfully unadorned, and he was on fire to sweep kisses down that creamy throat and find the pulse in the hollow at the base of it.

That scenario had an even more unfortunate effect, given that his body was now demanding more than was respectable for the theatre. He hastily scrutinised Cleo's unique features instead, but that only completed the spell, as an intricate memory of exploring her mouth with hungry kisses demolished his last resistance as the lost cause it was. He had to get closer to her; preferably so close that Rowley Afforde would take his ogling eyes back to sea and stay there.

Chapter Five

Although she was looking in the opposite direction, Caro knew to the second when Rob headed for her. Fleeing the building the way she was dressed would only invite disaster, she told herself. So she gave the gallant Captain a languishing glance and tried to look as if she hadn't a care in the world besides her own enjoyment.

'Why do they call you Rowley, Captain Afforde?' she asked in an effort to divert herself from the encounter with her husband that was sure to come very soon. 'I thought my friend said that your name was Charles.'

Charles Afforde was shocked to find that telling the story with his usual panache was beyond him. Something stopped him admitting he had gained it by seducing as many beautiful women as he could fairly lay his hands on, even if a more ridiculous idea than an innocent whore he had yet to come across.

'It was a nickname given to the second Charles Stuart, the Merry Monarch, y'know?' he added and, hardened womaniser that he was, he almost blushed as her amber eyes widened with shock. 'As we share a first name, I suppose I was christened after him—or maybe it's because I'm a sailor and he was said to be very fond of rowing.'

'I dare say that must be it then,' she agreed, but somehow even her censored knowledge of his infamous namesake led her to doubt it.

'I hope *you* will call me by my proper name, beautiful Cleo,' he whispered, redeeming himself a little in his own eyes by leaning far too close to the red-gold curls clustered round one very pretty ear to make himself heard above the din that had scarcely moderated when the farce began.

'Maybe I will, Captain Afforde, when we are better acquainted,' she replied, deftly seizing her fan again and pushing him away with it.

'Cruel creature,' he protested.

'Not so, sir, just a wise one,' she told him with a roguish smile that she was rather proud of, especially as she managed to bestow it on the gallant Captain at the very instant she felt Rob enter the box.

No need to turn and look—the involuntary shiver running down her spine told her he was close. She would *not* turn round and give him a welcoming smile. If he wanted her attention, it was high time he put himself out to earn it.

'Pray, who is the lady with the lorgnette, Captain Afforde?' she said, nodding towards an elderly dame who was wearing a very exotic turban and peering at Caro as if she was an exhibit in a specimen case.

'Curse it, that's my grandmother, Lady Samphire. I thought she was settled in Buxton!'

Captain Afforde paled noticeably under the tan that highlighted his bright blue eyes and sun-bleached hair. She wondered crossly why she could not have fallen for this rogue, instead of the one she was tinglingly aware was standing behind her. Captain Afforde was so much easier to read for one thing.

'Evidently you were mistaken,' Rob's deep voice mocked and she allowed herself an artistic start of surprise.

'Colonel Besford! What a shock you gave me.'

'Did I, Cleo? And there was I thinking you knew exactly where I was all along,' he said drily.

The knowing glint in his green eyes had that annoying flush tinting her cheeks again, but she fervently hoped that now the lights were a little duller the paint would do its job and hide her confusion.

'You are acquainted with this scoundrel, fair Cleo?' Captain Afforde enquired rather distractedly, trying hard to ignore his grandmama imperiously beckoning him to her side.

'We have met before, yes,' she replied cautiously, perfectly aware that both gentlemen remembered what they believed was their first meeting in the frosty darkness a week ago.

'Then 'ware him—not only is he the biggest rogue in Wellington's army, but I watched him get wed mere months ago.'

The Captain gave his friend a challenging look, and for a moment the rivalry between them seemed only half in jest.

'I know,' she said, and could not quite keep the sadness out of her voice.

'Best to stick to the Senior Service then, we're more reliable and less likely to wilfully commit matrimony,' the handsome captain said virtuously, as if his intentions were not just as dishonourable as his friend's.

'Are you, indeed? Now kindly be gone or be quiet, sirs. The play is about to start.'

They sat down, one on either side of her, but, between their antics and Lady Samphire's annoyed glare, she took some time to settle into the action on the stage. First the Captain stole her fan again and refused to return it, despite her vexed look. He just laughed and proceeded to fan her gently, watching her profile rather than the actors below. Then Rob edged his chair even closer, until she could feel the heat of his body through her gown. She pondered uselessly on the nature of obsession, or whatever it was she felt towards her husband, then forced her attention back to the players. Maybe she could pick up a few tips about pretence from the professionals, if she concentrated hard enough.

When the curtains closed for the interval, Caro came back from the world created for them on the stage to find Rob so close she was all but in his arms. She shuffled her chair forward and looked brightly about her, pretending an interest in the company she certainly did not feel.

'Lady Samphire is beckoning you again, Captain,' she said, after the old lady had pointed rudely to herself, then nodded emphatically at her grandson—as if demanding the return of a large and dilatory parcel.

'So she is, the darling old besom,' Captain Afforde said with a rueful grin, 'I had best go and see what she wants then, before she cuts me out of her will again.'

'Pray don't let us keep you from such a necessary errand, then. Nothing less than a handsome inheritance will do for a fellow who lives as you would like to.'

Rob's voice might sound all light mockery, but his look was challenging.

'*I* know when I ain't wanted, my friend, but what I said to you t'other night still applies. I shall give you a run for your money, make no mistake about it.'

'If you intend to discuss racing form, pray go and do so elsewhere, gentlemen,' Caro told them impatiently, forcibly reminded of two stiff-legged dogs challenging one another over a bone.

'You misunderstand, Cleo. We were discussing a pearl beyond price.'

Rob gave her a hot look she remembered from their last encounter, and knew he meant to silence her with the scorching desire in his green eyes. She raised her chin defiantly. Just the feel of him next to her might make her knees turn to water, but she was sitting down and there was no reason anyone should know about that apart from herself.

'Then I suggest you adjourn to Rundell and Bridge first thing in the morning,' she told him acerbically.

'An excellent idea, although I really don't think pearls would do you justice. What do you say, Afforde?'

Oh, insufferable! 'I have no use for jewellery,' she declared crossly.

He obviously believed that for a sufficient inducement in diamonds she would grant him the favours he suddenly wanted so badly and, despite her intention to make him think just that, she hated it.

'Then you are not just rare, my sweet, you are unique,' he told her and there was a spark of laughter in his eyes, as if he understood all too well that she wanted to hit him, but dare not do so in such a public place.

Captain Afforde looked questioningly from herself to Rob, then turned his head and encountered an adamantine stare from his grandmother. Seeming to accept the inevitable, he bowed gracefully to Caro, then took her hand and kissed it lingeringly. She looked down at his fair, curly head as he saluted each finger in turn once more, and had a suspicion he did it as much to annoy Rob as to woo her. No doubt if they were ever secluded together the temptation to try to steal more than a mere kiss would be irresistible, but for now he was content to irritate his friend and rival.

'I am ever at your service, lovely Cleo. Just crook a finger and I will come running.'

'I will remember, Captain, that gentlemen promise much today and forget even more extravagantly tomorrow.'

'So cruel, Cleo, but so bewitchingly lovely with it,' he said and his blue eyes laughed down at her with far too much understanding in their depths.

Then, with a neat bow in Alice's direction, he was gone. Other men came, ostensibly to greet Alice or Will, but Caro felt their greedy eyes running over her as if she was some coveted object and was grateful Rob's formidable presence at her side forbade open approaches.

'Do you truly wish to see this play?' he whispered as soon as the interval was over, employing his friend's ploy of leaning far too close to whisper in her ear.

'Yes, of course I do. I should not be here otherwise.'

'I can think of something that might amuse us both a great deal more.'

'Can you, sir?' she asked coolly.

'Of course, cannot you?'

'No, I particularly wanted to see this performance and have every intention of doing so.'

'What a waste when it will still be here tomorrow and next week, but the night, the moon and the stars will never be the same again.'

'I dare say they will be just as bright another night—pray adjourn to the King's Observatory at Greenwich if your fancy is for astronomy, sir, for you do not seem at all interested in the play. I am told it is an excellent venue for those who find stargazing more to their taste than the drama.'

'You are my taste, Cleo, but why not come outside and see if your sister comets are gracing the heavens, instead of a stuffy theatre?'

'Comets fade away all too soon, do they not? I had far rather be a mundane earthbound creature than a shooting star.'

'Just be yourself and I shall be content.'

For a moment he caught something close to agony in her lovely amber eyes, but when he leant forward in concern it was gone and they were frustratingly unreadable again.

'And being myself, sir, I am too wise to venture into the darkness with you a second time,' she said lightly and moved her chair a little further away.

'Still so cruel, Circe?' he asked lightly.

'No, still so prudent rather, Colonel.'

'In your situation, is that altogether possible?' he asked her with the appearance of genuine interest.

'I should say it is of the utmost necessity, for me more than anyone.'

'Excellent, then we may dispose of this dancing about and talk terms. I will have you. You are "a lass unparalleled" and may name your price, fair Cleo.'

That brought her eyes back to him and she regarded him with an odd mix of caution and ironic amusement over his evident frustration. 'As you seem to remember your Shakespeare so well, sir, you will recall that, "there's beggary in the love that can be reckoned" so I shall not yield.'

'Then you will be the least employed wench in your profession.'

'So be it, I can always seek another.'

'What, slave for a sour-faced dame? Scrub floors, trim bonnets, or teach ungrateful brats to despise the very learning you wear so well? No, you were made for love, Cleo, not to eke out your life in some garret while your looks wear away for sheer lack of appreciation. Anyway, no sane woman would employ you, for you are far too beautiful.'

'Am I?' she asked and her smile threatened to wobble. 'Then no doubt time will see to that as well.'

Considering the biting scorn he had often poured on his wife, she found it difficult to believe such extravagant flattery now. She knew perfectly well that she was not classically beautiful, but perhaps the Cleos of this world did not need to be. No doubt they held the allure of the forbidden for a man such as Robert Besford, whose duty clearly lay elsewhere.

'It will see us all off sooner or later,' her husband was saying lightly enough, 'but you were meant for something better, my Cleo.'

'And this is better?'

She could not help some of her bewilderment and anger showing, and suddenly he was looking at her as if he wanted to read her thoughts and get to the very essence of her. She bowed her head and would have veiled her eyes from him, but he put a hand beneath her chin and lifted it to look intently into them.

'Look at me, Cleo!' he demanded. 'Coward,' he whispered as she kept her eyes lowered and pulled away, but at that taunt she stared back at him.

'Not so,' she said proudly, although a voice nagged that he was right, or she would never have run away from him in the first place.

'So I see. I would never leave you abandoned and alone. Indeed, it will be my privilege to look after you, my dear, and I doubt I shall ever let you go.'

'You will—once possessed, an *objet d'art* soon loses its allure,' she said in a hard voice. Robert Besford had left her forlorn and lonely once already—she would be a crass fool to give him the chance to do it again.

'Do not insult either of us by likening yourself to a possession, however lovely,' he said sternly. 'I am not the sort of man who acquires something exquisite and then learns to despise it for being familiar, and you are not a thing to be picked up or put down so lightly, Cleo. You are too much your own person for that.'

'Am I? Yet I do say so. You are a married man, sir, and owe your loyalties elsewhere.' There, that had put the shadows back in his eyes. Perhaps he had a conscience about her after all, but, if he had, he put it behind him quickly enough.

'You will not suffer for my duty, trust me for that. Wherever I am, there will always be a place for you.'

His eyes were intent upon hers, as if he had forgotten the existence of an entire theatre full of people and great bustling, dirty London outside it, as well as his lost wife. Despite the fact that it was her own existence he was ignoring in his haste to claim a mistress, it was beguiling. Caro forgot the game for a moment and almost let herself be seduced by the passionate sincerity on his intent face.

'I don't believe you,' she said at last, examining the sticks of her fan as if their proper arrangement was of the greatest importance to her.

'Very well, then, we must have a contract between us. Have your man of business draw up the document and I will sign it.'

'You said that before and it is very rash of you, Colonel—one day I might take you seriously and then where would you be?' she chided, concentrating on the intricate pattern of shells and fanciful sea creatures on the face of her fan.

'Your terms will be reasonable enough, I dare say.'

That they will not, she thought uncomfortably. In the eyes of the law it would be a sentence for life, and he would never forgive her if he found out.

'I will consider your offer, sir,' she managed to reply coolly. Then, allowing herself to employ a few of the tricks Alice had taught her, she turned a little way back to the stage and sent him a coquettish look from under her eyelashes. 'I believe we are to drive in the park tomorrow.'

'Then I will meet you there.'

'How can you when you have no idea when we intend to set out?'

Her attention was once again upon that fascinating fan. He caught her restless hand, soothing it as if he would quiet the unease he must have sensed through her slender fingers. She slanted a glance up at him, and was surprised by the tender humour in his eyes as he smiled down at her.

'I shall just have to camp out on your doorstep until you do.'

'Pray do not, it would cause even more gossip for my friend. How could I serve her such a backhanded turn when she has been so kind to me?'

'Then appoint a time, and I shall only need to saunter about the Park, waiting for you. For if you are on time, Miss Tournier, you will prove yourself an even more remarkable female than I think you already.'

'Very well, we will be there by three of the clock.'

'Then so will I. Now, if you truly wish to see this play you really must pay it some attention, my lovely,' he teased and she sent him a look of reproach. He responded by insinuating himself closer to her than she found at all good for her peace of mind. 'Consider it my consolation for the loss of your exclusive attention,' he murmured, his teasing fingers busy with hers, until she rapped his knuckles with her fan. Little wonder she found it hard to concentrate on the drama being played out below once the curtains parted again.

In the end he had to go back to his mama and his duty. Oppressed by a sudden weariness, Caro was glad that Alice and her viscount were silent all the way home, too wrapped up in their own romance to remark on her latest encounter with a man she should avoid like the plague. Once they were home, the luxurious room waiting for her, with a welcoming fire glowing in the grate gave her a dangerous sense of comfort. She reminded herself that it was temporary, and there would be no rosy future with her Colonel, as either his wife or his mistress.

She sighed and fought a hot rush of tears. Her likely destiny of humble governess or lowly companion to an elderly lady suddenly seemed unendurable tonight. Was that because she would never meet Robert Besford in such a menial position, or because he would never want to see her again if he found out what she had done?

Once upon a time such a quiet and measured life had seemed a blessed haven from the unpleasant realities of her life—now it looked more like purgatory.

'Are you unwell, Miss Cleo?' the maid who came to dismantle Cleo Tournier and restore something closer to Caro enquired rather hesitantly.

'Of course not,' she said, stiffening her shoulders and raising her chin to challenge the poor, wilting female looking back at her from the dressing mirror. 'I am very well indeed.'

'Good, then I'm sorry to have troubled you, miss.'

Regretting that her reply might be construed as a rebuke, Caro pushed her doubts aside and concentrated on the moment. 'It is never a trouble to be asked after with kindness,' she said with a smile.

'Thank you, miss.' The girl hesitated, then seemed to come to a decision. 'Do you mind if I asks you a question then, miss?'

'Of course not, pray ask away.'

'There's a whisper as Mr Will—his lordship, I mean—is going to wed, and he'll give up this place. So can I come and work for you, miss? Miss Aleysha has Melby, so she doesn't need me and I don't want to go back to Vale.'

Caro paled. She had witnessed Alice's happiness tonight, and the thought of Lord Wrovillton contracting a marriage of convenience seemed like a brutal betrayal. Were all men so coldly logical when it came to marriage, then? Of course they were, she chided herself crossly. Rob had married her for money and his lordship would wed a débutante of impeccable reputation to breed his heirs, while he consigned Alice's loving heart to the devil once again.

'There, I knew I shouldn't have said anything tonight. You're white as a sheet now and I dare say that nasty theatre was hot and noisy. You bide there quietly, miss, while I go and fetch one of cook's possets.'

The girl bustled out of the room as Caro tried to tell herself that such was the way of the world, but it did not stop her raving silently at the injustice of it all. Alice was for ever condemned by the polite world, while the unspeakable rogue who had abducted, abused and then abandoned Alice Stoneleigh at the age of sixteen still had entrée to the fringes of society. The double standard that regarded a gentleman as proving his manhood by sowing his wild oats, while a lady must remain as inviolate as driven snow, stiffened her backbone. She had almost been regretting what she was doing, but this news braced her.

If she was truly Cleo Tournier instead of Caroline Besford, Rob's attentions to her were no better that his friend's in making poor Alice tumble headlong in love with him, then deserting her for a débutante. She conveniently forgot that money was deeply enmeshed with love in her friend's relations with her protector. Sometimes wilful ignorance was necessary to maintain the sanity of a pair of females dangerously adrift from the world they had been brought up in, and without the luxury of family or any friends besides each other.

For the first time since Alice suggested this infamous imposture, Caro took on the role thrust upon her and began to truly live it. From now on she would forget despised little Caroline and truly become forward, desirable Cleo, she told herself militantly. Then she would trample all over Rob's deepest feelings and humble his pride, just as he had destroyed her hopes and mocked her dreams without a qualm. And wasn't he doing so still? Losing him a second time might hurt her far more than his rejection and stony silence after their wedding ever had.

She was too angry to examine the idea that her feelings might be perilously close to Alice's for her Will. Nothing could have survived the cruelty of that treacherous kiss on their wedding day, she reassured herself. No, she was going to take revenge for herself and all the unfortunate females taken in by a gentleman's easy smile and pretend affection, no more and no less.

By the time the maid returned she had herself under control again and accepted the posset gratefully. She would never sleep without it, and she must be in looks tomorrow if she was to lure Robert Besford ever deeper into her gossamer web of lies. It didn't occur to her to wonder what she would do with him once she had extracted his plea to share her bed, the one she had threatened him with on their wedding day.

'I'm not sure if I shall be in a position to employ you, Emily,' she told the maid as she quietly cleared away the fine plumage of a bird of paradise, 'but I can give you a good reference. Although even the most glowing testimonial from the likes of me is unlikely to get you employment in the best households.'

'Oh, no, miss, I want to be like Melby and dress the high-flyers.'

Caro doubted if working for other courtesans was as comfortable as doing so for Alice, but she was too tired to argue. She was glad to just sit as the girl gently brushed out her newly auburn curls. Her eyes began to feel heavy and her racing mind started to slow. At last she was in a warm bed with the candles snuffed and the fire banked for the night. She nuzzled her face into the lace-trimmed pillows and just let her lazy thoughts drift for once. The trouble was they drifted back to the first time she ever set eyes on Robert Besford, one memorable evening that had begun like all the others.

The music had been loud, the ballroom stifling and, out of sheer boredom, Miss Caroline Warden had eaten too much at supper again and felt rather sick. How she had longed to walk out of the Countess of Foxwell's splendid ballroom, but the thought of her father's anger if she did kept her playing the wallflower. She was sitting out yet another dance with Lord and Lady Littleworth when his brother came to join them.

Until that moment there had been little to mark the ball out from all the other tedious, uncomfortable evenings since her father's money had launched her into society. Then, between one second and the next, she fell in love with a scarlet coat, a powerful masculine physique and a pair of laughing green eyes. Apart from that, it had just been an ordinary evening. Did she truly wish herself back in the past to undo it and become Mrs Cordale Westman, as her chaperon and Mr Westman's godmama had intended? Not even for the peace of mind that eluded her now, she thought drowsily, and finally fell asleep.

In her dreams she was dancing in Rob's arms. Helpless to control the fantasy she drifted on, enclosed in a bubble of happiness her everyday self knew was fragile as a cobweb. She muttered something incomprehensible into her pillows and tried to hold on to that delightful feeling, even as it drifted out of reach. Rob had pulled away from her now, and was regarding her as if she was a creature from the lowest pit of hell. He was laughing, and there was an empty cruelty in his eyes.

'You thought I loved you?' he asked incredulously. 'I told you I would get a moll from the Haymarket to warm my bed before I lay in yours. I could never love you!'

Waking up in a cold sweat and a tangle of bedclothes, she lay gasping with relief as those phantom words echoed round her head. Her nightmare had reminded her of her wedding day, and there could be no surer way of destroying any lingering romance the dreamer in her might harbour. She forced herself to recall every detail of that bitter scene to make her less-practical self abandon all hope of a happy ending. Her waking dealings with the noble Colonel were all about deception and revenge, and she would do well to remember it every time the silly romantic girl she had once been tried to linger over lost dreams.

Chapter Six

Just before three that afternoon, two dazzling Cyprians descended the steps to Miss Watson's barouche, regally ignoring their disapproving neighbours and gawping idlers alike. Miss Watson was in her finest looks, and glowed with health and high spirits as she stepped into her elegant carriage and turned to smile encouragingly at her protégée.

'Pray hurry, Cleo dear, or we shall be late after all,' she urged, as if she had no idea that her friend was having second thoughts about their outing.

'Maybe we could send Addey with a note,' Caro replied, standing on the pavement and trembling cravenly at the very thought of encountering Rob and temptation once again, whatever plans she had made for his downfall the night before.

Despite her dreams of revenge, when he was close and warmly teasing, she was in danger of agreeing to anything he wanted to keep him so. Once they wandered down that path there could be no quiet annulment for them. She flushed at the very thought, and Alice laughed out loud, as if she could read her racing thoughts.

'Oh, come along, do, or we shall be late. If I ever met such a ditherer, I am pleased to say I cannot recall them. Pray hand Miss Cleo up, Addey, before our neighbours are finally carried off by the apoplexy.'

Caro finally climbed into the barouche and Alice gave the order to move off before she could change her mind again.

'Just remember that he wants you, love, and you want him. You are too good at letting silly scruples get in the way of what you most desire, and tomorrow it might be gone.'

Caro wondered if this advice didn't pertain to Alice's situation as much as her own, but she was still right. She would enjoy this golden spring day, and the novelty of being beautifully groomed, exquisitely gowned and desired by at least two handsome rakes. The moment held too many attractions not to be seized as eagerly as her friend suggested.

Of course, her disdainful chaperon had taken her for drives in the park during her come out, but this trip was a different matter altogether. Where once the fashionable throng had overwhelmed and ignored her, today she and Alice majestically disdained the 'quality' and greeted the stylish *demimondaines* with smiles and nods, cool or friendly according to their temperament and aspirations. Alice pointed out the notorious Harriette Wilson, and Caro wondered what the fuss was about, but, as she was not a gentleman, she supposed she could be no judge of a coquette's charms.

'She is not half as beautiful as you,' she said loyally, and the cluster of gentlemen who besieged their carriage as soon as it halted evidently agreed with her.

'Would you care to take a stroll away from the chattering magpies, Miss Tournier?' drawled the one voice she could have singled out in the Tower of Babel itself.

'It would be pleasant to stretch my legs, Colonel.'

How fast to be able to claim possession of such outrageous nether limbs, she decided with a quirk of her painted lips, she could only suppose innocent society belles were commonly held to run on wheels!

He bowed rather ironically, held out his hand to help her descend, then led her towards a secluded grove Miss Warden would never have dared visit, even if she had possessed a beau stalwart enough to lure her into it. Content for once to take what she wanted, Caro let her small hand lie in the crook of his arm and felt singingly alive in every curve and extremity. The feel of his well-muscled arm beneath hers and the tender half-smile on his firm mouth were enough to blot out all else as he guided her towards dangerous solitude.

'You look even more ravishing than usual, my dear,' Rob told her and watched her blush, telling himself how lucky he had been to find such an exotic bloom with some of the dew still on it.

Today she was dressed in a shade of amber that matched her lovely lioness's eyes, and her pelisse was beautifully cut to reveal rather than conceal her delicious figure. The dancing plumes on her frivolous bonnet now and then curved down to kiss her cheek, and made him fantasise about doing likewise, before moving on to ravage the artfully reddened mouth beneath.

It was all done so tastefully that a man might forget he was being driven to the edge of reason by the artful promise of future delights. A cynical voice whispered that such exquisite presentation was designed to extract the maximum amount of cash from a rich man's pockets. The idea of his Cleo grown hard and ruthless brought a grim frown to his brow, and she struggled to regain her hand.

'Forgive me,' he said gently. 'I was thinking of something else.'

Caro found that she could not bring herself to twit him about the odd whisper that she had heard was doing the rounds: that his wife had run away rather than retreated to the countryside as the Besfords claimed. Luckily, most people apparently believed the family, but some were always eager to think the worst. The shiver that ran down her back was a mixture of fizzing excitement and chilly apprehension—the first from being with him, the second because the consequences, if ever she was found out, did not bear thinking of.

'You are cold, my Cleo? I would very much like to kiss you into warmth right here and now, but I suppose I must wait until we are a little more private rather than cause a scandal and a hissing.'

'That you must, sir, if I ever permit such liberties,' she gasped, quite forgetting for the moment that liberties were a courtesan's stock in trade in her hurry to deny the flush of heat that scorched through her at the very idea.

'I think you will, though, Cleo,' he replied, as if they were discussing some abstruse problem of logic. 'It's my belief that our previous encounters have haunted you as persistently as they have me, or am I even more of a want-wit than I thought?'

He looked as if her answer was a mere matter of curiosity, until she finally found the courage to meet his eyes, blazing bright green with barely contained passion. She gazed back, the flippant reply that would hold him at arm's length suddenly unsayable. All the same, mischief sparkled in her tawny eyes for a moment as the sheer novelty of their situation occurred to her. Who would have dreamt Robert Besford would ever want plain, dumpy Caroline Warden so badly?

He laughed triumphantly as her eyes boldly met his, and the sound turned a good many heads towards them as they continued towards those very improper trees. The fact that the gossips soon turned away to exchange scandalised whispers, took some of the gilt off Caro's gingerbread. Very soon the whole town would echo with the news that Robert Besford was hotly pursuing a mistress, while his wife went to the devil in some unspecified fashion.

If they only knew how right they were, all the scandal would be suddenly be directed at her, but she shrugged the idea aside. Society had disapproved of Caroline Warden ever since it reluctantly became aware of her existence, so she told herself she could live without its approval now. Yet even so a qualm still threatened to spoil her idyll. Rob had been accustomed to the acceptance of his peers since he was out of short-coats, and had stalwartly endured the adulation of so many of the aristocratic young ladies who looked on her as an ill-bred upstart. If her secret got out, he would be publicly pilloried along with her and how could she do such a thing to a man she had so wanted to love once upon a time?

She reminded herself that this was her golden afternoon, and nothing so solemn as portents of doom or scruples should dim it for her. She snuggled her hand into the pocket of Rob's great-coat, and made no protest when his large one crept in to join it. The moment would be over all too soon, and she intended to wring the last ounce of pleasure out of it before it vanished.

'Will you, Cleo?' Rob asked in a low, husky voice, as those alluring trees grew ever closer.

She stopped watching her own steps and looked up into his face, seeing he desperately wanted her answer to be yes from the white strain around his firm mouth, and the blaze of need in his eyes as they met hers, unguarded by his usual cynicism. Could she do it? Should she take such a ridiculous risk with her heart after what he had done to her?

Yes, she could, and, no, she should not, but she was suddenly afraid that she would. It was too soon for her to tell him so, though. Firstly, there was no need to give him more cause to hold a higher opinion of himself than he already had. And, secondly, she could not resist the temptation of teaching *him* how it felt to be unsure of the object of one's desire, even if that was all she would ever be to him.

'I am not sure. Could I have a week to decide?'

She briefly saw disillusionment flicker in his eyes, before his austerely handsome features assumed the sardonic expression she was more used to seeing.

'I suppose you mean to play your admirers off against one another and see who will come up with the best offer?' he said, his chilly expression making the question all the more hurtful.

'Is that not the custom of my profession, sir?' she said, struggling to remove her hand from a grip that was suddenly punishing.

She wondered if she had tweaked the tiger's tail a little too briskly this time, but there he was off again and it behoved her to listen, even if it was to her *congé*.

'What, then? You cannot pretend you are not attracted to me after our first two meetings.'

'Sometimes I wish I could forget you existed, Colonel. Even you must admit to being something of a stormy petrel,' she said lightly.

'And you think you are alone in that wish? Sometimes I dream of what my life would have been like if I never laid eyes on you, and thus stayed sane,' he ground out, unsportingly refusing to play along, and looking like a man driven by demons. 'Let us finally take the gloves off, Miss Tournier,' he said brusquely. 'You know how I am situated. I should not be here at all, but heaven help me, I cannot stay away from you. Being hopelessly in thrall to you, I am in sore need of an answer.'

Caro did not know what to say. There was a driven frustration in his voice that made it seem unlikely he was simply playing the rake. Yet, try as she might, she could not believe he felt any more than a passionate attraction towards an outwardly sophisticated and available female. His enjoyment of her kisses and his need of something even more intimate and passionate from her was self-evident, given those two encounters he spoke of, but what of her mind?

It seemed to her that her true self was as closed to him as it had ever been, but on the other hand, did even she know who she was any more? A confusion of hurt, exhilaration and fascination had made her stay and parley with him, when she knew perfectly well she should be in Bath, learning how little to expect of life as a schoolmistress. The silence stretched as she stood contemplating him as if he was a puzzle she might solve if she looked hard enough, when he groaned as if he was in pain.

'Say yes to me, Cleo! I am burning up with need of you and you must grant me relief.'

If things were as they should be, he was right. She would have had to overcome this anxiety about a deeper intimacy between them, if she had truly been his convenient wife. Well, she would do it and nobody but herself and Alice need be any the wiser. Who would protest if Robert Besford petitioned for an annulment, when everyone knew he and his wife had never lived together? She was beyond the pale as a wife, but why not take what he offered as his mistress, especially when she wanted it so much herself?

'I am so tempted,' she finally admitted in a voice so low that he had to bend closer to hear it.

She saw triumph blaze in eyes now darkly green and mused at how perfectly they mirrored his emotions, where once she had found them cold and impenetrable. Not knowing whether to laugh or cry at taking this final, awesome leap in the dark, she held up her hand.

'But not yet convinced, Colonel Besford.'

Sensing the hard tension in his impressive body as she added this caveat, she sent him an appealing look.

'I am new to this game, sir. Would you rush me like a mere amateur? I had thought better of your skills as a lover, but first impressions so often lie, do they not?'

Now that was mischief with a vengeance. She wondered if she had used up all her leeway, but it was so heady to feel in control that she stubbornly maintained her square, continuing to look limpidly into his compelling eyes and hoping he could not read her thoughts.

'You, madam, are a minx,' Rob told her, trying not to laugh because he knew he was being subtly informed he had not yet won a mere doxy to his bed. However lovely she was—and she was driving him crazy with her allure, her subtle scent, her closeness—he assured himself that was all she was. Well, not quite all, as she would soon unman him with a mere glance under those curling lashes of hers if he failed to impose rigid self-control on his baser impulses.

'And you, sir, are a fraud. Here was I, convinced you were the devil of a fellow who would sweep me off my feet, and it turns out that you are only a mountebank after all.'

'You will not divert me twice by teasing me into a temper, termagant. Give me the answer I crave, or I will haunt you night and day like a bad oyster.'

She chuckled unaffectedly at that—he was serving her with her own sauce and she liked it far better than his assumption that she would fall on the ground at his feet on demand like a circus horse.

'What a fate, but even bad food may be got over with a little care and good nursing. Why, even such feelings as you claim are but a passing sickness, and I have heard the recovery rate is astonishingly rapid.'

'Then you have been misinformed, my Cleo. I am one of your constant fellows who tumble at their adored one's feet, struck straight through the heart with a dart from her flashing eyes. I fear I shall never recover from my wounds.'

'And I that you are a mere Romeo who forsook his lady love at a glance from Juliet—he was a fickle youth to stand as the example of man's fidelity to his love, was he not?'

'Yet he died for it.'

'Ah, but did he die for love or for folly, I wonder?'

'Better an ounce of honest folly than all your wise logic-chopping, fairest Diana.'

'So now I have been promoted to playing a goddess? One no man could look at because she was chaste as the moon? Hardly apposite, I think you will agree, Colonel.'

Some of her bitterness at her ambiguous situation crept into her husky voice, and his eyes were intent upon her, his powerful intelligence suddenly concentrated on that very dilemma. She cursed herself for a bungling idiot, and forced her eyes to meet his with only a hint of cool irony in their amber depths. The very last thing she wanted was for him to wonder about her motives for seeking the half-life of a courtesan.

'Outside Arcadia things are never quite as they ought to be,' he said gently, seeking to comfort a lightskirt for the fallen status he was hot to make full and satisfying use of.

Yet that hint of vulnerability she sometimes let show was enough to pluck a man's heart from his breast, Rob thought, and he could not help wanting to protect her in the real sense of the word. He thought of his past amours and wondered ruefully if they would recognise their carefree lover in the besotted fool he had become.

The truth was that she engaged a part of him no other woman had ever managed to touch, and he wanted to explore the intriguing twists and turns of her acute mind—as well as her fabulous body and that wicked, generous mouth so temptingly close to his own. He could not envisage a day when he would grow bored with her questing intelligence and quick wits, in the unlikely event that they one day managed to wear out this driving need to explore every curve and crevice of her delicious body in pursuit of their mutual ecstasy. He pushed the idea that he was in deeper than he had ever been before to the back of his mind and concentrated on the moment. Somehow her answer was too important to allow either scruples or reservations to get in the way.

'You seem to be mistaking me for something I am not, Colonel,' she told him as if her words held a significance he could not even guess at.

'No mistake, I knew you at first glance,' he told her in an intimate whisper and felt the fine-boned hand jerk in his as if she intended to pull away from him at the last minute. She gave a rather forced laugh and her smile went awry.

'Knew me for what I am, you mean.'

'The woman I need, the one who needs me,' he managed finally, yet his mind was racing.

Now he considered the matter coolly, he had never met a Cyprian less at ease with her strange world, for all her wit and laughter. Some mystery lay behind the shadows in her lovely golden eyes, and he suddenly needed to explore it as well as the delicious secrets of her lovely form.

'A woman's needs are so seldom in tune with a gentleman's,' she was saying, and he forced himself to concentrate on their verbal duel, instead of the unplumbed depths of his siren's artfully enhanced eyes.

'Yet yours would prove so to me,' he replied smoothly—why should he not serve her with her own sauce while he considered his next move?

'How can you say so when you have no idea what they are?'

'Easily, my Cleo—what you need and desire, I long for too. Come now, my lovely, I am no green boy to be lost in a maze created by your ready tongue and there is a fire burns between us hotter than any I have ever known—even when you attempt to deny it.'

'Perhaps not deny, sir, but I have the sense to fear the flames lest they immolate me.'

'Then let me look to your safety, Cleo, and promise to be mine, before we are both consumed by frustration instead of passion.'

He tugged her hand out of his pocket and impudently stripped off her glove to place her naked fingers on his brow. She was glad they had wandered into one of the more secluded walkways, away from the eyes of a censorious world at last, although tongues were probably wagging busily enough as they disappeared into the forbidden shadows. Even her legs felt weak now, as the feel of his skin against her slender fingers shot heat right through her.

She remembered vaguely that they had been talking of just such dangers before he chose to demonstrate their power. To explore his features with her hands, to search every pore, every laugh line and sharply defined contour was a luxury of singing temptation, and blood thundered in her ears as she fought for control. He was making such fine ideas a mockery, for now both his gloves were off and the touch of his bare, questing fingers on *her* face was light as thistledown; he aroused a fever everywhere he caressed her so gently. Now his index finger was, oh, so gently, exploring her rose-tinted lips, and she gasped as the raw power of sensation dragged at her very core.

If he set his own mouth where his fingers lingered and teased her, she would surely flame out of control, or sink to the ground and let him do whatever he pleased. Fortunately for both of them in such a very public place, he had self-control and experience enough to resist such dangerous possibilities. She reminded herself that he was very much a man of the world, as he carefully stepped away without touching her further.

As the gap between them increased, misunderstanding widened with it. For him to provoke such a response with the mere rub of his long finger across her face, to dally and dip into her mouth like a lover and then depart like a stranger—Surely that made him a hardened seducer, to possess such finely honed self-discipline that it left her own at the starting gate?

'My point, I think, Miss Tournier,' he told her coolly, for all the world as if they were a pair of octogenarians playing piquet in front of the parlour fire, instead of potential lovers burning with unsatisfied desire.

'No, say mine rather, as you have just proved yourself a rake, sir.'

'Any self-respecting rake would take such a willing lady behind the nearest tree and have his way with her right here and now to their mutual satisfaction, like the upright man he is. I prove myself to be myself,' he said, but the idea had appeal all the same, and he had to look away lest he carry out that shocking programme and undo them both after all.

Caro felt herself turning bright red and averted her head as well. Did he truly believe he might tumble her whenever and wherever he pleased, as if she was a receptive parlourmaid and he an underemployed footman with time to spare for seduction? Yet by this masquerade, she had set herself up for such assumptions, and a wanton part of her cried out with need and curiosity to let him do just as he threatened. Well, she wasn't about to be ruled by such dim-witted impulses, she decided militantly, and turned away from her ungallant suitor to march towards Alice's carriage with her nose in the air.

Maybe this terrible need to be near him, to take whatever crumbs he bothered to offer her, would be sated if passion no longer ruled them. Maybe, but deep down she knew better. Her need went much deeper than a desire for a quick tumble in this man's bed, or out of it. It was unfair, but her infatuation with her handsome colonel had not been the product of loneliness and an over-vivid imagination. After what he had done to her, she should despise him, yet it seemed that her silly heart was firmly fixed on loving him, and reason was useless in the face of such determined folly.

'What a stinging revenge you have wrought upon your errant husband, Caro,' she told herself scornfully.

Railing at the gods for granting her what she had once longed for, in a form she could never truly enjoy, would do her little good when she still had to face the world, and her husband, with a courtesan's careless composure. She owed her pride the appearance of cool detachment at least, even if all pretence of it had fallen away in the face of reality.

With his longer stride it did not take him long to catch up

with her, so she swiftly got her emotions firmly under the airy control Alice had taught her was the armour of a successful Cyprian. The sobering effect of discovering herself to be disastrously besotted with a rake of the first order, she supposed, and glared at him accusingly.

'I am so glad you have finally slowed down, my lovely, you will have the gossips thinking I threatened to ravish you on the spot if you had continued to march back at the double,' he told her with an irrepressible twinkle in his eyes.

'Sir, you are impudent,' she informed him haughtily.

'Lady, I am not alone,' he drawled.

'Then you soon will be, for I am going home.'

'Are you, Cleo?' he asked quizzically and, all on end as she discovered she still was, the irony in his question brought weak tears to her eyes.

She had no home. The only place she had ever felt any sense of belonging was in the spartan little room she, Alice and two other girls had shared at school. Refusing to feel sorry for herself, she fought a sudden sense of desolation and met his eyes defiantly.

'Yes, and when I get there I shall give orders not to admit you, for I have no desire to consort with rufflers and scoldrums.'

'Very commendable—it would never do for a lady to associate with those who use thieves' cant.'

'You are no gentleman, sir.'

He seemed quite unruffled by this conclusion.

'No, I am a mere soldier and, as such, I leave poetry and posturing to those who have more time to practise them. Come, Cleo, admit you want me as badly as I do you, and this shilly-shallying is nothing but a carefully wrapped-up negotiation. Well, I give up—you can have anything you want.

Except you may not have my favourite horse, for I like him very well, and he would be too strong for you anyway.'

'You make a jest of everything, do you not?'

'Only so I do not cry at the moon, like a crazed dog on fire for his—'

Dreading to hear a word she could not admit herself to be on his lips, she hastily clamped her hand over his mouth. She drew back as soon as she realised what she had done by touching him so publicly, looking about in horror in case anyone else had seen such a betrayal of intimacy.

They were lucky; the Prince Regent's curricle had just arrived, and all eyes were intent on the lady at his side. Not Lady Hertford today, but the glint of a determinedly golden curl against a carefully shaded cheek heralded the arrival of the Countess of Foxwell herself. Caro had never thought she would be thankful for her mother-in-law's presence, and decided her world must indeed have turned on its head.

Chapter Seven

'I was only going to say on fire for his lady love, you know,' Rob murmured and turned her away from the spectacle fascinating the crowd.

'I am neither a lady nor your love, and well you know it.'

'Loathe though I am to argue with a lady, for you are one unless I am very much mistaken, you know nothing of the matter if you think I would beg for mercy from a mere passing fancy. I have my pride, Cleo, even if it is occasionally to be found lying face down in the dust.'

She was sure that was a reference to what, or rather who, had just passed in the Regent's carriage and compassion made her look enquiringly into his eyes at last. What she saw there left her breathless, and a little bemused. It was true—the intensity of his gaze seemed as if it might burn her with the strength of his feelings. She moved him in some way beyond the heady desire that ran between them like wildfire whenever they were together, and that extra pull was nearly impossible to resist.

'It may seem to you I know all the tricks of the game you would play with me, sir, but in truth I would know you better before we…before I… Oh, you know perfectly well what I mean,' she ended rather crossly, because his look of pent-up need had given place to one of amused exultation.

She had capitulated and they both knew it. Triumph blazed in his eyes, a careless, boyish smile lifted his firm mouth and only added to her dazed enchantment. Such a wicked little boy he must once have been; she wondered if his nurses and tutors had found as much difficulty resisting the knowing rascal's laughing eyes as she did now. She imagined him, ever knee-deep in mischief, and almost laughed aloud herself, her troubled conscience silent for once in the face of his obvious elation.

'I do, perfectly, and it seems it is just as well that one of us does. You shall have your week, lovely Cleo, and I will court you as carefully as the most devoted lover in history, but I warn you not to expect a second longer.' He took out his watch and examined it closely, 'I have the exact measure of it, so do not try to cheat me, or my revenge will be terrible indeed.'

He laughed down at her, and she decided that he both bemused and bewildered her in this mood. If she had not fallen head over heels in love with him at their first meeting, she might well have done so now she saw the man nature had intended him to be.

'Can I have my hand back?' she said, dazed by him and unable to think of anything more significant to say.

He looked puzzled for a moment, and then looked down and registered the crushing pressure he was putting it under.

'I am sorry, my Cleo. I was carried away, but I dare say I have made you black and blue. Promise me never to put up with such villainy again.'

'I promise, and if only all vows were so easily given,' she said carelessly, then could have kicked herself as she saw a shadow in his eyes.

Maybe he remembered the uneasy, angry ceremony that lay between them like a pall after all.

'You are a woman of your word, I hope?' Rob said. 'If not, I shall be forced to kidnap you and carry you off to my lair. Once I get you there, I give you fair warning that you will probably never even see another man, for I intend to be a very possessive lover, my Cleo.'

'Then it is just as well my honour is as important to me as yours is to you, is it not, sir?'

She caught the fleeting mockery in his extraordinary eyes before he veiled it, but that was enough to make her frown.

'I believe you,' he said softly and she looked up to see steadfast sincerity in his gaze this time. 'My only caveat is that you learn to call me Rob, for I will not be just "sir" to you of all people.'

'Very well, Rob, if that is what you wish.'

'As *you* wish, Cleo,' he corrected with a look that could easily have melted a heart far harder than her own. 'Just so long as you are mine, everything shall be just as you wish.'

'Good,' she said, merriment rising to the surface again out of sheer joy at seeing him smile down at her, however deceived he might be and however skilfully her rake of a husband had been stalking his prey. 'Then there is indeed a first time for everything.'

If Rob was surprised by her request to visit the Tower of London on the first day of her week, at least he did all he could to make the excursion memorable and, as her father had kept her very close since her return from school, she was as curious about her own city as any bumpkin up from the country.

At Rob's side she marvelled at the Mint and the Armoury and shivered at the sword the yeoman guardsman insisted was used to execute poor Queen Anne Boleyn. She was less impressed when a green curtain was whisked aside and a portrait of the lady's great daughter revealed, like a cheap tableau at a fair. Then the set of rooms where the then Princess Elizabeth had been imprisoned by her elder sister Mary Tudor had her grasping Rob's arm for comfort, glad to be close to the reassuring warmth and strength of his tall body.

'How very close she came to death, that poor lonely little princess,' she exclaimed in horror. 'No wonder she has such a secret look in her portraits.'

'Whatever the reason, her experiences certainly honed her into a great queen, so perhaps Prinny could have done with a similar sojourn in his youth to put a little backbone into him.' His laughing eyes invited her to share his ludicrous fantasy of that most petulant and charming of princes, living anywhere that was not luxurious to the point of excess.

'Shush! You will get us both locked up in the nearest tower.'

'Then my mother will have to intercede with his Highness upon our behalf, will she not?' he remarked with bitter cynicism, and Caro nearly quailed at the uncomfortable thought that she was as busy deceiving her husband as her mother-in-law was at cuckolding the Earl.

'Could we not change the subject? I have no liking for being confined at the best of times,' she said, and that much was true at least.

'I should imagine you have an excellent pair of lungs, my dear, so you could always scream the place down if anyone tried to lock you away.'

'Of course they would not dare to imprison you in the first place, you being such a fearsome military gentleman!'

He twisted a set of imaginary whiskers and Caro smiled as

he swaggered in the wake of their guide, so she could picture the strutting braggadocio he was imitating. She laughed joyfully, and even the stoic old soldier who was guiding them thought it worth putting up with his nonsense to hear such a happy sound enliven the gloomy old place.

Rob agreed, and would have made a fool of himself ten times over to prevent that wistful, haunted look returning to his inamorata's lovely eyes. Heaven alone knew what caused her to take up her imperfect new life, but if he ever found the man who had put the shadows in her honey-gold gaze he would destroy the crass oaf without mercy.

The Menagerie was less amusing than Caro had expected. She felt sorry for the poor beasts pacing their cages and the stench was enough to bring on a fit of the vapours in one more susceptible to such maladies.

'I imagine they would have been much happier left in their natural state,' she said at last.

'I am sure of it, but perhaps the local inhabitants wished otherwise,' he reasoned gently.

'I suppose lions and tigers might make uncomfortable neighbours, and I dare say it is good for us all to know that there is life in this great world beyond little England. I would far rather see such magnificent creatures roaming about in the wild, though,' she said wistfully, certain that she would never do so.

'Speaking as someone who has had that dubious pleasure, I am not quite so sure I would,' he said ruefully.

'Were you with the Duke in India, then?'

'Yes, I even had the privilege of receiving a royal tongue lashing from him for taking part in an illicit night-time tiger hunt with some of the sepoys.'

''Ere, was you Ensign Besford of the 33rd, sir?' their guide questioned, suddenly abandoning his dignified aloofness.

'I was once in the 33rd, but that was a long time ago,' Rob said with a frown that told Caro, if not his new friend, that he didn't wish to relive past deeds, or misdeeds.

'Former Colour Sergeant Bradley, sir. You saved my life at Assaye,' the old soldier informed him and saluted smartly.

'I am very pleased to hear it, although I must say I do not remember you. It was a long time ago, and the action was devilishly hot that day.'

'That it was, sir, hot as it comes and very glad I was to get this billet after I was invalided out. From what I heared, yours ain't been anything like so soft neither.'

'I doubt if the Beau believed any of us were in the army for the sake of our health, do you, Sergeant Bradley?'

'Very likely not, sir, but I heared as you transferred to that newfangled Light Division and they're always sent wherever the action's hottest.'

'Oh, we usually let the Rifles take the worst of the fire while we watch their backs,' Rob said, looking hunted, but Caro nodded encouragingly at the yeoman. After all, she was unlikely to learn about the unimaginable reality of a soldier's life from her husband.

'I suppose your regiment are known as the Fighting 52nd because you sit behind the lines and hold tea parties, Colonel?' she asked mildly and her new ally laughed delightedly.

'That they do not, ma'am, their officers is all come-ons.' Seeing her look of bewilderment, he explained, 'Two sorts of officer, ma'am, them as says come on, you b—men, let's up and at 'em, and them as stays behind and tells us to go and get 'em while they keeps their dandy uniforms nice and clean like.'

'What a time you must have had of it in such a regiment, Colonel. Dodging all those bullets and hiding from the French.'

'Oh, I did, it was devilish inconvenient at times, I might tell you, and I fear I am no more than a brevet colonel playing at staff officers. There is only one man who deserves the Regiment's leadership apart from Sir John Moore, God rest his soul, and that's Colborne.'

'Ah, well,' said Sergeant Bradley, nodding sagaciously at this attempted diversion from a discussion of Rob's more daring deeds, 'you gentlemen always would have your little joke, and they always said you was worse than most, sir.'

'I warrant he was, Sergeant. How very glad I am not to have been his unfortunate commanding officer.'

'I cannot tell you how fervently I agree with you, my dear,' he said, having his revenge by eyeing her laughing countenance with bold appreciation.

Caro flushed and hardly knew where to look, and the old soldier compounded her embarrassment by chuckling at her discomfiture.

'Yes, well, we must be getting on if we are to meet the others for luncheon, must we not?' she said brightly.

'Must we, my dear? If you say so,' Rob said, his teasing look telling her how much he enjoyed turning the tables on her.

'Then I'd be honoured if you would shake my hand afore you goes, sir? Been wantin' to thank you ever since that day you stopped me hoppin' the twig.'

'Of course,' Rob replied and solemnly did so, before re-possessing Caro's hand as if their contact was precious to him and wishing their new friend a pleasant goodbye.

'Good luck to you both, sir and madam. I hope you'm blessed with a pack of little 'uns as lively as mine before very long,' the man said in the way of a farewell, and it was Caro's turn to feel discomfited.

The gallant old soldier took them for a respectable couple

when, in the eyes of the world, they were so much less. The facts did not make any difference. Rob thought she was Haymarket ware and so did everyone except Alice, who with the best will in the world could do nothing to protect her from the contempt of so-called 'good' society.

They soon reached the inn where they had left the dashing high-perch phaeton, and the superb pair of greys were harnessed in double quick time. Caro was still trying to catch her breath from being boosted up into the high vehicle by Rob's strong hands about her slender waist, when the groom sprang up behind and Rob took the light carriage out of the narrow inn-yard with the quiet assurance of a master whip.

She was acutely conscious of his lithe movements in the restricted space, as he controlled the spirited pair with the lightest of touches on the reins. The greys knew as well as she did that there was formidable strength behind his gentleness, and she wondered impatiently if she had developed a fascination for the knife-edge of danger. Mrs Besford knew the perils of goading her husband until he lost hold of his more primitive instincts, so why was foolish Cleo Tournier wilfully toying with his formidable self-control?

Was it because she could then blame his fiery emotions for provoking her own improper desires? Or because she had sensed the deep reserves of passion behind his cool façade the first moment she laid eyes on him? If so, she certainly had a tiger by the tail now, she decided. Today the fire between them threatened to burn through her at the slightest touch of his gloved hand on hers, and she was helpless to control the way her breath hitched with excitement every time his gaze touched her.

While he was preoccupied with the lively team, she cast his austerely handsome profile a wondering look. Today he had behaved as a gentleman would in the presence of a lady of impeccable reputation. If she was not beginning to know him, she might have thought there was a fine thread of mockery running through that polite restraint. No, he was treating her with respect because he thought her an honest whore and she didn't deserve it.

She cast him another thoughtful look as she mused on such a transformation of feeling as she had undergone since she embarked on this infamous masquerade. Was it really only after her visit to the play that she had resolved to trample on his finer feelings as ruthlessly as he had on hers? Two days later and he possessed that rash promise of hers, along with her silly heart. What a devastating revenge this promises to be, Mrs Besford, she chided herself with a quick frown, but, fleeting as it was, he still noticed it.

'Tired, Cleo?' he asked, eyes once more on his cattle and the busy street.

'Not I,' she replied and flashed him a smile that she hoped would dispel the idea that she was such a paltry creature.

'Then keep your chin up, my lovely, and pray don't frown at me as if I dragged you out against your will, or my already rather tarnished credit will soon hit rock bottom.'

'You are beforehand with the world, Colonel. Being a hero as well as an aristocrat and a man of means, even I know that you have a deal more tolerance to call upon than the rest of us mere mortals.'

'Even if you were right, which I dispute, I think you may safely say I am close to the limits of it by now,' he said ruefully and she found it impossible to smile and look carefree in the light of such a conclusion.

Half of her wanted to spend every possible minute with him, while the other part warned that being seen with her did his reputation no good at all. She should make him stop away, or meet him in secret. Instinct alone stilled her tongue from even suggesting it, for he would never agree. Somehow she knew that just as surely as if they had actually gone through the arguments in favour of stealth and he had proved immovable.

She cast him a look that was as much made up of exasperation as admiration and spent the rest of their journey thinking up ways to circumvent his ridiculous notions of honour.

When they arrived back at Alice's neat little house, Rob told his groom to take the equipage back to Berkeley Square and the man gave Caro a bold, knowing leer as he handed her down from the high carriage.

'If you wish to lose your place, Webb, go on behaving just as you are now,' Rob snapped as he intercepted that impudent grin.

Instantly the man was impassive, his eyes never veering from the road as he took the reins from his frowning master and drove the elegant carriage away with neat precision.

'I can only apologise, Cleo. He has been my groom since I joined up and has often proved himself to be as brave as he is impudent.'

'It would be foolish to blame the man for showing openly what everyone else just thinks,' she said in a hard voice and stalked ahead of him with her nose in the air.

No doubt Webb imagined they would spend the afternoon in some sinful fashion she had not yet quite got sorted out in her mind, and who could blame him, considering what she was pretending to be?

'I will set you up somewhere else, my sweet Cleo. We can pretend to be man and wife and it will save you all this,' he told her, catching up with her and seizing her arm so she had to look at him. 'Truly, you were not made for this game,' he told her and pulled her into the empty morning room to look down into her troubled eyes with concern in his own.

'And how long do you think it would be before our imposture was discovered, Colonel Besford? Better to be an open whore than a secret jezebel, in my humble opinion,' she said, aware she was flying in the face of her own resolutions not to cause him public harm, but now in the grip of her own stubborn nature.

'Humble, Cleo? Were you ever so, I wonder? You have as much pride as any duchess I ever came across, so why not let me buy you somewhere quiet? A private villa in the country, perhaps, where I can visit you discreetly and you need not suffer so much over our liaison.'

It was a tempting notion—to be removed from this invidious position and enjoy his exclusive attention, before they inevitably parted and she dwindled into the lonely life she had mapped out as her future. She reminded herself sharply that he had obligations to attend to, and that she was a coward to even consider it.

'We cannot—you have your family and your duties to think of, Colonel.'

'Curse it, so I do. You are right and I cannot go off for days on end without leaving word of where I am. Who would have thought you would become keeper of my conscience, Cleo?'

He was regarding her with such a potent mix of tender concern, rueful amusement and banked desire that she shivered. If he had so much as an inkling of who and what she really was, all that would fade in an instant to be replaced by the bitterest contempt. Then she forgot everything else, as he took advantage of their solitude to kiss her. Her doubts melted away as her body responded enthusiastically, without the slightest pause for permission from her confused mind. Indeed, she went from fairly rational being to a creature of fire and passion from one minute to the next as his mouth opened on her eager one.

Everywhere he touched her, she flamed into heat and an exquisite arousal soared within her the like of which she had never dared dream existed, until she met him. His mouth was the only reality she needed, his long fingers trailing over her sensitised skin lit wildfire. In the quiet room the only sound was their accelerated breathing and the shush of her silken skirts, as even they moulded themselves to him, much as her profligate body longed to do.

Emboldened by his groan of need, she closed the gap he had been careful to preserve between them and let her wanton limbs have their way. Unable to maintain any distance, he deepened their kiss, ravishing thought away as waves of sensation poured over her. She found the heat of him, the unmistakable arousal of his mighty body as new and yet as familiar as this feeling of being on fire in her own skin.

She could feel him breathing, feel the hum of sound as he murmured something into the soft skin between her jaw and her throat, then scorched kisses down the sensitised line of her neck to the hollows at its base. Every time he kissed her, every time he touched her with such driven ardour, such gently fierce persuasion, she became a creature beyond her everyday self. Yet every time he did it, that creature became more powerful, more needy, and the hunger at the heart of her grew until Caroline seemed in danger of disappearing altogether in Cleo's fiery passions.

Not yet willing to lose herself irretrievably, she might have struggled in his powerful hold, if he had not already been gentling it as he eased away. Now his lips against hers were their only contact and he gave another of those lovers' inarticulate sounds that was half-groan, half-sigh, and lifted his head at last to watch her with eyes heavy-lidded with desire.

Flushed with passion, her perfect skin was glowing like pearls lit by candlelight, even under the modest amount of powder and paint she had deemed suitable for today's excursion. Rob longed to see her without either, as he had that first day, and wondered why she bothered with such artifice when her fish was well and truly landed. He toyed with the idea of telling her how much better she looked *au naturel,* but was distracted by the novelty of her trying to close the gap he had created between them with such an effort. While her confidence in his self-control was touching, it far exceeded his own. He eyed her lips longingly and almost lost himself in the warm depths of her eyes all over again.

'Ah, Cleo, I shall not be able to stop at kisses if we are alone any longer,' he told her unsteadily, and opened the door for her before he gave in to his baser desires and threw her on the *chaise* to take her to their mutual relief and delight.

Escorting her upstairs with enough distance between them to satisfy a dowager duchess, Rob was shaken to the core by her capacity to turn him into a besotted fool. She was dangerous, and he had to remember the sphere she gilded was not his. He could not let himself love her, but he would value her and dignify their relations with care for her pleasure and deference for her obvious inexperience. The lover who had driven her to this pass must have been clumsy indeed, or she was the finest actress he had ever encountered, for her response to him had been as untutored as it was fiery.

Moving at his side with the fluid grace Alice's relentless teaching had finally released in her, Caro knew she had committed the ultimate folly. Falling deeper in love with him every time they were together would be tragic, if she was not such a besotted fool she no longer cared. That old schoolgirl infatuation was a poor weakly little thing by the side of the deep feelings for the real Robert Besford that now racked her. Under the fizz and exhilaration of mutual desire was something that felt frighteningly permanent. Her arrogant, rackety, short-tempered love had flattened her careful defences with no effort at all, and how would she face the day when he walked away from her again?

Such uncomfortable conundrums made the beautifully prepared food awaiting them taste more like dust and ashes on her tongue. In the end she was almost glad when Rob said a polite good day, gave his friend Wrovillton a rather twisted grin and departed to attend to his duty, wherever that lay today. When his lordship departed as well, Caro paid little attention to Alice's homily on the subject of never allowing a gentleman to become too sure of his conquest, in case he grew bored. There seemed to be very little risk of ennui developing just at the moment.

Chapter Eight

Refusing to be confined to his room any longer, Lord Little-worth had sought refuge from his well-wishers in the library at Foxwell House. He greeted his brother cordially, but must have envied the excess of energy that set Rob pacing the room after yet another frustrating day.

'Webb said you had given up your bachelor lodgings and come home at last, little brother, but surely it's a bit late to start throwing sops to the gossips now?'

'I'm not quite sure if that constitutes a welcome or a rebuke.'

'I am always pleased to see you, Colonel—being so closely related to one of Wellington's heroes adds a glow of reflected glory, don't you know? But if you cannot sit still, why not take a gallop on that resty young devil kicking the stables to splinters and get rid of both your blue-devils for a while?'

'Because I have far too many for it to make much difference, I suppose,' Rob said with a rueful smile and subsided into the chair across the hearth at last. 'I think I need your help, Jas,' he finally admitted.

'Oh, dear, now my ears have started deceiving me.'

Rob grinned at his brother's sardonic comment and silently acknowledged a hit.

'Well, I have tried everything else,' he acknowledged ruefully.

'To ask for my help you must have done. I presume you still have not located your wife, otherwise the mighty Colonel Besford would have no reason to call on a weakly breakdown like myself.'

Rob shook his head.

'I always had more need of you than I let either of us realise. Look what a confounded muddle I have made of things while you were at Reynards with the Earl if you doubt that.'

'Leaving aside the fact that you have revived the family fortune since I left our tangled affairs in your lap, treating a good woman so badly that she has run away from you constitutes a little more than a muddle, I believe.'

'I used the poor girl appallingly, and then left her to the Countess's tender mercies, which was a backhanded turn she almost certainly did not deserve, but I must find her and negotiate some sort of compromise we can both live with.'

'Considering how much you hurt her, you might find that a bigger challenge than you think. I don't believe she wishes to be found.'

'Her wishes are irrelevant.'

'Are they, indeed?'

'As she is barely nineteen years old and at the mercy of every conniving rogue who crosses her path, then they have to be. Are you seriously telling me that you can stomach the idea of the silly chit starving to death in a ditch somewhere?'

'No, but it had occurred to me that you might be able to.'

'Then you should have known better,' Rob replied, his mouth setting into an ominous line that did not seem to impress his lordship in the least.

'Maybe I should, but you must admit that you have shown precious little concern for her well-being thus far.'

'Your wife has already told me that I am culpable,' Rob replied stiffly.

'Yes, my darling does seem to have expressed herself with unusual frankness,' James said with a fond smile.

'How can you both defend the chit when she wormed her way into your confidence, just to find out what likelihood there was of you succeeding to the earldom?' Rob rapped out and started pacing again at the very thought of one day having to step into his beloved brother's shoes.

Not only would he never fill them half so well, he had not the slightest ambition to be anything more than a country gentleman once his soldiering days were finally over. Until Warden had decided to use him for his own ends, at least he had always known his friends liked him for his own sake rather than for his expectations—a gift denied his brother from birth.

'Neither Jane nor I are fools, Rob, and Caroline would never consider the acquisition of a title a valid reason for marriage.'

'So she actually believed I would make her a congenial husband?' Rob asked incredulously.

'If she did, she has doubtless discovered her error.'

There was something in the way James avoided his direct gaze that made Rob think his brother was not telling everything he knew, but what more could there be? His wife had to be more mercenary than James and Jane believed. Yet if her father only saw her as a means to acquire a titled grandson, he supposed he could not really blame her for trying to influence her own future. After all, an arranged marriage was a fair enough proposition, if both parties agreed to it. So what if she had not known that he was a reluctant bridegroom indeed until it was too late?

Pacing once more, he finally saw what he had been too lost in pig-headed self-pity to see at the time—she had been ignorant of Warden's ruthless manipulation of his family's debts and James's setbacks until the very moment when she arrived at the altar. His great-aunt's revelation had left his bride white and shaking, and, now he looked back, he remembered that she had made her vows with something more akin to blank shock than triumph.

While he had suffered a few stabs of unease before, now he realised that the poor girl was truly innocent, his treatment of her suddenly appalled him. There had been a scrap of magic in the kiss they had shared in Henry Warden's bookroom, and he had snuffed it out so brutally that James was right—his wife would never willingly live with the man who had treated her with such casual cruelty.

'You should have talked to her, Rob, got to know her properly.'

'Yes, it might have saved us both from disaster,' he acknowledged in a hollow voice as he tried to take in this new reality.

Thanks to his actions, his marriage was over before it had begun and he would be an idiot to think falling under the spell of a lightskirt could improve matters in any way.

'I suppose a man of your varied experience could persuade her to listen to your suitably abject apologies when you track her down,' James offered encouragingly.

'I might, if I had not made very sure I am the last man on earth she would want to hear out, let alone forgive.'

'You have been busy, brother mine. Seriously, though, Rob, why did you treat poor Caro as you did?'

'I was over-hasty in my judgement of her, but, as I badly need some advice on finding my wife, I hope you will come down from your high horse and give it to me rather than constantly twitting me on past follies,' Rob returned with an effort at lightness.

His brother just raised his eyebrows and looked unimpressed.

'Damn it, Jas, I can't stand watching you suffer. I thought that I was taking the strain off you by marrying her to get the mortgages back.'

Lord Littleworth darted his younger brother an impatient look. 'When I want your protection, or your pity, I shall be certain to ask for them,' he replied with a haughty pride Caro would definitely have recognised as a family trait.

Tension crackled in the air of the quiet library and even the tick of the clock sounded unnaturally loud all of a sudden.

'I don't pity you, damn it. I love you,' Rob finally burst out as if that admission had been torn out of him.

James grinned at his glowering sibling. 'And I quite like you for some odd reason,' he replied, then laughed as temper flashed in Rob's eyes. 'Lord, those red-headed furies of yours used to get us into so much trouble, little brother,' he gasped, as laughter threatened to turn into a coughing fit.

'And continue to do so, but as I am at least three inches taller than you now, we will have less of the "little", if you please.'

Rob poured them both a glass of cognac and watched his brother sip at his with ill-concealed anxiety.

'Enough skating round the subject, Rob. We must resolve this mess you have got yourself into, before it becomes an open secret that Caroline has gone.'

'So I cannot interfere in your affairs, but you feel free to delve about in mine to your heart's content?'

'Something like that, but stop trying to steer me away from trouble, I just told you how little I like it,' James said quietly, the hectic colour fading from his thin cheeks at last.

'Very well, then. If it's trouble you want, I have it in spades.'

'That you do, but I committed our last penny to my venture into trade of my own free will, Rob, knowing there was nothing left to do but risk all to gain all. Yet you refused to blame me for mortgaging every asset we possess. Mama spent every penny she could lay her hands on by fair means or foul, with no assistance whatsoever from your unfortunate wife, but I cannot recall you railing at her or our father over the fact. In a way I have to admire your bull-headed loyalty, but I cannot help thinking it ought to be tempered by a dash of logic. If only it had been, maybe you would not have taken out your feelings on a vulnerable girl with nobody to defend her, while I sat at Reynards cosseting myself and just let you.'

At last his brother had to pause for breath, and Rob knew it was no good citing the illness that had sapped his brother's vitality in his own defence.

'We brought about our own downfall, Rob,' James insisted, 'whereas Caroline did little to deserve hers. If I was her, I would not want to be found either. Your wife has an unusually acute mind and a strong sense of justice, little brother. Take that into account for once and you might stand a better chance of finding her.'

'She would never have let herself be married off to me if she possessed a single grain of common sense,' Rob returned wryly, wondering for the first time why Caroline had not jilted him at the altar.

'There is a subtle difference between intelligence and common sense, little brother. Good women have a habit of undertaking the redemption of rogues, whether we deserve it or not.'

'I doubt if my wife thinks I do now.'

'Considering you worked so hard to disillusion her, what else would you expect? Speaking of which, I hear that you still have a reformation to accomplish if you do finally manage to find her and to persuade her to come home.'

Rob avoided his brother's acute gaze, for renouncing Cleo was a step too far. He would feel as if the French had put a bullet in him on one of those bloody skirmishes somewhere in Spain or France, he suddenly realised. Such wild emotion would have horrified him, even before he realised Caroline was innocent of the sins he had slated her with.

'Never mind the state of my conscience just now,' he said uncomfortably. 'Finding my wife must take precedence over my future redemption.'

'Even if you are currently in hot pursuit of another?'

'Even so, Jas,' he replied and held his brother's gaze at last with a fierce challenge in his own that did not seem to surprise the Viscount in the least.

What was new in that emerald gaze was the steadfast resolution to keep his ladybird, and Lord Littleworth's grey eyes sparked with some of his old energy. The spectacle of his haughty brother in thrall to a woman of the night was a novelty he could not help but savour.

'In that case, you will have to find a way of pacifying one woman while you bed another. I fear that I cannot offer you any useful advice on that particular dilemma,' he replied blandly.

Rob knew he was being subtly informed that his conduct was ungentlemanly and, as he was already well aware of the fact, it stung. He sometimes longed for the days when he had watched such besotted fools as himself with amused contempt, then remembered his Cleo hesitating between acceptance and denial of the fire and need that raged between them. No, he would not exchange her for ten times the fortune he possessed now. She had turned his world upside down since that smoky night in St James's. He had no intention of letting her go just to appease the proprieties, nor to preserve the honour he had once held so dear.

'Then you might as well offer me some help in finding Caroline instead,' he replied calmly enough. 'You must admit she would be better off with me than wandering the world on her own, even if I am a devilish unsatisfactory husband.'

His brother looked far from convinced, but drank his cognac and raised a questioning eyebrow at the decanter and his brother's empty glass.

'I think the demon drink has caused me enough problems to be going on with,' Rob said with a reminiscent smile that intrigued his brother.

He left shortly afterwards, sure that James knew more than he was admitting. Perhaps a gruelling training session with the half-wild animal he was hoping to turn into a civilised officer's mount one day might be advisable after all. Somehow or another he had to work off the frustration he had to keep in check for another six days, or prove himself a liar as well as a rogue.

Yet even as he tried to convince the skittish animal he was to be trusted, and weathered his determined efforts to unseat him, he knew how impossible it would be to pacify his wife, and keep a mistress. At the end of their efforts he should have been as weary as the young horse, but even physical exhaustion did not seem to make him forget his dilemmas in sleep nowadays.

He thought of the seven very lonely weeks Caroline had

spent under the family roof, and knew that he deserved every sleepless minute. Yet, when he eventually slept, he dreamt of a very different female indeed and woke with an urgent longing to be with Cleo, which boded ill for his obligation to Caroline. Trying hard to forget both women, he was relieved when his duties kept him tied to Horse Guards all day with little chance to brood on his lost honour.

Caro was so busy with her strange new life she should not have time to miss a man who had humiliated and despised her before deserting her, but annoyingly she still did. Even while Alice was teaching her the finer points of becoming an accomplished ladybird, her thoughts would drift away as she tried to puzzle out Robert Besford, gentleman, hero and unwilling husband. Why not just forget him and carry on with her life, she asked herself for maybe the hundredth time? Then a picture of him, transformed into the ardent man she had so stupidly dreamt of after their first meeting, slotted into her mind, and reason flew out of the window again.

For Cleo his eyes sparkled with warmth, and a wicked invitation to share his joy in life. His curling chestnut hair was often dishevelled nowadays as he ran his fingers through it while puzzling how to get her into his arms. The teasing smile on his firm mouth stole her breath, and any vestige of good sense along with it. She just couldn't bring herself to banish wicked, wayward Cleo, and watching *him* play the supplicant for once was too satisfying to forgo lightly.

'Pay attention!' Alice rapped out like a drill sergeant.

'Hmm?'

'He is doing what you wanted, so for Heaven's sake stop moping,' her friend ordered on an exasperated sigh.

'Whoever can you mean?'

'As if you don't know. The "he" you think about morning, noon and night, of course—the one who treated you like something unsavoury he had got on his boots. The husband you said should be out looking for you instead of treating with a mistress? You know, the man you daydream over like a silly schoolgirl whenever he is not with you and you should be paying attention to your lessons?'

'I do not.'

'Then what did I just say?'

'Something about using my hands to express myself?'

'I really should give up on you. I was trying to show you how to recline properly, or should I say improperly? I might as well go downstairs and instruct the kitchen maid; I would probably get a deal more sense out of her than I do out of you, even if that is not saying much.'

'I'm sorry, Alice, I promise to do better from now on.'

'You will never manage it unless you forget that wretched husband of yours for five seconds at a stretch.'

'Somehow he is not that easy to forget.'

'So it seems, but if you followed your conscience and went to teach in Bath after all, would you be able to do so there, do you think?'

'No.'

'Then stay here and remember. He deserves a few sharp reminders of how a gentleman should treat a lady, especially when that lady is his wife.'

'Very well,' Caro agreed meekly, thinking that she might just as well when there seemed so little alternative.

After all, she would need all the resolution she could muster when it came to the imperfect realities of being her husband's mistress.

* * *

The next day Colonel Besford sent an order that Cleo was to be available for a carriage ride in the afternoon. She read his note again in the hope it might contain some soft word she had overlooked, but, no, she might just as well have been a subaltern guilty of some breach of military etiquette! If he had used flowing periods and dramatic flights of fancy she would have doubted his sincerity, of course, but his abrupt summons set her teeth on edge. It reminded her too readily of Colonel Besford the husband and not enough of Rob, her supposedly eager lover.

So Caro presented herself for duty at the appointed time—and spoiling for a good argument. She might not be able to make herself turn him away, but if he thought he could order Miss Cleo Tournier about in the same perfunctory fashion as he had his wife, then he had better think again!

Coming downstairs dressed in her amber pelisse and a very smart new bonnet, she heard Rob's voice below and frowned at the sight of Alice's smart barouche drawn up against the pavement. She would have preferred to ride in a closed carriage, not one where they would be a mark for all the world to gawp at. He was making something too close to a public declaration of intimacy for her peace of mind.

'And just where do you intend to take me in that?' she demanded crossly.

'Back to school to learn some manners, I should think,' he said, handing her up with infuriating composure and giving the coachman the office to move off.

Despite an urge to stick out her tongue, her heart jolted with fear. How could he know she had been to such a place? Her tension must have betrayed her shock, for her gave her a wry grin.

'Come now, Cleo, I am not entirely a fool,' he said, in reply to her unspoken question. 'You have obviously been very well educated—in fact, I'm quite sure that you were born a gentlewoman.'

Which was more than he knew, she thought militantly. His opinion of her lack of breeding had been branded into her mind for ever.

'I came into the world in the same state as the rest of humanity,' she informed him crushingly.

'Yet, if I am not mistaken, you did so hosed and shod,' he replied, not in the slightest bit abashed as she tried not to show the panic his speculative look was causing her.

What if he took it into his head to find out more about her? If he really set his mind to it, he could soon find out who Alice really was—and that her best friend at Miss Thibett's Academy for Young Ladies had been one Caroline Warden. If he then put two and two together, she would be properly unmasked.

'That makes two of us, does it not? And at least you have been lucky enough to stay that way, Colonel Besford,' she managed calmly enough.

'Which explains why you are reduced to enduring my obnoxious attentions, I suppose?'

'Of course it does—why else would I dream of doing so?'

'Then I suggest you stop regarding me as if I have been washed up by the last tide. Lady Samphire's carriage is coming the other way and I have no wish for rumours that I abducted you to start doing the rounds.'

'She would not tell such whoppers, would she?'

'The lady is bored and you know what they say about the devil and idle hands, or, in this case, tongues.'

'I do, but I still don't believe you, Colonel.'

'Rob, my dear, only ever Rob to you.'

He gave her a smile of such warmth and complicity that Lady Samphire clicked her tongue disapprovingly.

'In my day a gentleman kept his lights 'o love hidden away, yet Robert Besford brazenly flaunts that creature while his poor little wife is heaven knows where, doing goodness knows what. I dare say she could not endure the nauseating spectacle of her husband treating with a demi-rep, but if she has been ill, why is he still in town? Surely the boy can see that such public indifference damages them both?'

'I presume he has duties to attend to, Gussie, and men only ever see what they wish to. They usually see it in the eyes of a painted jezebel, what's more.'

Her companion today was a peppery little lady who had never forgiven the dashing officer who had engaged himself to her, then run off with her younger sister.

'Y'know, Beatrice, I doubt Penny could be called a painted jezebel with any degree of truth, even by you.'

Ignoring the annoyed glare of her old schoolfriend, Lady Samphire raised her lorgnette once again, staring at the bird of paradise who was sitting laughing at her lover's antics while they waited for the knot of traffic to unravel. For an instant an expression of arrested attention flickered across her face, followed by a very satisfied smile, but both were gone before her less acute friend could catch sight of them.

'Looks to me as if that girl is having a great deal more fun than you or I ever did, Trixie,' she observed with an about-face that left her old friend gasping, despite being acquainted with the contrary countess for longer than either of them cared to remember.

'Well, really, Augusta! How could you compare us with that…that strumpet?'

'Easily—we should have kicked over the traces years ago.

Might have made Samphire sit up and take notice, aye, and your captain of dragoons as well.'

'The very idea—really, Gussie! I swear you grow more indelicate every time I see you. I believe I shall walk from here, if you will just order your footman to help me down.'

'Suit yourself,' said Lady Samphire equably, pleased with herself for besting her girlhood sparring partner.

She even went so far as to nod graciously to Caro for helping her do it, before turning her eyes to the front and keeping them there.

'Did you see that?' Caro exclaimed.

'Yes, and what a magnificent old baggage she is, but pray don't count on the acquaintance. She is as likely to cut us both dead tomorrow as smile, but I never take it personally. She does the same to the rest of the world, Rowley included.'

'So I see.'

Rob turned in his seat to see his friend riding towards them on a handsome grey gelding. Justice made him admit Rowley made a dashing picture in his immaculate riding gear, but jealousy made him clench his fists by his side as he wondered how long he could go on restraining this primitive urge to lash out at his rival.

'Quite the social gathering ain't it?' drawled the Captain and bowed over Caro's hand with the grace and charm that had won him so many conquests, and that well-deserved nickname.

'Afforde, I thought you were busy preparing for your next voyage?' Rob greeted his friend without noticeable enthusiasm.

'Oh, we seamen like to bid a loving farewell to the glories of dry land whenever we take to the waves again, old fellow.'

Damn him! Rowley was gazing soulfully into Cleo's face and sighing like some damn poet, and she was colouring up and laughing at the coxcomb in return.

'Just as well you have been ordered back to sea, then; doubtless you have outrun the constable as usual,' Rob declared severely, sounding more like a pious member of his father's generation than as big a renegade as the object of his strictures.

'Now there you are mistaken, for my gracious relative yonder has stumped up the dibs like the handsome old darling she is.'

With this he bowed to Lady Samphire, and kissed her hand. He laughed joyously when she glared at him and shook her head, as if she knew very well what they were talking of and wished she hadn't thrown good money after bad.

Chapter Nine

Caro could easily see why Lady Samphire had succumbed to her grandson's charm, and wondered yet again why she could not have fallen in love with such an uncomplicated, laughing rogue herself. The complex creature at her side would never take dependence on a capricious old woman so lightly, and that conclusion suddenly made her see their marriage in a different light.

She flinched as she realised the depth of revulsion Rob must have felt on being manoeuvred into a marriage that compromised honour, pride and whatever hopes he had cherished for the future. She should have fought harder when her father informed her she was to marry him; indeed, she should have run then, rather than long after the ceremony. A small voice whispered at the back of her mind that she had only complied with her father's orders because she had wanted to do so rather badly.

If so, it had been a very poor sort of love; if the barouche had not begun to move at that very moment, she might have got down and walked into the bustling streets to pursue her own damnation. Even loving him more every time they met, she was set on a course that would bring disaster and scandal down on his unsuspecting head if it were ever discovered. The trouble was, she also had an ungovernable desire to spend every minute she could in his company, and she wouldn't get much of that commodity if she finally resorted to telling the truth.

Having no idea of Cleo's dark thoughts and chaotic emotions, Rob sat back in his seat with a contented sigh when his so-called friend was left behind doing the pretty to his grandmother.

'I was beginning to think I would never get you to myself,' he said, seizing her gloved hand and carrying it to his lips.

'Oh, pray do not,' she cried, wrenching her hand away before he could wrest her glove from her again. 'You said I might have my week,' she explained rather lamely when he looked at her with astonishment that did not quite hide a hint of hurt.

She had come so near to giving herself away, she almost sobbed with relief as she recollected herself. He had no idea of the turmoil of feelings that were tearing her in contrary directions; indeed, why should he care one way or the other what she thought when she was just a fleeting object of desire to him?

'So that we could get to know one another better, not to pretend we are two octogenarians at a tea-drinking. I did not scheme to get you alone so we could pretend polite indifference to one another, my dear. Or perhaps you feel no need to pretend?' This last came out somewhat haughtily.

Ashamed of her weakness though she was, she still could not let him believe he was right. It pushed her back into her deception and she relaxed into the character of Cleo Tournier, amateur seductress, with a mental sigh of relief.

She gathered up every shred of dignity she could muster. 'I would not give myself without feeling, whatever else I may do.'

'Whatever else you may be is the most enchanting creature I ever came across, queen of my heart,' he said lightly.

For now, she added mentally, but allowed him to possess himself of both her hand and her glove without offering any more resistance. To her surprise that was all he did, holding her small bare hand in his large warm one under the travelling rug all the way to Richmond Park, and refusing to relinquish it even then as he pointed out the vistas and views to her with his other.

The trees were still bare and the air was clear and sharp, but Caro was cocooned in warmth and enchantment. With hot bricks at their feet and a thick rug over their legs, they were as secure as if in a nest. Added to which, Robert occasionally looked at her as if he was in the company of the woman he wished to be with above all others. Which, she reminded herself rather caustically, was probably true enough, for now.

She made herself forget her newly tender conscience, and allowed some of the bittersweet happiness she felt in his company to show on her glowing face. Nothing had really altered. Nothing would cost him more than it already had, so long as she stayed in character. When he tired of her, she could fade out of his life and he need never be any the wiser.

'Tell me what life is really like in the army,' she said, as eager to store up knowledge of her love as a squirrel making ready to weather a long winter.

He shrugged and turned to gaze at the parkland with a frown it did not deserve, as if weighing up how little he could tell her about his profession.

'It is often hard, sometimes terrifying even, and in Spain we probably enjoyed ourselves more than we should have when we were off duty, considering we were at war with a dangerous and determined enemy,' he said abruptly, as if discussing the past was bringing it back too sharply.

She could not help persisting; if she did not know something of what he had been through, she would fail to properly understand him, and she very much wanted to know what had honed privileged Robert Besford into the powerful man now beside her.

'All my life we have been at war with the French and now we are to be at peace together, it does not seem real yet,' she mused.

'Perhaps it is not.'

'Surely it must be? Nobody would wish to see Europe in chaos once again, just so that Napoleon Bonaparte could call himself Emperor of half the world again. Oh, no, I cannot bring myself to believe anyone would want all that suffering and brutality back. With Bonaparte in exile, surely we must be safe from his ambitions at last, Colonel?'

'For now at any rate, but I thought I asked you to call me Rob.'

Her turn to frown. She knew he was trying to get her to fly from the scent, but he did not realise she had a streak of determination, if not downright stubbornness, that closely matched his own.

'Rob, then, but is it truly possible the French could loose that on us all over again?'

'Despite the fact that fat Louis is wiser than many think him, he cannot control the hotheads around him who are determined to rub their enemies' noses in the dirt. Whether revolutionary or royalist, the French are still not sure if they hate one another or the English the most. Wellington did his best, yet it is more by good luck than good judgement that he is still alive—so many plots were hatched against him while he was our ambassador in Paris.'

'I know about the Field of Mars—do you mean there were other attempts on his life?'

He did not answer her directly, which made her suspect she was right.

'Plot and counterplot are the lifeblood of Paris,' he finally admitted. 'If Bonaparte returned he would soon hold the army in the palm of his hand, and whoever commands the loyalty of its soldiers, commands France.'

Caro gasped in horror and even Alice's stoic, and tactful, coachman seemed to flinch on his box, despite the pretence they all indulged in that he was deaf.

'I am sorry to have alarmed you,' Rob said impatiently.

'Why? I wanted to know; if I don't like the answer, I should not have asked. Pound dealing is always better than polite pretence,' she said and felt herself flush.

Pound dealing had stopped for her the night she had inadvertently flung herself into his arms, but luckily he didn't notice her guilty colour as he considered the awful prospect of renewed war.

'Disarming with such haste might yet turn out to be a mistake,' he said ruminatively, as if he had finally forgotten he was not talking to one of his friends at his club. 'If Bonaparte raised the army, he could catch us napping before half our troops were back from the Americas, or we could recruit more to take their place.'

'I know he is a great general and achieved some extraordinary victories, yet surely he was failing in the last few years of his rule?' she said hopefully.

'When he deserted his men in Russia he was certainly no Hannibal, but even at his worst he's capable of greatness and he recovered from that débâcle remarkably well. Good Englishman though I am, even I have to admit that the man is a genius and still quite a young man as emperors go.'

'Well, he has never fought against the Duke of Wellington,' she reminded him stoutly.

'True, and his Grace has as cool a head as you would find anywhere, but even he cannot conquer his foes without an army.'

'Then we must pray he has time to find one if he has need of it.'

'Indeed, and I had no intention of discussing either war or soldiering today, Mademoiselle Cleo, so, pray, why am I doing so?'

'Because you cannot stop yourself thinking, sir, any more than I can prevent myself wanting to know the truth of matters you gentlemen believe to be beyond the capacity of the female mind. Despite the fact that a lady is deemed unfit to do anything more strenuous than paint watercolours and sing sentimental songs, some of us do possess *something* in the way of brains, you know.'

'And you have rather more of that commodity than your more fortunate sisters, do you not?'

How to take that? It might be a compliment, but he could be implying she was freer to use her native wit than the débutantes ever would be. 'Thank you, sir, I think. Although my so-called sisters might not appreciate your saying so.'

He laughed. 'Best to know your enemy, don't you think, even if only to anticipate their next move?'

'They are too well brought up to acknowledge my existence, but as the débutantes share your breeding, am I your enemy too?'

'Never, you are my darling.'

'I have heard gentlemen often say so when they woo, but are quite otherwise when they get what they want, to find they only desired it while it was withheld.'

How shocked the world would have been to hear such pert opinions fall from mousy Caroline Warden's lips. Yet a fallen woman was supposed to be sharp and full of stratagems, as anyone else choosing to live beyond the pale must be, if they were not to fail disastrously.

'But when could a man ever know you, Cleo? I have wanted women in the past, even thought I needed them, but you? I long to explore the twists and turns of that acute mind of yours, even while I am on fire to learn each delectable inch of your lovely body.'

His voice had sunk to an intimate murmur, but she flushed like a poppy and cast a conscious look at the coachman's carefully oblivious back.

'No man ever fell in love with a woman's mind,' she protested.

'And does that work the other way? Could you love a man smashed half to pieces? Some of the poor devils who came out of the breaches at Badajos are so scarred and maimed that they would frighten strong men—what if I was such a one?'

A stab of pain dissipated the warm glow he had ignited with his whispered seduction. If he ever suffered such a fate she would feel every bullet, every shot and sabre slash drive into her own flesh as certainly as it did into his. Maybe something of her inner turmoil showed on her face, or her stricken silence gave her away, for suddenly the tension seeped out of him.

'I should not talk of such things. The horrors of war are not for such as you.'

'Are they not? Then they should be, Colonel. Women who sit snug at home while brave men fight for their safety deserve only contempt if they shun those that return hurt. I cannot tell what would happen if you were mutilated, but I doubt you would let me near you to find out if you considered yourself less than perfect.'

'Acute of you, my Cleo,' he said slowly, acknowledging his own stubborn pride with a rueful grin.

More than anything in the world she wanted his respect and

for a moment she had it, if only for her shrewdness. Then she remembered how little he would admire her if he knew the truth and some of her radiance dimmed.

'What is it about you, Cleo? I think I have the measure of you and then you surprise me yet again. What ails you this time, my dear one?'

'A goose just walked over my grave,' she said lightly and smiled into his questioning eyes.

He smiled back and she wondered if she could even try to hold him at arm's length for much longer. Yet she needed the time he had promised her to be sure, to salve something in her that demanded he be as securely wound up in the toils of wanting and needing as she was herself. Not vengeance now—certainty, perhaps? Then he gently carried her hand to his lips, and the touch of his mouth on her bare skin shot such a jolt of poignant longing through her that she was surprised to find the world had not turned on its axis after all when he raised his head.

'More likely it is growing colder and I should not have kept you out so long,' he told her and she did not argue.

To admit that her latest shiver was born of nigh over-whelming love and desire for her supposed protector would be a step too far just yet.

'Maybe,' she murmured.

'Certainly, I should say,' Rob said, and ordered the coachman to turn about and take them back to Alice's home.

Sunset was already beginning to tint the sky with a blaze of rose and gold as they turned out of the park and once Caro had shrugged off her reflective mood she felt surprisingly content, despite the delicious tension of desire not yet fulfilled that sang between them. Worn out by too many disturbed nights, she was finally lulled into serenity by a subtle gentling of the tension that constantly sang between them. Now she thought about it, Rob seemed more concerned with entertaining her than seducing her today and, unable to decide if she was pleased or disappointed, she promptly fell asleep against his broad shoulder.

Travelling back through the city with Cleo lying warm, relaxed and trusting against him, Rob could not bring himself to push her away, even though it was a refined form of torture to hold her so close and not make love to her. Looking down at her drooping head and tumbled red-gold ringlets as she tried to find a comfortable place to rest, despite her fashionable plumed bonnet, his smile was surprisingly tender. He gently undid the ribbons and removed that rather *outré* triumph of the milliner's art, whereupon she muttered something indistinct and burrowed contentedly into his shoulder before going back to sleep.

'I am undoubtedly a fool,' he muttered to himself and thought grimly that, with several days to go before he could pleasure both himself and the tantalising woman in his arms, he would be fit for Bedlam before relief finally came.

Even when they drew up outside Alice's home, Caro refused to wake up. She was having a delicious dream of being safe in the arms of a man who loved her to distraction, and it was hardly surprising that she was not at all inclined to wake up and face hard reality. Rob sighed and carried her inside, looking stonily at an amused Lord Wrovillton and his lovely paramour as they came forward to greet him.

'If you will tell me where her bedchamber is, please? It seems to me that Miss Tournier would be best left to sleep it out,' he said in a low, harsh voice that gave away some of his frustration, and his anger at them for knowing of it.

'Gone to sleep on you, has she, old chap? Must be losing your touch,' Will remarked cheerfully, then recoiled at the sight of black fury blazing in his friend's eyes. *'Pace,'* he said, holding his hand up, 'I'm sure Alice will show you up directly.'

'Indeed, pray follow me, Colonel,' Miss Watson said with regal politeness and a distinct chill evident in her fine blue eyes.

He wondered grimly what ailed the lovely baggage, and hoped she had no plans to make mischief between himself and the bewitching little creature nestling so contentedly in his arms. Dismissing La Watson's hostility for the time being, he followed in her wake into an opulent chamber. It was done with taste, as everything in this house was, but the light amber gauze that draped a canopy lined with gold silk drew attention to the large bed set on a dais and spread with golden satin shot with flame. Just the right shades to highlight Cleo's lovely tumbling auburn curls, he decided crossly.

Aleysha Watson drew back the covers to allow him to lay his delicious burden down on the snowy linen sheets. Almost savage with need, he wanted to set aside his ridiculous promise, and climb in beside the delicious little doxy and wake her in the most effective way possible. To his shame, he could not control the eager reaction of his body to that delightful scenario and had to hastily avert his gaze from her heart-shaped face as the seductive mass of her auburn curls tumbled on the snowy pillow.

He met the knowing eyes of Cleo's friend and wondered if she had some real cause to hate him. For a moment her expression was almost gloating and he shook his head in an attempt to clear it. By the time he looked back, she had veiled her feelings and was looking at him with cool mockery again.

'I think you will have to possess your soul in patience,

Colonel. You seem to have quite tired poor Cleo out with your attentions,' she said, in a fine parody of innocent sympathy.

He could hardly challenge her openly. Cleo was her protégée, partaking of her hospitality and cared for as a valued friend. Considering the depths a woman could be reduced to when alone and unprotected, he had good cause to be profoundly grateful that Miss Watson had taken her in when whatever disaster Cleo had suffered struck.

Unfairly, he thought the courtesan might have set her friend on a more respectable course but, as he himself had pointed out, respectable employment for a lady was hardly likely to equate with either safety or financial security for someone so enchantingly lovely. Contrarily he wished his Cleo was both respectable, and scandalously available to his most ardent seduction all at the same time. Indeed, he could hardly blame the lovely Aleysha for disliking him when he found it rather hard to like himself. At any rate he must bite back his frustrated fury over his own vulnerability and her knowledge of it for now. All the same, he promised himself that when he finally got Cleo into bed at long last, it must be under any other roof but this one.

'I have become a very patient man since I made Miss Tournier's acquaintance, Miss Watson,' he said smoothly enough.

'It has been my observation that gentlemen are seldom particularly patient with their womenfolk,' she replied cynically.

'Do you not think so?'

Alice heard the dangerous tone in his deep voice as he considered his reckless promise to the girl in the bed, and decided she had gone far enough. It would be foolish to make the ungallant Colonel suspect she had real reason to hate him at this stage of the game.

'I know so,' she told him with a roguish look.

Rob wondered why her singular beauty and undoubted witchery had left him unmoved from the moment he encountered Cleo. He was not besotted enough to think the girl nestling her face into the lace-edged pillows with an inarticulate murmur, as if searching for a comfort she had recently lost, more lovely than her infamous friend. Yet seeing Cleo seeking him out in her dreams, he felt as if his insides had turned a somersault and looked sharply away, before Miss Watson's acute blue eyes could discern the fact and mock him for such vulnerability.

'I will bid you a good evening, madam,' he said tersely and turned upon his heel to leave the room.

'Good night, Colonel,' Aleysha Watson's husky voice followed him.

He heard amusement in it and a hint of triumph, and turned about at the door to give her a long, considering stare. She faced it with dignity, for all the hard challenge in his eyes must have come as a shock to her. At last he could discern what his friend Will wanted so badly in her that he was prepared to do almost anything to keep her. He nodded slowly—she was obviously intelligent and her pride seemed strong as steel as she held his assessing look unflinchingly.

'I fully intend to look after Miss Tournier, madam. My lawyer will meet yours when he has drawn up a deed of settlement, and I shall find her a suitable house before the end of the week.'

'To remove her from my pernicious influence, Colonel?' Alice challenged him over Caro's sleeping head.

She was unable to help herself when she remembered how little heed he had once paid to the sharp, sensitive mind that animated the girl he had now decided to want so badly after all.

'To give her security. You forget that I am still a soldier, perhaps? Or do you think I will abandon her when I am under orders to join my brigade again?'

'I have no reason to expect anything of you, sir.'

'No, but for some reason you always anticipate the worst, do you not? Sometimes I cannot help but wonder why,' he said and his eyes narrowed speculatively.

'I have seen too much of the world to expect anything else,' Alice said, and just managed not to show how uneasy his shrewd gaze made her.

'Maybe, but in this case you are dealing with a gentleman, madam,' he said quietly, then gave a curt nod and left the room.

Alice listened to his steps recede as he went downstairs. A murmur of sound reached her as he said a cheerful enough farewell to Will, then he was gone. A gentleman, he had said, and, against all evidence to the contrary, she believed him. She looked down at Caro's curly head and sighed. Ringing for Emily to undress her sleeping friend as best she could, she eventually went to join Will with a thoughtful frown knitting her fine brows.

Meanwhile Rob had met Lord Wrovillton coming out of his lover's drawing room and gave him a hard look, as if expecting to see a similar challenge in his old friend's intelligent grey eyes. There was nothing but the usual humour and an unspoken question to be seen there, and he conceded another point to the haughty piece upstairs. At least she had no plans to destroy a friendship that had withstood years of soldiering by spreading her antipathy to her lover.

'You remember we are engaged to dine with Afforde tonight?' Will asked warily, obviously wondering about that challenging stare.

'I'm hardly likely to forget. A sore head come morning will

be a small price to pay to get rid of Rowley for a few weeks. High time he made himself useful for once.'

'I thought he was your friend, Rob.'

'So did I,' Rob replied gruffly and Will grinned at him.

'This love business is the very devil, ain't it?' Will replied and Rob opened his mouth to deny such tender feelings, then shut it again.

It wasn't love, he assured himself stoutly, this protective, passionate desire to have Cleo safe and thoroughly satisfied in his arms. It could never be love when he was entangled with a courtesan and leg-shackled to a lost wife. Anything more than fascination and mutual desire would lead to disaster and he refused to permit such a possibility, lest he be forced to give up his extraordinary Cyprian, or put her second to his duty to the elusive Caroline.

'Whatever it is, it's a devilish nuisance,' he said crossly.

'If that's all it is, then you ain't far enough gone yet,' Will said cheerfully and sauntered upstairs, whistling.

Chapter Ten

Lounging back in his comfortable chair in Captain Afforde's bachelor chambers a good many hours later, Rob could not forget that disconcerting question of Will's. Love and lady-birds did not go together, he told himself sternly. Despite this conclusion, his senses harped on Cleo's faint rose scent, the delicious sensation of her fluid curves moving against him and the echo of her heartbeat wild against his chest, even while his brain was ordering them not to be so idiotic.

Then there was the insidious memory of his wife and that one, brief, shaming moment when he had been tempted to just take her, as the unforgiving drive of desire urged him to do. To distract himself from his two conundrums, he looked round Captain Afforde's untidy sitting room to discover that he and Will were the only ones left conscious, even if he would be rash to claim sobriety for either of them. He briefly envied the others their easy repose, then shifted uncomfortably under his friend's contemplative gaze, hoping his thoughts weren't plain to read on his face for a man who knew him so well.

'She can't be s'bad as all that, Rob,' Lord Wrovillton declared hazily.

'Who, Janey? You know very well that she lost the babe day before yesterday. She's inconslobab…incos…dammit, she's beside herself. Third or fourth time it's happened and she despairs of giving Jas the pack of brats they always wanted.'

He aimed a disapproving glare at the recumbent figure of Captain Afforde, who was giving vent to a penetrating snore that must make him deeply unpopular aboard ship.

'Hope Rowley only does that when he's drunk,' he observed sternly.

Even in the face of the intriguing idea of a whole shipful of resentful ratings, unable to get their required beauty sleep thanks to their famous captain, Lord Wrovillton clung stubbornly to his chosen subject.

'I know that. Don't mean Lady Littleworth, not that she ain't got m'sympathy, of course.'

His lordship contemplated the unfairness of his friend's sister-in-law losing yet another child and Rob emptied his glass in one long swallow.

'That girl, she's the one I meant,' Will managed, as if his cryptic words explained everything.

'Oh, *that* girl.' Rob finally understood and glowered darkly.

'Aye, y'wife.'

'Wish I'd never married her,' Rob said gloomily.

He might not hate his unfortunate wife any more, but her existence made Cleo square very ill with his conscience. Even if he found Caroline, her flight and determined disappearance had made her low opinion of her husband very plain, and who could blame her for that?

Lord Wrovillton looked about him furtively, and, seeing their companions were too fast asleep to hear the last trump sounded, bent nearer.

'I'm goin' to marry Alice,' he confided, pressing an unsteady finger to the side of his nose, 'but that's strictly tween you and me.'

Rob laughed, then met his lordship's grey eyes and saw burning sincerity in them, if not much in the way of focus.

'You can't, she's an impure,' he protested, rather proud that he had put it so politely, given his current state.

'Don' care. I love her; she loves me. Why wed some silly society ninny who'll fill my nurseries with bastards and then run off with her lover? Alice'll never play me false. Knows the rules.'

'Of being your pillow mate, yes, but the tabbies would never accept her, she'd be condemned to inhabit the fringes of society.'

'She's used to it, and I don't give a fig for society.'

'I know that, but what about your children?'

'What of 'em? Have a loving mother. More than most men of our acquaintance can say for their offspring.'

'True.'

When he was a child Rob's mother had appeared now and again to show off her handsome boys to her glamorous friends, then she would ignore them as if they were nothing to do with her for the rest of her stay. One of his first memories was of walking in the gardens at Westmeade with his father, and hiding behind him on seeing her.

'Who's she, Papa?' he had whispered, with a mix of terror and fascination.

The lady had looked like the beautiful wicked queen in the bedtime story that his nurse told him, on the rare occasions when he was good enough to deserve such treats.

'Your mama, Robbie. Just make her a neat leg and she'll be happy enough.'

'If she's my mother, why doesn't she live here with us, sir?'

'Why indeed?' the Earl had said with a funny smile that did not look amused at all. 'Still, I have my brats, she has her parties and I know which of us has the best of the bargain.'

Years later he admired his father for making the best of a bad job, and wondered why he could not have done the same himself, then he felt Will's intent gaze on him as he tried to marshal his wandering thoughts.

'Children would suffer,' he finally announced. 'You know what the tabbies are like, and there's a dashed puritanical mood coming over society of late.'

'Maybe, but they won't hear any whispering if I don't send 'em to school. Anyway, now the Continent is open again I want to explore it properly.'

Rob was sceptical; Will's travels would bear no resemblance to the staid progress of an English milord. He was more likely to drag his wife and children around Europe as if they were a band of gypsies, stopping wherever his interest was piqued and turning his hand to any wild scheme that took his fancy. Seeing how serious Will was, he considered the idea properly and thought perhaps Aleysha Watson might be the ideal wife for him after all—she was certainly no faint-heart and might well relish such an eccentric progress.

'You saved my life too many times in the Peninsula for me to do aught but support you, but think about it some more, Will. Marriage ain't an easy matter, take it from one who knows.'

'That's where you're wrong, y'know. Find the girl you want to marry, wed her and start a family as soon as nature allows. That's it.'

'And what about her family? Females don't come full grown out of the egg, y'know.'

'That's the joy of it; they cast her off years ago. No need to fear a pack of spongers hanging on my sleeve.'

'I think they might change their mind when they know the girl has netted herself a viscount,' Rob said cynically.

'Not a chance.' His lordship looked about him again, then moved closer and whispered, 'She's a Stoneleigh.'

'Good Lord! Is she, though?' Rob's voice rose in astonishment and Will shushed him nervously, but luckily the crack of doom would have gone unheard until their companions had slept off their potations.

'True, niece of Gronforde's. Sent to school in Bath when she was orphaned. Some damn rogue abducted her when she was little more than a child, despoiled her to blackmail her uncle into consenting to their marriage and deserted her when he got nowhere with the old curmudgeon. Gronforde needed whipping for not hunting the carrion down and making him eat grass before breakfast, of course, but I have to admit the poor girl would have had the devil of a life if she'd married him. Devil of a one anyway, I suppose.'

'And when did she tell you this affecting story?' Rob asked cynically.

'D'you know you've got a nasty suspicious mind? Found an old letter addressed to the Honourable Alice Stoneleigh by some schoolmistress. Went to Bath and the tabby who runs the school told me the tale, after I camped out on her doorstep for nigh on a week. I had to convince her I truly wanted to marry Alice before she'd say a word on the subject.'

'If you were ready to go to Bath and spend a sennight making up to some naggy old schoolmistress, then it must be love.'

'It is—you should try it sometime.'

Rob muttered something unrepeatable, then reached for the bottle and gave an impatient curse when he found it empty.

'Damn all women, more trouble than they're worth!' he said, trying hard to forget his lovely little lightskirt, yet finding that picture of her searching for him in her sleep impossible to dismiss.

He wanted her, he told himself irritably, and tried to put her to the back of his mind, since she refused to be banished from it altogether.

Lord Wrovillton rightly ignored such a ridiculous assertion.

'So will you support me, if I ever manage to persuade Alice she ain't goin' to ruin my life if she accepts me?'

'Aye, of course I will. Even if I think you're a bigger fool than I was.'

'Devil a bit. I ain't intending to mislay my wife, supposing I ever get her to the altar,' Lord Wrovillton said cheerfully.

Rob gave a bitter laugh. 'Told you they were trouble. Now where's the next bottle?'

'There ain't one, we've drunk poor old Rowley dry. We'll both have a head come morning as it is, and I've got to persuade Alice I was only escorting a pack of drunken sots about town out of the kindness of my heart.'

'If you can convince her of that, then she's a pearl beyond price.'

'And so she is.'

Rob rose unsteadily to his feet and gazed about him. 'Pack of jug-bitten noddlecocks,' he condemned roundly, and lurched towards the door in search of a more comfortable place to sleep off his excesses than Rowley's floor.

'Tell him?' Caro said, startled into pushing her breakfast away from her the following morning as if it suddenly revolted her, 'Have you run mad, Alice?'

'I'm not sure, but last night your Colonel spoke to me seriously for the first time and I realised what we were about. I must admit it frightened me.'

'Frightened you? What has he been saying? I shall revoke everything I promised if he has been bullying you.'

'No, it was nothing he said, or at least not in the way you mean. Just that when he assured me that he intended to behave like a gentleman towards you, I suddenly realised his code is different. He and Will live by another set of rules from the likes of most of the society bucks and that poltroon who abducted me.'

'Do they? Then they both seem perfectly willing to avail themselves of our services without feeling a pang of conscience about it, despite their so-called honour,' Caro said out of her own bitterness, and then could have kicked herself as she saw Alice flinch. 'I'm sorry, Alice, I truly like your Will and he is indeed a gentleman, as well as a nobleman.'

'But that is just it,' Alice persisted, and Caro saw that this was one subject she refused to treat as lightly as she usually did the uncomfortable realities of her life. 'Both he and your Robert were good soldiers, so they lived by a code of honour. Not in the way my stuffy Stoneleigh cousins think of the word, but as an everyday reality. I admit that I don't know exactly what I mean—going on when every instinct told them not to, I suppose. Refusing to leave the worst job to someone else, however much they would have liked to. They were both in a position of sufficient power to abuse it and chose not to do so. It's my belief that they still live by that code, on or off the battlefield.'

'And if they do?' Caro said calmly, refusing to show that she was shaken by the idea, especially as she had prated to Rob of her honour that day in Hyde Park. He lived by a creed that must have demanded things of him it would turn her stomach to even think of.

'Do you not see, love? Because they live by such a code, would they not expect the same of any woman they came to love?'

'What, even the likes of us?'

'You are just a wife in search of her husband where he ought not to be.'

'No, I cannot acquit myself that easily. I set out to deceive him, to bring him down even. Don't look at me like that, Alice. You are far better than I am. At least *you* are honest.' Alice laughed bitterly. 'In the truest sense of the word you are, and I am a charlatan,' Caro insisted.

'You know nothing of charlatans if you believe yourself to be one, you goose. Your husband owed you a fair hearing at the very least, and instead he bullied and reviled you, then deserted you without a backward glance.'

'It wasn't that simple, indeed. I am not sure anything is straightforward any more. When we are together, I have to admit that thoughts of revenge are not uppermost in my mind.'

She flushed and found it an effort to meet her friend's level gaze.

'Do you know, I had a suspicion that was so,' Alice replied and the spark of mischief was back in her eyes again. 'In fact, it was abundantly clear to me from the first moment you met him again that something far warmer than vengeance was afoot.'

In spite of her unease, Caro chuckled as she looked back to Rob's scandalous meetings with Cleo, wondering how he had restrained himself from taking her, say she yea or nay, when he had received such enthusiastic encouragement. She saw what Alice meant about that honour of his, and the future looked blacker than ever.

'And just what do you believe he would think of me if he found out who I really am?'

'He would be furious of course, for a while. Afterwards he would probably be glad he was married to you after all. Far better than what was between you before, and even what is between you now, trust me on that.'

'No, it is you who insist on the fact he lives by a code. Can you not see how he would react to the news that his wife had lied and deceived her way into his bed in the guise of a kept woman? I can assure you he would *not* insist we set ourselves up in wedded bliss post haste.'

'How can you know?'

'Because I see much about him now that I did not allow myself to notice in the past, both when I adored him from afar and when I believed I hated him nigh as much as he did me,' Caro said with a bleak smile. 'He already believes I insinuated myself into his brother and sister-in-law's sympathies to secure an eligible marriage for myself. I dare say he looks at my father's example and thinks I never spoke or acted honestly in my life. Then I am to take him to my bed and let him do whatever it is husbands do, and it quite vexes me what that might be, for you will never tell me,' she told Alice with a stern look. 'After that I suppose I am to greet the morning with the happy news I am really his wife, and by that act he has chained himself to me for life, will he nil he. I will not do it, Alice. Indeed, I cannot.'

'But I thought you had almost promised yourself to him,' Alice said diffidently, as if she was reminding her friend of some distasteful duty she had committed herself to in a weak moment.

'Not that, you ninny. I have every intention of fulfilling the one promise I feel free to make him, for I am not a saint after all. No, I will never tell him who I really am, and neither will you.'

Alice sat silent and looked mulish.

'You will not, Alice, because he would turn against me for ever and I doubt if you wish me to run quite mad. Let me have my few weeks of forbidden paradise, then the brouhaha over my disappearance will have died down and I may seek out Miss Thibett and convince her to help me find a situation.'

'Oh, Caro, no! Such a little life when you could have had everything.'

'Nothing, it would be nothing, Alice. Can you imagine what it would be like to become another such as my mother-in-law? She does not appear to care or even notice, but her life is as empty as that of any poor governess. Oh, she has jewels and fine things aplenty, but nobody loves her and even the Earl has finally agreed to publish a disclaimer of her future debts, so she cannot even gamble to fill the void. I would rather live alone than endure seeing my husband and family despise me in such a fashion.'

'You are nothing like your mother-in-law—you could not be so unfeeling if you tried for half a century—and you could bear his children, share his life,' Alice argued half-heartedly.

'And you think it a good thing for them to grow up with distrust and dislike the only bond between their parents other than themselves? Of course not, and don't forget that I already know what it's really like to be despised by a father. God send no child of mine ever has to face that ordeal, although He need not trouble, for I shall not have one.'

'You might—after all, you *have* agreed to take Rob Besford to your bed,' Alice said with a hint of defiance.

'I will not, because you are going to tell me precisely how I go about avoiding such consequences.' She looked her friend in the eye and continued firmly, 'And don't try to tell me you have just been fortunate. You know perfectly well that I am determined enough to follow you about morning, noon and night until you tell me that, and a good many more things I need to know.'

'It is not proper for me to do so, you are not one of my sisterhood.'

Caro succumbed to a fit of the giggles over this piece of chopped logic.

'Don't be such a widgeon, Alice. I never thought to hear such a piece of mealy-mouthed nonsense come from you, of all people.'

'I vow I don't know what you mean,' replied Alice, on her high ropes.

'I mean that you are being either nonsensical or devious, and I have no intention of letting you get away with either. So you just sit right back down in that chair and tell me what I wish to know, Alice Stoneleigh.'

'Shush! Anyone might come in.'

'Let them—if I am to confess, then I swear I will take you down with me.'

'You would not?' Alice said reproachfully, and, seeing Caro's militant expression, sighed. 'Very well, then, but I refuse to discuss such matters at the breakfast table. You had best come to my boudoir as soon as we have finished here.'

Several hours later, Caro's mind was still reeling from the information Alice had imparted. Maybe it was just as well Rob had sent a vast bouquet of flowers and a note telling her he was engaged on business today. She concluded that this must be one of his wife-hunting days, and fervently hoped he was making no progress on that front whatsoever. Meanwhile, Alice looked a little anxious at the lingering shock in her friend's tawny eyes.

'With love, or even strong passions involved, it is truly the most wonderful experience, Caro, but I knew that I should not have told you,' she finally said, rather hesitantly.

'No, stupid to let silly girls go to the marriage bed in a state of ignorance and well you know it, Alice. I dare say a good many débutantes would think harder about choosing a husband if they knew what marriage really entails.'

'Maybe that is the very reason they are kept in ignorance.'

'All too probably. The idea of such intimacy, even with Rob, could have given me the vapours if I had been unprepared, so what must it be like for some females?'

Caro was so indignant she momentarily forgot what a dreadful awakening to the true facts of what a man and woman did in bed together poor Alice must have had.

'Unthinkable,' Alice said with a shudder, revulsion raw in her voice.

'Oh, Alice, love. How very much I should like to bite that creeping toad.'

Caro hugged her friend, and was relieved to see Alice's eyes clear of memories as she came back to the present.

'Ah, but toads taste so foul. Anyway the best revenge is to live well, is it not? And I certainly intend to do that.' Alice looked uncertain for a rare moment. 'Will has asked me to marry him, Caro, and I confess that I don't know what to do.'

'Marry you?' Caro fought to keep her incredulity out of her voice, because of course Lord Wrovillton could not find a better woman if he spent a lifetime searching, but marriage?

That honour Alice spoke of was a marvel indeed if it had led to this.

'How wonderful! I wish you both very happy.'

But Alice still looked uncertain.

'I said no, but he keeps asking and I don't know how much longer I can hold out, for I do love him so, Caro.'

'Of course you do. I could tell that the first time I set eyes on you together.'

'But it will ruin him in the eyes of the world.'

'Nonsense, his real friends will accept you for his sake.'

'A scarlet woman? Don't be naïve, love.'

'His wife, the woman he loves. Your Will is not a man to trifle with.'

'But what about his position? His seat in the House—oh, I don't know, everything?'

Caro smiled at her friend's tragic expression.

'One, I cannot see Lord Wrovillton carving out a political or diplomatic career, whoever he marries. Two, he does not care a fig for his position, nor anyone who is taken in by his title. And three, he loves you, Alice, so stop looking so Friday-faced and be happy about it.'

'But to *marry* me?'

'How else can you have children together? He is not the kind of man who would relish hearing the sons and daughters he loved stigmatised as a pack of bastards.'

'They will be so ashamed of me, Caro, and their school-friends will taunt them that their mother was a whore.'

'Then they can tease them back. A good many so-called respectable wives are bigger strumpets than either of us, and *they* don't give it up when they marry, either.'

'Very true, Miss Tournier,' a deep voice said very quietly from the doorway.

'My lord…' Caro let her voice tail off, looking up and seeing Lord Wrovillton looking back at her with amusement and speculation in his eyes.

'I have to thank you for putting my case so eloquently. Your friend Alice can be stubborn as a mule when she gets a notion fixed in her lovely head.'

'And I suppose you are not, my lord?' Alice said with a decided snap.

'Me? I am so reasonable you could pour me over troubled waters,' he said, which was an outrageous lie and they all knew it.

'Reasonable? You have run mad and I should send for a lunatic doctor rather than a priest.'

'Ah, but you won't, will you, my darling? For you're as mad as I am.'

'Oh, Will, I quite think I must be.' Alice gave him a look compounded of resignation and an incredulous, dawning joy.

Caro felt it was high time she left them in peace. His lordship was astute enough to take full advantage of such a promising opening, so she retired to her bedchamber to give him the chance to do so and pondered on the contradictory wiles of fate.

That night the unrest that had been growing in the city over the new Corn Bill kept Colonel Besford away, but the next day a terrible piece of news put the furious London mob into the shade. Bonaparte had landed in France, the army had welcomed their beloved emperor enthusiastically and his re-instatement was a foregone conclusion!

Alice took one look at Caro's white face and dilated eyes and rang for a bracing dose of cognac to counteract the stark shock she saw there. Lord Wrovillton had sold out after the Battle of Toulouse, but Rob Besford was still a serving officer and would no more sell his commission now than he would fly to the moon.

'Come now, *Cleo*. You must compose yourself,' she said with a significant glance at Lord Wrovillton, who had been the bearer of ill tidings. 'You will *not* faint on us like some spineless bread-and-butter miss.'

'I won't?' Caro asked, managing a faint smile as she shakily abandoned her sofa.

'Decidedly not.'

'Very well, then. It is faintly ridiculous to start indulging in an excess of sensibility at such a time, I suppose, but it means war, does it not?'

She looked at Lord Wrovillton with vain hope in her eyes, knowing she was an idiot to wish he would deny it.

'Since the French army have welcomed Boney with open arms, Miss Tournier, it is inevitable. No point denying the truth just because we don't like it.'

'No, and with so many of our regiments either in the Americas or disbanded, it will be hard for us to stop him, will it not?'

'It will be the devil of a struggle, especially if Bonaparte intends to pick off the Allies one by one as any wise strategist would choose to do.'

'Then you will wish to discuss the matter with my friend,' she finally managed to say, as coolly as she was able.

She must try to justify Alice's faith in her stalwart character by composing her jangling nerves, so she headed for the small sitting room on the ground floor where Alice sometimes totted up her accounts to do so. There was no point expecting Rob to remember her at such a time, she decided glumly, and sat down at an old spinet that had been consigned to this limbo, and let her fingers wander half-heartedly up the scales.

There must be some way of convincing her husband that a mistress would prove indispensable to him in the days ahead, she decided, and tried out various airy phrases that should make it impossible to turn down her confident expectations. He could hardly take his wife when he had no idea where she was, and Caro was not brazen enough to turn up in Berkeley Square with a suitcase full of improper gowns and an apologetic simper. Simpering was not in Cleo Tournier's style, and Caro Besford didn't have any style at all, so she could just stay buried in the unhappy past where she belonged.

Chapter Eleven

$\sim\!\!\!\sim\!\!\!\sim\!\!\!\sim\!\!\!\sim$

Rob finally dashed into the little house in St James's late that afternoon, and Alice tactfully left them alone as he seized Caro's cold hands in his warm ones. She only just managed to resist the temptation to cling to him like some weak vine winding itself round a strong oak as she feasted his eyes on his vital features, as if storing them up against a potential drought.

'Well, my Cleo, am I vain to hope you have missed me a tenth as much as I have you?'

Tears threatened, but she refused them passage and smiled up at him as if it cost her nothing.

'Indeed, I might have wondered where you were and what you were at just once or twice,' she told him with mock-solemnity.

'Sweet rogue!' he laughed, then released her hands only to pull her into his arms, as if to hold her close had been his burning desire ever since he heard the news of Bonaparte's escape. 'Liar,' he murmured and kissed her with such passionate need that she shuddered, and gave up trying to be strong and self-sufficient.

She flung her arms round his neck to pull him yet closer

and tried to insinuate herself against every beloved inch of him, as if only by doing so could she reassure herself that he was still alive, and perhaps shield him from harm. With his lips on hers she forgot everything: scruples, the self-styled Emperor Napoleon, discretion, promises, the lot. His mouth on hers was her world, and his hands on her tingling, willing body the only reality that mattered. Sensation was confined to her lover's body cradling hers and it was close to bliss, as his hands and mouth soon roamed to such effect that they were both breathless and shaking.

Caro wondered fleetingly if they could get any closer, so lost to the world as they were. Then a hot flowering of need told her otherwise, and suddenly the facts Alice had imparted to her the other day seemed not just possible, but infinitely desirable. At that moment she would have consented to anything he demanded. Unfortunately for this gnawing heat that had rushed so completely and demandingly to life within her, his control was infinitely greater than her own. He raised his head at last and thrust her a little further away from him.

'Not here and not now, I fear, my Cleo. I must go back to Horse Guards very soon, and the first time we pleasure each other will be with a whole night before us, and nothing and no one to interrupt.'

For a full minute she could not speak, and was taken aback by the fact that he could not only string sentences together, but sound so composed while he did so. She began to wonder if it was true that love was indeed a woman's life, but only a man's pleasure. Love? Of course he felt no such thing for a lightskirt and never would, she reminded herself impatiently. She must not mistake his regard for her pleasure, and his skilful seduction of her senses, for anything deeper. He was a considerate lover, yes, but although he wanted her and, at the moment, probably needed her, love was hers alone.

She rose from the *chaise* they had tumbled on to so precipitately and wondered at herself. To be so cosily snuggled against his muscular body that she had forgotten they were in Alice's sitting room in broad daylight once again did not auger well for her ability to calmly walk away when he tired of her.

'I would never keep you from your duty,' she said.

He saw her white face and cursed, then took her back into his arms, despite her efforts to escape him. This time he was offering comfort rather than ardour, and she fought that too for a moment, before subsiding against him to accept whatever he had to give.

'I can see for the first time why a man would put a woman before his honour, sweetheart. I would swap an hour with you for a year with any other.'

There was such sincerity in his voice that she felt a glimmer of hope, but stifled it conscientiously. However much he might want her, it didn't mean he loved her, and, as Cleo Tournier was no more real than a character in a play, perhaps that was just as well.

'You say that now, sir,' she told him lightly, 'but in a year from now you will have forgotten me and be happy in the arms of another.'

'Never—I swear you are the only woman who exists for me.'

'Promise me nothing, Colonel, in case you tarnish what we have. I think you have a wife who deserves better than that.'

For some obscure reason, she was angry on her own behalf. If she were not his wife pretending to be someone else entirely, would he now be making such sweet promises to another houri? Her romantic side hoped not, but the cynic in her wondered if she could believe anything a soldier said to his ammunition wife.

'Don't throw my disreputable past at me just now, Cleo, for I have more to regret than a dying politician might feel moved to confess. I admit that I am a rascal, but I promise to be a considerate one to you at least.'

She saw the irrepressible twinkle was back in his eyes, that beloved quirk to his firm mouth, and could not help but laugh in response. He was right; turning comedy into tragedy, or melodrama, was a pitfall to be avoided at all costs.

'I grant you will try to be, sir, and who knows whether you will succeed or not? Until the time comes for you to begin such a mighty endeavour, I suppose I must bid you farewell, but until when, pray?'

'As soon as this panic is over and order set in its place.'

She sighed heavily. 'That long?'

'Maybe just the panic then, my lovely shrew.'

'Good, and I will give you back your other promise in return, if you want it,' she offered with a rosy flush on her formerly pale cheeks.

He understood her, for heat turned his eyes a glistening emerald, but he shook his head all the same.

'No, I have plans to fulfil before we make good on that pledge, and this latest commotion means it will take until your week is out to complete them, but take fair warning that you may expect no mercy from me then, my darling.'

'Shall I see you before that?'

'Maybe, but since we patently cannot keep our hands off one another, perhaps it would be better if you did not.'

'Very well,' she offered stiffly.

Three days seemed like eternity after what had passed this morning.

'Chin up, my Cleo. Remember *your* promise and be good.'

'Since you give me very little choice in the matter, I shall have to be.'

'I doubt anyone could force you to do what you do not wish to, but pray try, or I shall be in hell thinking of all those other fools leering at you and wanting you.'

'I think I shall go to Vale with Alice and your friend. Lord Wrovillton is keen to see the local militia properly prepared, in case they should be needed.'

'Good, but be sure you are back by the end of the week.'

'Why, what happens then?' she teased, and tweaked the tiger's tail with a vengeance this time.

'This,' he muttered thickly, and tugged her back into his arms, as if he could not help kissing her with a passion that, for once, forgot her inexperience and let her know that releasing her took a supreme effort of will.

All the same he managed it, then strode from the room without looking back. Which, given the fact that her hair had tumbled down, her gown was in complete disarray, and her mouth was swollen and moist and wanting, was probably just as well. Her life might have drifted hopelessly beyond control, but she had command of her appearance at least. She fully intended to make sure Cleo was so irresistibly chic from now on that Robert Besford would not dream of going off to war without his mistress!

Between his duties at Horse Guards, Rob paid a flying visit to James's estate near Brighton. He had to suborn his brother and sister-in-law to agree with the tale that his wife would be staying with them until he was sure what was to do on the Continent. Jane was very stiff with her former favourite, but James managed to hide his feelings as well as ever.

'I suppose there is nothing I can do or say to stop you going to fight Boney again?' he asked as soon as the brothers were left alone after dinner.

'No, the Beau will be short of experienced men without the ones he has to hand staying at home. The Duke of York has it in his head to send me off to Belgium to help stop Slender Billy invading France on his own anyway, so I can hardly cry off afterwards, always supposing the young hothead doesn't get us all killed before Wellington even gets there.'

James nodded, looking unusually solemn. 'Father tells me York can't stop you going, so he might as well make use of you. Can you tell me with your hand on your heart that you are not so eager to get out of your marriage that you would gladly march away, Rob?'

Here was straight talking with a vengeance and Rob shook his head, rather surprised to find his one-time loathing for Caroline Warden thrown at him when he had forgotten it himself. Until Bonaparte's fate and his own were decided, his marriage was probably the least of his worries, but in the meantime his brother deserved an answer.

'No, and I have every intention of surviving the battlefield and coming back to plague you all, I assure you. I should have tried to make the best of a bad job,' Rob finally said gruffly.

'All I will say is that while you may take after the Earl in looks, you have certainly got the Countess's temper,' the Viscount observed, but he looked visibly relieved at that reassurance.

'I suppose you think I have got what I deserve then, Jas— neither my wife nor my freedom?'

'Of course not. You are my brother, right or wrong, but your bride had to endure a number of things she did not deserve at all.'

'I know it, ' Rob acknowledged stiffly. 'But I cannot set things right when she has put herself beyond reach.'

'You can be discreet. To cause her more pain and a public scandal would be ungentlemanly.'

'I will conduct my affairs as a gentleman should,' he finally said, poker faced, and his brother turned aside to hide a rueful smile.

'Well, that will make a pleasant change,' James said mildly and watched that famous temper flare in his brother's eyes. 'Caroline has suffered enough,' he warned abruptly.

'I will do what I can to protect her from scandal, but I cannot promise you anything more. As you trenchantly observed when we last met, she obviously has no wish to be found and I am involved with another woman,' Rob ground out, as if wringing the admission out of himself was like getting the proverbial blood from a stone.

'A woman of Miss Tournier's stamp is hardly the stuff great love affairs are made of,' his brother said with a bland smile.

'You think not? She certainly has me caught as fast as a tiger in a trap.'

'Dear me, you had best take her into your keeping, then maybe you will get over her all the quicker.'

'You make the girl sound like a fleeting sickness.'

'What else can she be?'

Rob thought of his amateur enchantress, and his hard eyes softened as he fought back a smile.

'She is unique,' he finally replied quietly, and failed to see the unholy light in James's own dark eyes as his top-lofty brother finally admitted his fascination with a woman beyond the pale in every possible way.

Lord Littleworth thought Miss Tournier was probably the most unlikely Cyprian either he or his brother had come across in their colourful careers, but somehow held his peace. He even managed to prevent Jane treating her former favourite like a pariah for long enough to take tea with them, before his brother left to attend to his duties once again.

Rob might loathe the idea of stepping into his brother's shoes, but James had never quite learnt to live with the fact that the next letter might tell him Rob was dead on some distant battlefield, or wounded and beyond his help. He lingered at the window long after his brother's powerful form had been swallowed up in the twilight.

'We shall just have to pray, love,' his wife said as she came up behind him and slipped a warm hand into his cold one. 'After all, you always did swear he had a charmed life.'

'But this will be a mighty struggle, Janey.'

'Yes, and I cannot help but wish that he and Caro were reconciled before he went to play his part in it. This will be a terrible blow to her, wherever she might be.'

To her surprise James smiled ruefully at the thought of their lost friend.

'D'you know, I think she will find a way of keeping close to her husband, Janey love.'

As he rode back to town through intermittent moonlight, Rob let his thoughts dwell on his unwanted bride once more. His regret and shame had come too late, he decided ruefully. If he ever found his wife, she would doubtless meet him with the contempt he deserved, and then there was Cleo…

He had a passion for the wench that was slowly driving him to distraction, or indiscretion, or both. Jas was quite right; a woman ready to embark on a career selling herself to the highest bidder was hardly the material great romances were made of, yet he was perilously close to needing her beyond reason. A family and children with plump and homely Caroline seemed in retrospect a haven of tranquillity set against the mad, passionate—and he could not flinch from the word for ever—adulterous affair he was about to embark upon.

Yet he only had to think of holding his Cleo—warm and willing in his arms, and the whole night ahead of them as he had promised—and he was like a green boy promised wondrous delights. Maybe a few weeks in her arms would cure him, as his brother had implied. When the inevitable battle was over he could return home, God willing, then finally sell out and set about retrieving his wife. Once he was living with her in mundane respectability, few would be tactless enough to remember his shady past.

Except the idea of getting over Cleo, as if she were a tropical fever that was so fierce it must burn itself out, was laughable. Some things just were and Cleo was his, no cure and no term they could just live out, then walk away. If only he had never met the wench on that wild night in St James's, how very much simpler his life would be—yet how very much less worth the living.

However many times she told herself not to be a ninnyhammer, 'Cleo' missed her lover very badly indeed. She tried to remember that sooner or later she must learn to manage without him altogether, but the very idea made her life seem such a desert that she rapidly dismissed the voice of reason. Common sense never had done her an iota of good when it came to Rob Besford, and she had a lowering suspicion that it never would.

The planned visit to Vale had not materialised after all, and she had no taste for the places open to a courtesan once there was no prospect of seeing Rob in any of them. After two days spent playing gloomy pieces on the pianoforte, and annoying the gardener by pottering about his small domain looking for something to do, she decided that the life of a fashionable convenient was deeply tedious when her protector was otherwise engaged.

To make matters worse, Alice and Lord Wrovillton spent the whole time arguing. A stern look seemed to have settled permanently on his lordship's handsome face, while Alice became more defiantly sulky by the hour.

The morning before her week was supposed to be up came with no sign of Caro's supposedly ardent lover. However, Lord Wrovillton strolled into his lover's morning room while they were at breakfast, fidgeted with his elegant cane as if he were far more uncertain than he looked, frowned darkly and finally cleared his throat.

'Come, my dear, pray tell your friend what we are about, so you can both put on your best while I repair to Cavendish Square and get tricked out like a Bond Street beau on a spree.'

Alice gave him a mulish look and folded her arms across her chest, pursing her lips and glaring defiance.

'Before God, it's just like trying to humour a naughty child!' he burst out.

Traitorously, Caro felt a certain amount of sympathy with that view as Alice snapped, 'Then humour me by not coming back.'

'Much more of this, my girl and I might do just that. Heaven knows, Old Nosey will need every experienced officer he can get, so I might just as well rejoin and go straight to the devil if you refuse to see reason.'

'No! Oh, no, Will, you must not!'

Now there was no mistaking the anguish in Alice's voice. It held the same thread of terror Caro felt at the thought of Rob exposed to enemy fire once again.

'Then get yourself to church by noon, you stubborn female, or I shall go straight round to Horse Guards and sign up this afternoon. If you will not have me, I might as well go where I am needed.'

'Never—I would brave all the harpies in England rather than risk that. But you could do so much better.'

'No, there is no other wife for me. If you refuse, I shall stay a cross-grained bachelor all my life and am quite willing to swear it here and now in front of a witness. I, William Wrovillton, will live and die a lonely, embittered man if you, Alice Stoneleigh, refuse to become my lawfully wedded wife. There, Miss Tournier, that is a solemn enough oath for any man on his wedding morning, do you not agree?'

'Why, yes, sir, I rather think it is,' Caro replied, with a smile of complicity, openly delighted at the mention of the word wedding, and Alice gave an exclamation of disgust.

'Traitor!'

'Guilty as charged.'

'I should have been able to rely on you of all people to read him a lecture on the consequences of an over-hasty nuptial,' Alice told her bitterly, then clapped her hand to her mouth, and looked from one to the other in horror at giving part of Caro's secret away.

'Oh, I am so sorry, I let my temper fly away with my tongue. Forgive me, Caro love?' she exclaimed, compounding the crime in her haste to apologise for it.

'Of course,' Caro replied with a resigned sigh.

His lordship's shrewd, speculative grey eyes were hard

upon her now. She had been so close to attaining her stolen idyll, and now Rob's friend would surely insist the sorry truth came out after all.

'So, Alice, I have to deduce that your guest is not a Miss Tournier but a Mrs Besford after all,' he drawled with an artistic look of surprise that made Caro deeply suspicious.

'Surely that is a rash conclusion to draw, my lord, just on the strength of a slight change to my forename,' Caro replied, with her chin in the air and her backbone ready stiffened against the blow that was sure to come next.

'But such a singular one, ma'am. Coincidence is rarely quite as random as it is made out to be in my experience,' he replied with an elegant bow and an enigmatic smile.

'Will, please, please do not tell him. I beg of you!'

Alice sounded frantic, but made good use of some of the arts she had tried to teach Caro by clasping his arm as if it was her only support in life, and letting her large blue eyes fill with slow tears that only made them look more beautiful than ever. Unfortunately, he was amused rather than moved.

'There's no point playing off your tricks on me, minx. I have seen 'em all before, after all.'

Alice flung away. 'I knew I should never have become entangled with a rake.'

'Considering that you are La Belle Aleysha, I fail to see how you were going to meet any hymn-singing methodies, m'dear. Indeed, I wonder you meet anyone *other* than rakes. You are to be congratulated on your ingenuity.'

'You are insufferable, sir, and now you're going to ruin my dearest friend's happiness. I hate you—do you know that? I really and truly detest you.'

'All the same, you will meet me in church at noon, or I shall be off to inform Rob that his wife has been right under his nose all the time he was making a fool of himself searching for her up hill and down dale.'

'Not even you are such a bad ha'penny as to resort to blackmail.'

'Oh, but I am, my dear. Unless you agree to marry me, of course.'

The names Alice then called her would-be husband were largely unknown to Caro, but she watched fascinated as Lord Wrovillton shrugged them off his broad shoulders.

'Your answer, if you please?' he finally said coolly.

'Very well, I will marry you. Then make you regret it to your dying day.'

'I'm quite sure you will try,' he told her and Caro saw him turn aside to hide a smile of pure triumph. 'Twelve o'clock sharp then, Miss Stoneleigh—one minute later and I shall visit Berkeley Square first, then Horse Guards.'

'I gave my word,' Alice told him between gritted teeth, 'even if you cannot act the gentleman, a true lady does not break her promises.'

'How refreshing. Very well, then, I shall see you in church, my dove, and don't forget to be on time.'

'And afterwards, I'll see you in hell.'

'Very probably,' he told her and, whistling under his breath, he quit the room with such a broad wink for Caro that she only just managed not to burst out laughing.

She was tolerably certain that he had never had the least intention of giving her away, but it would never do to let Alice know it. At least not until after Will's wedding ring was safely on her finger.

Despite her complaints, Alice was dressed in a very fetching ensemble in plenty of time for the ceremony.

* * *

'You ordered this days ago, did you not?' Caro chided as she helped the bride into her barouche and fussed over her friend's fine pelisse and matching satin gown as befitted her duties as chief, and only, bridesmaid.

'Yes,' Alice admitted on a sigh. 'I hope cream trimmed with rose pink is not too much of a lie, but what do you think, Caro?'

'I think that it becomes you beautifully and is, like you, almost painfully honest,' Caro said with a slightly wobbly smile of reassurance.

'Well, I could not help but dream and plan just in case, although I knew it was ridiculous to listen to him.'

'Not ridiculous at all, love,' Caro told her with a hug they both needed for reassurance. 'Although I think it is traditional for the bride to be tearful, not her attendant.'

'I dare not give in to my feelings in case I think better of it all and turn tail after all. Anyway, it's no wonder if you cry at weddings, when I think how awful your own must have been—and me not there to fuss over you as we always promised to do for each other. What a fine pair we are to be sure, love—both in the wrong place at the wrong time.'

'We have swapped roles this time,' Caro said with a smile. 'Now you will be a respectable wife and I the scandalous woman. You will have to meet me in Green Park incognito, just as you used to me. Although I never knew what guise you would turn up in next. I thought the milkmaid's outfit became you the best, but turning up that time dressed as a groom was probably a little too daring even for you.'

'At least it made you laugh, and while I might be about to become a wife after all, I cannot see that I shall ever become a respectable one.'

'I don't think your Will does respectable,' Caro observed, seeing the apprehension still lurking in Alice's ultramarine eyes.

Her friend chuckled and her whole face softened, 'No, he goes his own way, just as I have always done.'

'Then now you can be blissfully original together,' Caro said smartly and, since they had arrived at the church, Alice did not argue for once.

Chapter Twelve

It was a bittersweet experience, witnessing Alice and Will's wedding at Rob's side. Stupidly, Caro had not expected to walk into the church behind Alice to find him acting as groomsman, although Will and Rob had such a tried-and-tested friendship she probably ought to have done. She thought it spoke volumes about Rob's feelings towards his own bride that he had not demanded Will's support at his own marriage.

The sight of her husband waiting by the altar when she and Alice arrived brought back a host of uncomfortable memories, and her heart gave a frantic jolt. Maybe it was a trick of the light that he looked more like the hard-faced cynic who had once awaited his despised bride, rather than her urgent suitor of the last week. Every line of his stiffly held body seemed as hostile as it had on their wedding day, and she nearly turned and ran at the very sight of him, just as she should have done the last time they met at the altar.

She hastily reminded herself that everything had changed between them now, but it proved little comfort when she considered how quickly he would assume that mask of disdain if he ever learned her true identity. She looked away, until the vicar was well and truly launched on the flowing phrases of the marriage service and she could risk a sideways glance. Now he was staring directly in front of him, as if all his attention was concentrated on the ceremony, but there was an air of tension about his broad shoulders that told her otherwise.

When the parson asked uncertainly who gave the bride to her groom, there was nothing for Caro to do but step forward and declare firmly, 'I do.'

All four of them turned and stared at her then, and even the organist swivelled round on his bench to stare at such an unusual sponsor.

'Well, who else is there?' she asked belligerently of the air just to the left of her husband's ear.

'Point taken,' he replied equably.

'Very well, then, perhaps we may proceed?'

The vicar cleared his throat and sailed on with this unconventional marriage, as if eager to get it done so he could grapple with his conscience over his morning's work. Caro duly entrusted her best friend to Will Wrovillton, and he spoke his vows with such sincerity even his bride wiped away a surreptitious tear or two. Then it was over at last, and Alice's slender hand was clasped within Will's large one, as if neither ever intended letting go of the other.

Following them out of the quiet little church, Caro remembered how she and Alice had planned the most perfect weddings for their adult selves when they were at school together, and almost had a fit of the giggles as she automatically caught the bouquet Alice threw at her.

'Well now, are we to expect another nuptial, Miss Tournier?' Will drawled and Caro did not know whether to grin back at the devious rogue, or stick her tongue out like a naughty schoolboy.

'I should not advise you to hold your breath, my lord.'

'Best not, perhaps, but who knows what the future holds for any of us?'

'Who, indeed?' Alice told him sternly.

'Ah, my pretty dove. I already know *my* future stretches before me in an uninterrupted stream of serenely happy days with my good and obedient little wife.'

'Pah! I want an annulment.'

'Tell me so again in the morning, and we will see if you may have it or not,' he told his furious lady with such pompous self-satisfaction that Caro had to look away to hide her smile.

'I had rather go to my bed with mad King George himself than share it with you, my lord.'

'No, but would you, indeed? I fear that his Majesty is already well and truly married, if those innumerable princes and princesses are anything to go by, my love, and who said anything about going to bed?'

'You can wait until hell freezes over for me, in bed or out.'

'Then you will burn before I do, my love,' he told her and seized her in a passionate embrace that seemed to leave her neither breath nor inclination to argue.

They finally recovered enough discretion to say a hasty farewell, climb into their carriage and tug down the blinds. Then the coach and four swept out into the traffic and Caro was left standing by Rob's side, wondering what on earth she was supposed to do now.

'Your week is up tomorrow, madam. Pray be ready to set out on a brief journey, and do not bother to pack more than you need for it. I fully intend to provide for you from now on.'

With that terse order Rob signalled to Alice's waiting

coachman, handed her up into the barouche, then touched his curly-brimmed hat with his cane and walked away, just as if he had encountered a chance acquaintance in the park.

For a moment she watched him saunter off with open-mouthed incredulity and wondered whether to fling the bouquet at his receding back. She had, she told herself crossly, half a mind to go and buy that ticket for the Bath stage after all.

It was lonely in the neat little house in St James's without Alice and Will, and Caro spent the rest of the day brooding over perfunctory gentlemen who were April when they wooed, and December after they won. Towards evening she began to feel wistful rather than angry, and by bedtime she was wondering mournfully if her tender lover of the last few days had gone for ever.

'And I will miss him so,' she murmured, as her maid gently brushed out her curls.

'What was that, miss?'

Had she really said it out loud? Maybe she was going distracted at last; she braced her shoulders and refused to even acknowledge the possibility. Colonel Besford and his unsuitable wife would never be rid of one another if she got herself locked up in the local madhouse for the insanity of loving a man who despised her.

'Nothing to signify, Emily. Is everything ready for tomorrow?'

'Oh, yes, miss, it's all bang up to the knocker,' the girl assured her fervently and Caro was glad one of them was happy at the prospect of going out of town and facing the unknown in strange surroundings.

Still, as Alice had said, a lady did not break her word, and she had promised herself to Colonel Besford. Then there was the fact that she wanted him just as fiercely as he did her. Indeed, if today was anything to go by, it was possible that she was more eager to succumb to his dubious charms than he was to exert them. Drat the man! She had known he was trouble the instant she laid eyes on him and should have run then, instead of when it was too late.

Her sleep had been light and disturbed the previous night, and she fretted throughout the morning, slowly realising that Rob did not intend to appear before the very moment she had dictated made up her week's grace. There was something implacable about his strict measure of the day, and instead of admiring his rigid adherence to his word, she was filled with foreboding.

'Wretched man!' she exploded as she lingered over a luncheon she hadn't even tasted.

'I beg your pardon, Miss Cleo?'

'Nothing, James—if anyone calls, I shall be in the drawing room.'

When her husband finally condescended to come and collect his mistress, he would soon realise that the highly finished article of no virtue at all he had picked out for the role had better things to do than sit about moping over her dilatory keeper. Sitting down at the piano, she launched into a complex piece of Herr Beethoven's that she was determined to master and put her tangled emotions into the music. If she concentrated hard enough, she might even manage to forget her so-called lover for more than thirty seconds at a stretch.

At exactly the appointed time, Rob ran up the steps. He ruefully noted a collection of bandboxes and a valise large enough to have supplied a man's needs for a fortnight waiting in the hall, and concluded that Cleo kept some of her promises after all. He handed his hat and cane to the footman on duty, but kept his greatcoat on.

'We shall not be staying,' he informed the impassive James, then raised a questioning eyebrow.

'Miss Tournier is in the drawing room and she said you should go on up, sir.'

'Did she, indeed? My thanks.'

'Thank *you*, sir,' James replied sincerely.

Life would be quieter but considerably tamer at Vale Court, he decided, and doubted he would come across many gentlemen who tipped as generously as the Colonel, at least not now that the missus had turned respectable.

Rob ran upstairs with all the impetuosity of an eager lover.

'So we come full circle, Cleo,' he said, with a light in his eyes that recalled their first encounter in this room as he met her honey-coloured eyes over the mirror-polished instrument.

'Do we indeed, Colonel?' she replied, her fingers coming down in a clash on the keyboard.

He came closer and she felt a prickle of unease slide down her spine, even as she flushed under his heated scrutiny of the flimsy muslin gown that had moulded itself so lovingly to her figure. It might be the most respectable of her day dresses, but trust Alice to insist on an invisible petticoat and the softest of material that would lovingly cling to her curves.

'Did you ever doubt it?' he said, when he could wrench his gaze from her figure to her face at last.

'Few things in this life are certain,' she replied coolly, proud of herself for refusing to melt before the fire in his eyes as he probably intended.

She wasn't just a graceful body and well-displayed curves,

any more than she was merely a wife or mistress and it was about time he realised it.

'And this is one of them,' he announced as if driven by demons and plucked her out of her seat to plant swift, impatient kisses on her open mouth.

Passion, complete and utterly demanding, swept over her in the tick between one second and the next. The suddenness of it, the uselessness of fighting her feelings for him, overwhelmed her, and tears pricked her tired eyes and crept down her cheeks, despite her exasperation at her own weakness.

'What is it, my sweet?' he asked gently, once again the lover she had dreamt of so uselessly during her sad career as Mrs Besford.

'You, me…this… Oh, I don't know.'

'Very lucid.'

'I don't feel lucid,' she informed him crossly, wishing his mouth back on hers to burn away the doubts that had suddenly sprung to life again now he had set several feet of cool air between them.

'Neither do I, but let's get away from here before you make a liar of me, Cleo.'

She looked a question at him.

'I said I would not take you under this roof, and I do like to keep my word now and again.'

'Well, *I* have been ready this age.'

'And you think me dilatory, do you not?'

'Umm, well… No, of course not.'

'In other words, yes, but now your time has run out, you must admit we are free to enjoy one another's company however we please. Your rules were *very* constricting, my dear.'

Caro tried to gauge his mood, and wondered how he could

look so frank and open while revealing so little of his inner thoughts. She shook her head in puzzlement, took out a thoroughly frivolous handkerchief and dabbed at her damp cheeks, then fussed over an imaginary spot on her travelling gown. Perhaps it was better not to attempt to work out the convolutions of his mind while her brain felt as if it was full of feathers.

'Come then, Miss Tournier. Or are you thinking of reneging after all?'

'I gave my word, that should be enough for you, Colonel,' she told him haughtily, before sailing regally past him and out of the doors.

She was halfway down the stairs and under the eyes of the servants before she realised that he had done it again. He had provoked her into forgetting her doubts; in fact, he had manoeuvred her into doing exactly what he wanted, as usual. He was, she decided, the most managing, ruthless, demanding, devious man she had ever encountered and he knew perfectly well that she could not tell him so in front of all these people. She shot him another furious look and swept through the front door and on to the pavement, even more infuriated when he had no difficulty keeping pace with her whatsoever.

'Here we all are then, sir and miss, and we'd best hurry if we're to get there afore nightfall,' observed Webb, indicating a fine travelling carriage and another behind it, loaded up with luggage and with Emily's eager face peering out of the window.

This time Webb's face was impassive as the Sphinx, but Caro flinched away from contemplating what he really thought of his master's choice of travelling companion.

'True, but before we set out, there are a few things we need to make plain,' Rob said and fell back to discuss them with his henchman in a confidential undertone.

Caro waited impatiently and wondered why her husband had made that choice herself. He might have been conveying a chance-met acquaintance for a promenade in the park for all the passion he was showing for her company at the moment. Was this how the future was to be? she asked herself despairingly. Was she to become a transient diversion for those times when he had nothing better to occupy himself with than his kept woman?

She shot him a fierce frown, only to find his eyes had been centred on her the whole time. Deciding crossly that every time she thought she knew him, she found that she had been allowed to see just one facet of his complex character, she concluded that nobody really knew Rob Besford, particularly not his wife. Tired of standing on the pavement, feeling as if most of London's idlers were eyeing her slightly *outré* garb and slender person with scorn, Caro submitted to being handed into the carriage only because she still wanted to be wherever Rob was. The look she gave him as soon as she was settled and he had given the order to be off was hostile all the same.

'I suppose it would be too much to expect that I might be informed of where we are going?' she enquired sweetly.

'Far too much, my dear,' he replied indolently and lay back on the squabs as if he intended going to sleep without further ado.

As Caro sat bolt upright in her corner, trying to think of something crushing to say, he opened one indolent eyelid, then closed it again.

'I suggest you emulate me. You will find precious little opportunity for sleep when we reach journey's end.'

And just what was she to make of that? He was hardly the impassioned cavalier of last week. Today he hardly seemed to care if she was with him or no, and she minded the loss of her ardent suitor very much indeed.

'I wish to be put down in Bond Street,' she told him haughtily.

'Wish away, my Cleo,' he replied lazily.

She could have kicked him, hard. Indeed, she would have done, if not for the fact that she only had light shoes on her feet and his boots were of a very different order. She made all too many mistakes, but rarely the same one twice she assured herself. Except that the worst one of all was sitting opposite her, looking as if he hadn't a care in the world!

'If you will not oblige me in that, then pray tell me where we are going.'

'No.'

'No? You are a bully and a braggart, sir, and I shall make such a fuss when we change horses that you will be glad to take me back to Alice's house and be done with me.'

'I thank you for the warning.'

'Then you will not take me home?'

'Oh, I shall do that, never fear,' he remarked and opened his eyes at last, and what she saw in them disturbed her more than ever.

Caro began to wonder if she had misjudged Lord Wrovillton's integrity. Had he informed his friend of her identity after all? No, she decided, his lordship at least was a man of honour. She looked down her nose at the contrary male opposite, and wondered what ailed him this time. From the banked fire in his lazy-seeming eyes, he desired her as hotly as ever, but something had changed and she lacked the experience to know just what it was. Perhaps all gentlemen behaved so with their kept women, in which case she was surprised they kept them as long as they did!

Dark looks seemed to make no impression on the wretched man, so she turned to stare moodily out of the window. No need for *them* to pull the leather blind to keep out prying eyes, and she told herself she was glad as the town fell behind them and fields began to outnumber houses. The landscape was not familiar to her, but she thought they were probably heading southeast. Was he taking her to the Continent, or merely intending to love her and leave her at one of the Channel ports, while he rejoined the Army of Occupation?

Either way, she would have liked a choice in the matter, even if the very idea of London without him seemed as bleak as the polar wastes. She sighed and wondered why she must persist in loving the monster, but love him she did all the same. The thought of even one night in his arms was enough to send a warm current of excitement coursing through her entire body, and make her tingle from head to toe. Flushed with guilty heat, and furious with her imagination for being so unruly, she tugged at the window to let in some air.

He leaned over and pulled the catch open with such ease that her temper ignited again.

She just managed to grit a 'thank you' between her teeth before staring resolutely at the view, as if her life depended on remembering every detail.

'You are very welcome, my dear,' he murmured and turned back into his corner to take up his catnap where he had left off.

Insufferable, arrogant, unknowable man! Why women put themselves to the trouble of loving and, even more rashly, marrying any member of his sex she could not currently imagine. She glanced at his sleeping form and wondered why she had committed the folly of falling in love with him, when she had been indifferent to far more handsome men. Indeed Will Wrovillton was more of an Adonis than Colonel Besford would ever be; yet he left her unmoved, just as all the pinks of the *ton* had done before she laid eyes on her husband. She granted herself the luxury of surveying her husband without his over-perceptive green eyes studying her in turn, and tension seeped out of her as she watched him sleep.

He was so much himself, she thought with such a tender smile that it was as well neither of them could see it. From the vantage point of a wallflower she had observed the eligibles night after night, and soon decided the most handsome young men were strangely interchangeable. It came of having similar backgrounds and education, she supposed, but they had seemed much of a muchness, until she met Colonel Robert Besford and found him unique.

Even in repose, he seemed to exude an air of suppressed energy, and she challenged any woman to resist the devilment in his true green eyes when they were exclusively focused on her. After all, that was why she was here, wasn't it? Because she could not resist the fire and promise in that gaze, especially when he seemed to be able to look into the very essence of her and communicate his secret self to hers. Really, she was just as silly as all the other débutantes—ridiculously in thrall to a handsome face like a rabbit to a fox, she told herself crossly, and brooded on the enigmatic nature of love for a while.

At last she began to feel unaccountably weary herself, and her eyelids started to droop so heavily she decided there was no point fighting it, any more than she could resist her obsession with the unknowable Colonel Besford. She snuggled into her corner of the luxuriously upholstered coach to sleep more peacefully than she had since he carried her into Alice's house in his arms.

Once her soft breathing became slower and more regular, her companion's eyes opened at last, and it was Rob's turn to gaze at *her* unguarded face. His brooding look lingered on the pure oval of her face, examining every feature until such heat began to warm his gaze he was surprised it did not wake her. He swept a scorching look over her delightfully curved person and her delicately moulded features, and finally forced his attention away from her unguarded face, to watch the passing countryside in his turn.

At the posting house she gave a murmur of protest at the noise, then fell back into that determined sleep when he reassured her quietly. The fewer people who saw Colonel Besford on his way to the coast with his mistress, the better, he decided. Jas and Jane would never forgive him if that particular scandal became public, and it would interfere with his own plans rather badly.

Waking at last, Caro caught a confused glimpse of a lake glittering in the last rays of sunset, and a sweep of gravelled carriage drive towards a neat Tudor manor. She rubbed her eyes and sat, blinking owlishly in the fading light as she tried to gather her senses for whatever onslaught they were about to experience.

'I seem to have slept the day away, but where have you brought me, Colonel?' she managed at last.

'Westmeade Place.'

'Really? How extraordinary of you.'

'Why should you think that peculiar when it is my home?'

'Mainly because I ought not to be here, I suppose.'

'I always like to spend at least one night at Westmeade before I leave England,' he answered her obliquely and she wondered once again about the mysteries he was brooding on.

'And I am to have no say in the matter?' she sparked back, her misgivings about staying at his house and meeting what should have been her staff in such a guise making her sound distinctly querulous even to her ears.

'Whether you have or not, nothing will prevent you saying your piece, I suspect,' he returned wearily.

'Even if you have no intention of listening?'

'Not when you chose to take a pet.'

'Take a pet? You make me sound like a silly schoolgirl,' she replied, inwardly squirming as if she really was the other woman in the case and this house his wife's true home.

'No, do I? And that would never do, would it?'

'Certainly not when you are aping the schoolmaster so ably,' she returned smartly, allowing herself to be helped out of the carriage by a suddenly respectful Webb.

So without really thinking about it, Caro found herself complying with Rob's wishes after all. Vexed with herself when she realised it, she forgot to look where she was going and her stiff legs went from under her as she tripped on a loose stone. She closed her eyes against inevitable disaster, but never reached the ground. Breathless with the suddenness of her rescue, she was borne up in her husband's strong arms to enter her home for the night as if she was a veritable invalid.

'Put me down!' she demanded crossly once he reached the venerable Tudor hallway.

'Madam is very tired,' Rob informed a couple of grinning footmen, who dutifully lit the way upstairs, despite 'madam's' very vocal protests that she was perfectly capable of walking and not in the least weary, thank you very much!

All the same, Caro was secretly rather impressed when they arrived in what was obviously the master bedchamber without him showing much sign of exertion. Thank heavens she was no longer the plump little squab she had once been, but she was still a healthy young woman and his great strength briefly awed her into silence.

'Emily!' she squeaked as her maid came towards her, smiling a welcome.

'Ma'am.'

'Pleased though I am to see that you have arrived safely, I believe we can manage all that needs to be done for ourselves tonight, thank you, Emily.'

'Very good, sir.'

'Oh, no, we can't, I…' Caro began, but it was no good; Emily had already curtsied and left. 'Deserter,' she muttered darkly as the door closed on her handmaiden.

The next moment she let out a surprised squeak of protest as Rob dropped her on the bed so abruptly that she bounced, and her skirts flew up with the speed of her landing. She glared at him in silent reproach, but he only looked indolently back at her and grinned.

'Well, you were getting heavy,' he said ungallantly, and went over to inspect the cold collation left ready for them as she groped for words pungent enough to express her outraged feelings and failed lamentably.

Chapter Thirteen

⁓⁓⁓⁓⁓⁓⁓

'We seem to be provisioned to withstand a siege, but if you are not hungry, then…' Rob let his voice trail off, and eyed Caro's exposed legs with wolfish appreciation, then made a determined move to join her on the bed.

'No, no, I am! Very hungry, that is,' she insisted breathlessly, and hastily slid off the opposite side.

'Will you sit then, madam, or must I consume my dinner standing up?'

'Of course not, what a ridiculous notion.'

Anything to have several feet of fine mahogany between them she decided and hastily sat. She reached for her plate and piled it up at random, winning an amused glance from her companion at her selection from the plenty on display.

'Wine?'

'Er, yes, I believe so.'

It might put a little heart into her, she decided, while marvelling at herself for behaving like the shrinking heroine out of a melodrama at the same time. After all, this was what she had expected, what she had been inviting one way and another ever since they met again. So why did she feel like an ill-prepared bride on her wedding night now it was upon her at last?

She ate her food and sipped her wine without tasting anything as she pondered on the nature of passion, and what would shortly take place between them. Then she wondered if she could face it after all, now he was strangely unlike the ardent lover he had been so recently and her heartbeat began to outrun her appetite. Should she confess, before he committed himself to her in the eyes of church and state all unknowing?

'I want to tell—'

But he did not wish to hear.

'Better?' he interrupted ruthlessly.

'A little, thank you, but that Chantilly cream looks delightful. I believe I shall try it with the apple pie.'

'I think you will find it tastes exactly the same as the spoonful you ate with your asparagus.'

'Heavens, did I? How very odd of me.'

'Indeed, almost as odd as the fact you appear to have confused me with Bluebeard. I really don't share any of his murderous tendencies, my dear, so you can refrain from eating every dish on the table to hold me at arm's length.'

'Is that what I was doing?'

'Undoubtedly,' he said and at last that teasing light was back in his eyes, and his mouth softened from the hard line she had been growing familiar with once more.

'Oh, dear,' she said rather inadequately and castigated herself as a widgeon of the highest order.

'Oh, dear, indeed, for I do not think I can bear a night spent chastely on the day bed, and you appear to have lost your nerve, do you not, my bold, bad Cleo?'

'Er…' she began and ground to a halt, nothing coming to mind but the facts that she was not bold, nor bad, nor even Cleo.

'Will this help?' he said in a driven tone and tugged her out of her chair and straight into his arms.

'This' was such a passionate seduction of her senses that all she could do was cling to his broad shoulders, like a shipwreck survivor hanging on to a rock. His mouth ravished her lips, her eyes and the curve of her chin, then came back to hers, as if he was desperate to centre himself on the only sure thing in life. Now she could not doubt the need in him, but she might have succumbed to maidenly terrors even then, if she not felt the fine tremor that had undone her before run through his long-fingered hand as he drew her ever closer.

Rendered defenceless in a breath by that hint of vulnerability, it was her turn to let her mouth explore his face and glory in the feel of his firm features under her wondering touch. Bliss to have such freedom—torture to feel such hot, driving need shoot through her body and not have it sated. Suddenly she was longing for some balm only he could grant her after all, as passion burnt and confused within her.

She raised herself on tiptoe and placed her hands on his broad shoulders, then daringly opened her mouth on his, darting her tongue inside his as he had taught her, and she shamelessly moaned her hunger as his muscular torso brushed against her sensitised breasts.

'I think I need you, Colonel Besford,' she gasped.

'As I am desperate for you, my enchantress, that's just as well, is it not?'

He took charge again, proving it with the urgency of his touch and swept kisses from her jaw to one ear, then the other, as she shivered with delight.

'I had no notion,' she murmured.

Even to her own ears, she sounded dazed and a little foolish after his master-class in sensuality. She had learnt so much since she ran away from her husband, but suddenly nerves were threatening to engulf her again.

'Then let me show you more,' he whispered back.

He stopped to place a lingering kiss on her eager mouth, then moved his questing one down her throat, even as his fingers parted the first buttons of the provocative amber pelisse he had fantasised over ripping off her for a sennight if she did but know it.

His lips followed his wicked, experienced hands down the growing gap he created, and she felt cool air against her skin, until he displaced it with hot kisses. At last, the pelisse fell away and the fragile muslin beneath did little enough to hide her aroused state. He ran an open-palmed hand over the spot where a shameless nipple stood proud through the fine material and her heart thumped a maverick beat as he caressed her through the gossamer stuff.

Her tongue slicked suddenly parched lips as her breath gasped, and he completed her undoing by catching her tongue gently in his white teeth and taking it languidly into his own mouth. By the time his busy hands had pushed the flimsy gown off her shoulder, she was as eager for his touch as he was to explore uninhibited by its scanty cover.

She tried for a brief moment to think about what she was doing, to hold back a little of herself, to remember she had to face him in the morning and pretend to be what she was not. Then he lowered his mouth and took her bared nipple into his mouth and there *was* no tomorrow, only now.

Pleasure shot through her, warm lethargy invaded her limbs and all she wanted was the freedom for them to explore each other endlessly. She looked down at his head at her breast and wave upon wave of love-stricken desire shook her. She moaned her need, and he left one breast for the other. It luxuriated under his hungry caress and she keened with pleasure, as his long fingers attended to the one he had just forsaken, still damp with his kisses and hard and full with an arousal so powerful she felt it would burn her up.

She was languorous with wanting him, yet so alive her heart sang with it, when it was not beating swift and hard in time to the flick of his knowing tongue on her beseeching breast. For a blissful instant he pulled her even closer, his hands running down her spine to rest on the rounded cheeks of her bottom and draw her into the heart of their desire. Now she felt no fear of the unknown, no shock at the rampant difference between them, evident in his hard arousal. She revelled in it rather, and longed for fulfilment.

All her inhibitions finally got up and left as she pushed his coat open and fumbled with the small buttons of his waistcoat, almost desperate in her need to get closer to his powerful torso. At last she got them undone and impatiently tugged at his shirt. She keened a protest as cold air intruded between them, but he just pulled the offending garment from his breeches and tugged her back into his arms, as if he could not bear the slightest gap of separation either.

Released, her hands ran under the fine lawn and over rigid muscles, caressed skin that felt like satin over steel, and explored the novelty of his eager response to her touch. She braced her palms against his torso and he moaned. Eyes feverish with triumph and the novelty of making him as needy as she was herself, she met his fiery emerald gaze without a hint of her usual reserve. She could hold nothing back in the face of a passion that burnt, cleansing and merciless, between them.

He pushed her gently from him, held her a few inches away and gazed down into her face with heat-hazed eyes, and the cold air made her question herself again. What if she did not please him now he had licence to see what no other man would ever see? What if he despised the amateurish touch of so unlikely a virgin?

Suddenly it had all crept back: the insecurities, the uneasy knowledge of what she was doing; what he, all unknowing, was doing to himself by wanting her. Panic made her shake under his restraining hands even more than desire had a few seconds earlier—maybe he did he not want her after all? Maybe her urgency revolted him? She twisted her face away from him, fighting his gentle grip on her narrow waist. The humiliation of knowing her craving for him had outstripped his for her was agony.

'Ah, no, Cleo, my darling. I want you, beyond reason I want you,' he told her, gauging the fear in her heart and gentling his voice, even when the wrenching grip of hot desire was driving him to take her and not count in her inexperience.

Cleo—there was the rub, was it not? Yet even that lingering sadness flew away as he spun a web of wonder and delight about her. The making of it had her marvelling that a man could be so gentle, so patient and yet ravage every sense, every inch of his lover with such sensuous demand. He pressed her gently down on to the edge of the bed and removed her soft kid boots, kissing the arch and curve of each foot, then working his way up her legs until he undid her garters and tugged off her stockings then, to her grave disappointment, stopped.

'Too soon, my lovely. There are so many things for us to learn about one another yet.'

Then he was cursing the elaborate fastenings of her gown and she succumbed to a breathless fit of the giggles and fell back on the bed, almost doubled up as he searched for hooks and laces.

'At last! You females truss yourselves up like chickens,' he said after a short struggle.

Caro felt the gown give, and stopped laughing to turn on to her back and raise her arms in welcome. He threw himself down beside her, and she wondered fleetingly if he might not need a new bed before morning, given the punishment he was inflicting on this one.

'This is a parlous state of inequality,' she told him with mock-severity after another breathless interlude. 'There was I, supposing a gentlemen at least took his boots off before he bedded a lady.'

'You, hussy, are lucky I got us as far as the bed,' he told her darkly, but nevertheless he sat on the side of the bed to tug off the offending articles.

'Let me,' she said, and darted up from her languorous pose.

After a struggle she ended up on the floor, with one boot held to her breasts and their eyes met in a long, needing gaze until neither could stand more delay. He threw his other boot across the room and ripped his fine lawn shirt over his head with one mighty tug and sent it after his mistreated footwear. Soon she would be as unpopular with Rob's batman as she already was with his groom, she decided ruefully, then turned her attention to their far more interesting master.

Caro watched with awe as her eyes took in what her fingers had already begun to know. She catalogued the muscles playing in her lover's powerful torso as he unbuttoned his breeches impatiently, and could not wait to view him in all his glory.

'Seen enough yet, little voyeur?' he asked in a voice roughened with hunger and only he knew what else besides.

'Not nearly enough,' she said confidently, then the sheer physical perfection revealed as he stripped off the last barrier made her admit to awe after all.

He laughed rather unsteadily as he took in her widened amber gaze and pulled her towards him.

'The inequality is now in your favour, Cleo, and it's high time we remedied it.'

He eyed her supposedly invisible petticoat with disfavour, removed it in one smooth movement and unlaced her corset and sent it to join the rest of her ensemble out there in the darkness beyond their magic circle of candlelight and passion.

'How many layers of provocation must a man get through to reach the heart of you?' he said in a much-tried voice, as her gossamer silk shift flew across the room.

'At last, the centre of the maze,' he remarked abruptly and pulled her down on the mistreated bed once more, as if he was quite beyond fine words or gestures.

'Love me, Rob,' she whispered.

'I fully intend to,' he managed in a husky voice very unlike his usual firm tone, and trailed a blaze of passionate kisses from her chin to her breasts, then worshipped them lingeringly once more.

At last he continued that downward path of excitement and arousal until she resisted, and he looked up into molten amber eyes with a plea in his own.

'Trust me,' he demanded, and she opened to him with all the banked fire of love and longing within her, deciding recklessly that she would let the devil take tomorrow if she could have tonight.

'I do,' she returned with aching need frank in her wide eyes as they met his brilliant emerald gaze.

Satisfied, he nodded, then used his wickedly knowing tongue to heat places she had never even dreamed she had to liquefied fire, and she gasped an incoherent appeal for him to salve the wild heat they had set ablaze before it burnt her up completely.

She ordered herself to trust him, parted her legs where the heat was now emphatic and surrendered up the demanding, dragging warmth he had aroused for their mutual pleasure. She received him, open eyed and joyful, as he reared over her and thrust into her with one powerful movement that new made the world for her. Her brief moment of pain as he entered stalled him briefly, but she rode it with feverish need. For a moment they were still as she felt her body adjust to his awesome possession, then, as the delightful sensation of fullness fought and overcame her hurt, she rose in unspoken demand.

She gasped her pleasure aloud as he almost withdrew, and then completed them again, groaning his satisfaction and watching her with molten eyes as he moved yet again, wary of hurting her, but nearly out of control with need of yet more. She brought her head up, met him gaze for gaze, eyes all polished, glowing amber as she kissed him full on the mouth, welcoming his thrusting tongue as her body flexed to demand he imitated its movements once again where they were so intimately joined. The ascendancy of lovers, the sensation of glowing, growing delight, obliterated her inexperience, and she moved hungrily, until neither knew who gave and who took.

Everything in her was centred where his ravishing, thrusting body melded with her ravished, demanding one. This was beyond anything she could have dreamt of. She revelled in the sensation of his great strength, his careful, rampant passion united to the very essence of her. His tender hunger had moved her outside her wildest dreams, and she wanted it never to end. Yet the relentless drive of mutual need demanded more. When he began to thrust urgently towards some unknown, but wondrous, destination, she suddenly needed to achieve it as badly as he did. She wrapped her slender legs round his mighty body and instinctively timed her own racing desire to this new, driven rhythm.

A great surge of delight opened up in front of them, and she was awed as they strove towards it, unified and outside the world, beyond time. With one last desperate thrust, he tipped them into molten fulfilment, and they both cried out involuntarily as they tumbled into rapture together. Convulsions rocked them, beat for blissful beat, and she revelled in every movement, every murmur. Now they were linked for all time, beyond time. Nobody could measure such endless, unknowable ecstasy— and why would they be fool enough to try?

At last she was back in his bed, returned from some golden world they had just learned together, and she heard her own breath sob as she smiled at him beatifically, her heart in her warm amber eyes. He was gasping for breath, his own eyes ablaze as he rolled their bodies over until she was cradled in his arms. Then he gathered the tempest-tossed bedclothes about them, and kissed her flushed, triumphant face.

'Oh you wonder, you enchantress,' he murmured into her mass of red-gold curls.

She buried her face in his chest and breathed in the tang of his heated skin, finding her own scents mingled with his, and highly satisfied that no part of them declared separation at last. He kissed the top of her head and his arms came up to cradle her, as if she was infinitely precious.

'Not a true red-head, though, I see,' he observed lazily, with a hint of teasing laughter in his deep voice, as if he felt the fiery blush that reddened her face against his still-labouring chest when she realised just what he meant.

'Unlike you,' she told him, refusing to raise her head from its haven on his muscular torso when its sprinkling of dark chestnut curls was brushing so satisfyingly against her cheek, as she listened to the steadying beat of his heart the settling of his breath.

'True, I'm red as a dog fox.'

'And are you as cunning?'

'Sometimes, and sometimes not,' he replied cryptically and she murmured a protest, as if she felt some sort of gap was opening up between them and resented it deeply. 'What of you?'

'The same, although more often foolish than fly.'

'Then we are much like the rest of hurrying humanity, are we not?'

'I never claimed otherwise.'

'Maybe not, but you are nevertheless unique.'

'How so?'

'In so many ways that I cannot think where to start,' he told her huskily and began to explore the byways of the ear closest to him in a way that made her forget the odd note in his voice.

In truth, she had never thought such a workaday organ could be the seat of such pleasure, she decided hazily, as her heartbeat began to quicken and heavy longing began to heat through her again like liquid lightning.

'I think you must truly be a sorceress, my lovely,' he whispered, and lifted her further up his prone body so he could set his mouth roaming down the cord of her neck, without wasting any more breath on idle conversation.

'You mean we can do it again?' she whispered in awe.

'As often as I have the strength and you the will.'

She pulled back and sent him a long, saucy look before replying, 'As I have more of that commodity than seems altogether proper, Colonel Besford, we could be here for a very long time.'

'Then all blessings be on such impropriety, if only you will stop your tongue and let me demonstrate how fervently I return the feeling.'

She put her head on one side, as if the outcome needed consideration.

'Very well, but only in the pursuit of scientific study, you understand.'

'Liar,' he accused, laughing up at her before taking her mouth in such a ravishing kiss that any attempt at coherent thought, let alone conversation, fled clean out of her mind for a very long time.

Later she recovered a little of her ordinary sense to wonder why happily married couples ever got up at all, then remembered the temporary nature of such delights for her and was suddenly close to tears. As if he knew it by some mysterious alchemy, he nuzzled her face into his strong neck and gently soothed her wildly tangled curls.

'Sleep, my sweet, everything else can wait.'

'Yes, the world can go hang, can it not?'

'Of course,' he replied with a wry twist to his lips, and then smiled at her as if she was just as crucial to his continuing happiness as he was to hers.

'That's good,' she murmured and slept at last.

Rob shifted her until she lay more comfortably in his arms and stared into the darkness for a while, savouring the feel of his lover as close to him as two human beings could be after so many nights spent racked by unsatisfied desire. If he had anything to do with it, there would be no more of them, he decided. All the same, he finally fell asleep with her still cradled in his arms, as if she might elude him even now if he did not keep her clasped to his mighty body.

Chapter Fourteen

Caro was not given the opportunity to wake in her lover's arms and dreamily savour the glories of the marriage bed the next morning. Instead she was awakened by the furtive sounds of her maid quietly collecting up discarded garments, trying to look as if it was quite normal to find an assortment of them cast to the four corners of the room.

'Your bath is ready in the dressing room, ma'am, and everything else is done. You have only to break your fast and then we can set out again,' Emily told her happily.

Overcome by the most ridiculous shyness, Caro just nodded and flushed as her maid held out her peignoir. She was lying back for a delightful soak in rose-scented bath water when the girl's words finally sank in.

'Set out?' she called, but only heard more bustling activity from the bedchamber as Emily whisked round it, gathering up traces of her mistress's occupation. 'What do you mean, set out?'

Her maid chose not to listen to her repeated question, and shortly afterwards Caro heard the door close behind her, so she had to contain her impatience while she dried herself in front of the fire. She had tried not to grow used to the ministrations of a maid, knowing she would have to look after herself as soon as she took up the life of a poor schoolmistress. Unfortunately she found that she had not succeeded very well in this laudable resolution, as she hastily donned the unfamiliar clothes laid out in readiness. Only when she finally had them on did she look at herself in the mirror, and found the daring cut and slightly *risqué* touches that embodied Cleo the seductress quite gone.

Instead a modest young woman stood in her shoes, and she tried to become reacquainted with Caroline. Her gown was soft amber again, but this time fine wool and buttoned firmly to the neck. She had to admit it was acceptable for a spring journey when worn with a velvet spencer of the same colour, and a dark blue pelisse was waiting to add further warmth if necessary. As Emily and the rest of the household seemed to have gone deaf, an elaborate hairstyle was impossible, so she wound her hair into a simple knot and secured it high on the back of her head. At least the rather severe style went with this new austerity, even if her dyed curls did not.

If it were not for the unmistakable air of quiet elegance, the superb cut that would inform a careful observer old money and good taste had been at work, she might have been the governess she had once determined to become. She wondered crossly why nobody seemed to trust her to choose her own attire, picked up the pelisse, the beautiful soft gloves and modest bonnet, and marched militantly downstairs to find the provider of her latest set of fine feathers.

She did not relish covering up her true status in Rob's life with yet another set of false colours. Without Cleo's panache she would look altogether too much like a good and obedient little wife, who had perforce to be satisfied with the few moments her husband deigned to offer when his mistress was so much more appealing. How he thought he could get away with the pretence, when half of Brussels would know Colonel Besford was there on government business, he alone might be able to tell her.

As he was not present to do so, and her stomach was rumbling, she was obliged to eat without him. She wondered if this was the common lot of women, whether harlots or wives, to be loved and left while their men got on with life. The thought of Rob's profession made her second slice of tender pink ham turn to dust and ashes in her mouth, and she poured herself more coffee to wash away the taste. Unwelcome reality descended on her like a pall whenever she thought of the battle ahead, and not even the afterglow of last night's loving could dissipate it. She was only Rob's brevet wife, in his eyes as well as those of the wider world, and after experiencing such extraordinary oneness with him, how would she find the strength to leave him again when the time came?

Then it occurred to her that there might be a child. In the heat of the moment, neither of them had done anything to prevent one being conceived last night, for all her hardheaded resolutions beforehand. The idea wrapped itself seductively into her racing thoughts and took them over. Once that would have been a disaster, but to bear Rob's child when she was a fading memory to its father? That small miracle might make life worth living after he was gone, and she could not bring herself to dread it.

She sternly reminded herself that a child needed to know its father and thrust the temptation to encourage such an outcome aside, along with her plate. Suddenly she could feel tension souring the atmosphere of this lovely old house, as if everyone was waiting for something significant to happen. As she rose the butler pulled her chair back himself, quite as if she was a fine lady, instead of whatever she might be now.

'The Colonel is awaiting you in the library, madam,' he informed her in a fatherly tone, quite as if he had dandled her on his knee when she was a baby.

'Is he, indeed? I am afraid I do not know your name,' she replied, puzzled by such a lack of condemnation for a scarlet woman when the man was obviously an old family retainer.

'Hadley, madam, and you will find the library three doors along the corridor and on your right.'

'Very well, Hadley, thank you.'

Despite his tardiness, she was eager to see her lover. He had chosen not to wake up by her side, but she wanted to spend every minute she could by his, even if nothing was on offer but his company.

Nothing was—she saw that as soon as she was ushered into the library and he turned away from the wide range of windows that lit the lovely old room. He came to meet her without a trace of the warm smile she had come to expect lighting his austerely handsome face.

Colonel the Honourable Robert Besford was his imperious, impeccable self again, with more blue blood in his little finger than circulated through her whole body. The beautifully tailored coat of the fashionable buck had gone, along with the impeccably tied neckcloth and the ease of the last weeks. Here was the man she had married once again—the stern officer, forced to carry out an unpalatable duty against both his inclination and instincts.

'Good morning, I trust you slept well?'

'You know that I did not, Colonel.'

If he intended to disown last night as a meaningless tumble

in the hay, she refused to collude with him. Something flickered in those icy green eyes and he seemed about to thaw into the man she so stupidly loved, before the frost set in again.

'I take it the marriage bed did not fill you with disgust then, wife?'

Wife? At first the word would not leave her mouth. She formed it with numb lips and then silently released it on an aching sigh.

'Wife?'

'What else should I call you now, Caroline?'

She turned her back and ordered herself not to faint or cry as she strove to fit Mrs Besford back together. The pieces would not mesh. The cowed little creature who had run from Foxwell House that memorable night had gone forever. Bold, bad Cleo had never really been. So what, or rather who, was Mrs Besford?

'I collect that you must want a divorce, then?' she finally managed in a distant voice and wondered if that was the Colonel's lady talking.

If so, she decided that she would find it hard to like the frigid creature.

'Last night would not have happened if that had been the case, my dear.'

His dear? Oh, no—she studied his hard face and rigidly set shoulders carefully and saw no hint of her ardent lover— she was not his dear. This man was merely Caroline Warden's unwilling husband and she felt more alone in his presence than she had ever been in a rather solitary life.

'You knew,' she whispered and, despite her determination not to let her feelings show in front of him, shuddered visibly.

Throughout their journey to Westmeade she had deluded herself the difference in him was the confidence of a lover, rather than the ardent hope of a suitor. Then he had initiated her into the marriage bed so carefully she should have suspected he knew too much about her. She had not been in any state to marvel at his self-restraint at the time, but he had undoubtedly known she was a virgin. And all the time he took her so tenderly to the heights of passion, he had been taking revenge—while she had been simple enough to think they were making love in the truest sense.

'As well for your sake that I did—were you going to announce your presence over the breakfast table this morning, Mrs Besford?'

Was that why he had stayed away?

'No.'

'Then you were waiting for a more momentous occasion, perhaps?'

'No.'

'You were never going to tell me at all, were you?'

'No!'

'More use of that word in our dealings last night and you would not be bound so inexorably to me now.'

'And when did you ever listen to a word I say, Colonel Besford?'

'When I held back from you like a lovesick fool, when you said yes to me and I felt ready to take on Boney on my own. When I believed you everything that you are not, madam wife.'

'You did not see me, only a convenient shadow. You do not want to know me now any more than you did when we first met. What have you done this morning? Why, donned your true self and brooded over the inadequacy of your low-born wife, while I lay oblivious. You have never listened to me, never wanted to know me. You no more wanted the real Cleo than you did fat little over-dressed Caroline Warden, did you, Rob?'

She heard her voice rise and turned to look blindly out at the ancient park in her turn until she had herself under control again.

'Then explain yourself to me, wife. Tell me how you were going to walk away from me as soon as you were bored with your game. How I would have perjured myself if I petitioned for a dissolution of our marriage all unknowing. If you can talk your way out of that one, madam, you are the best liar still breathing.'

She turned to face him proudly and saw from the rigid set of his mouth that he had already made up his mind. Well, far be it from her to disillusion him, when the truth revealed too much of her feelings for him. Yet the fact that he had been containing this vitriolic fury all the time he had so tenderly made love to her last night bit like acid.

'I might explain myself, if you tell me why you went ahead and consummated this wretched marriage when you knew perfectly well that I am your wife, and we are now shackled for life?'

'There's the rub, Caroline, I wanted you. Heaven help me, I still do.'

'After what you just said, and all you think you know about me?'

'Yes. Now tell me it's not mutual and confirm everything I believe.'

She opened her mouth to deny him, to deny them, and shut it again. It was not true, unfortunately, and something told her it never would be.

'Cat got your tongue?'

'No, it's true.'

'I am so glad you sometimes choose to embrace honesty in our dealings.'

'I adjust to suit my company,' she said and traded him hard

look for hard look, as she secretly mourned the teasing, ardent lover of yesterday.

'As I have orders to meet with the Prince of Orange and his father, you had best force yourself back into the role of a lady before we get to Brussels.'

'You are taking me to Belgium?' she said, too shocked to find that he proposed to take her with him to fire defiance back at him.

'As the House of Orange resides there, it seems like the best place to go.'

'You know perfectly well what I mean.'

'Then you wish to be left here, perhaps?'

Caro looked about her at the lovely room with its air of permanence and sunny comfort. She thought about what she had seen of this gracious old place so far and tried to imagine herself placidly living here, while he risked everything on the battlefields. Of course she didn't want to stay.

'Yes,' she lied.

'No, what you really want is the chance to escape again while my back is turned. Rowley Afforde may not be the type to take a serious interest in an untutored virgin, but thanks to me, you are no longer one of those are you, my dear? You are coming with me, Caroline, and if you play off any more of your tricks I shall make you regret the day you were born, let alone the one upon which you wed me. One strumpet in the family is quite enough to be going on with.'

'I already rue becoming your wife in every sense of the word, Colonel—how could I not when you laid a bear trap for me to blithely walk into?'

'Whereas your intention to make a liar out of me was innocence itself I suppose? Your father trained you very well in chicanery, if in nothing else.'

'My father trained me in nothing, as you would know by now if you had taken a scrap of interest in me, either before or after our marriage.'

'I took a great deal of trouble with you these last few weeks.'

'You were just investing a little flattery in a potential mistress.'

'And I dare say you had Afforde picked out as your lover before the ink was dry on our wedding lines. Is he the man you threatened me with that day?'

'No, but now you have pointed him out…'

She let her voice trail off and eyed his thunderous expression with a certain grim satisfaction. For all his heady wooing and apparent tenderness towards Cleo, she was evidently a closed book to him after all, and wasn't that just as well? If he knew how much he had just hurt her, he would be able to twist the knife in the wound again and again.

'And you expect me to leave you here to await Rowley's return? What an idiot you do take me for, Mrs Besford.'

'With good reason, but do *you* propose scouring the demi-monde for your next victim, while I am busy hoodwinking the *ton* that we have been unhappily married since January after all?'

If he recognised the implied threat that she might consider taking a lover if he did likewise, his expression gave no hint of it. Her inconvenient husband met her eyes as if it cost him nothing to do so and smiled cynically.

'Why look for a hack when there is a perfectly adequate one in your stable already?'

'What an extraordinary analogy, and how delightfully the next few weeks promise to pass, do they not? Between your barrack-room vocabulary and my dubious origins, at least we will never be short of insults to trade over the dinner table, but I can manage without your company on the journey, sir.

I dare swear I shall have more than enough of it to stomach when we reach our destination.'

'And when did you mistake me for a green fool, Caroline? From now on you will not be allowed out of my sight for long enough to draw in any more deluded idiots. You will sleep with me, eat with me and service me whenever I require you to do so. It is what a man expects of his brevet wife after all, so you might as well fulfil two roles at the same time, since you proved so eager to take them both on.'

Service him? He could call it that, after what they had shared last night? Cut yourself off, Caro; don't let him see how much that hurt.

'I am not some left-handed connection, I am your wife,' she defended herself, drawing on a pride that had cravenly abandoned her the last time she confronted her reluctant husband across a book-room.

He silently took her wedding band from the desk and placed it on the upturned palm she could not stop herself raising to meet his touch. His chill green gaze dared her to put it on, and accept everything it signified. She hesitated, as if resuming it was deeply significant and not just the symbol of ownership he was making of it. She had left it in her room at Foxwell House the night she ran away, thinking to relinquish everything it represented.

The gold ring lay in her hand, as cold and unyielding as the man who had given it to her, until at last she succumbed to the truth of it and slipped it on. It felt heavy on her slender finger, and she was even less sure that she wanted it there than she had been when he reluctantly slipped it into place in church, looking as if he would have preferred taking poison all the while.

'I was so much in thrall, Caroline, that you even called

yourself an echo of your own name and I was too stupid to notice. Too stupid and too damned enchanted by your bright lures and false promises, to think about anything but needing you almost beyond reason.' His voice rose on that accusation, his eyes flared with temper and, fool that she was, she preferred it to his icy self-control.

He briefly paced the room before getting his emotions under strict military discipline once more and faced her, more remote than ever after that momentary lapse.

'You once swore to me that you would see me down on my knees begging before you took me to your bed,' he said, as if the hard gold band reminded him of their disastrous wedding day as well. 'I hope it gave you satisfaction to see me so humbled?'

How dare he remind her of the burning humiliation she had endured in her father's study, as he twisted all she had ever felt for him into something new and vengeful? She realised that Cleo had been born then, long before she made her shocking debut *en déshabillé* in Alice's drawing room. A creature of revenge, and of a witless, ridiculous love that still refused to die under the frost of his displeasure. Yet she had learnt a lot from Miss Tournier, and she refused to let her eyes fall before the icy challenge in her husband's.

'Do my feelings and aspirations have any bearing on the matter?'

'Not when you embraced matrimony so enthusiastically just a few short hours ago, wife.'

'One thing I *have* learned since I married you is that it is always unwise to dwell upon one's past follies, husband.'

'Kindly be ready to leave in ten minutes, I am in haste,' he rapped out, as if her defensive reply had actually hurt him, which was easily the most ridiculous notion she had indulged in all morning.

He strode from the room before she could think of a reason not to do as she was bid. Which was just as well perhaps, as they had hurt one another quite enough for the time being.

'Hearts do not break, Caro,' she whispered to herself, and if the words were as lost in this vast old room as she was herself, she refused to be destroyed by the fact.

At least he had left her no time to wallow in self-pity, or to feel the sting of betrayal bite like acid into her secret dreams. Perhaps, if she never allowed herself the luxury of examining the wounds he had just dealt her, they would not prove to be as deep as she feared. After all, he had done it before and she had survived, but that had been a light skirmish compared to seeing last night's magic transformed to gimcrack. No, she would not give him the satisfaction of realising what he had done to her, and she had no intention of meekly going into a decline this time.

When she had finally accepted the burden of despair and anger that weighed heavy on her slender shoulders, and got all hint of emotion firmly under her control, Caro donned her pelisse, tied her bonnet with a jaunty bow and raised her chin resolutely. Then she swept out of the room, past the staff gathered for a sight of their new mistress with only a regal nod, and out on to the carriage sweep without a backward glance for the lovely old manor house.

From now on Mrs Besford would live strictly in the here and now, never in the might have been. Even so, she met a polite request from Webb that she was please to step lively on account of keeping the horses waiting with well-concealed disappointment. It was like turning up to fight a duel, only to find her opponent had not even dignified the occasion by leaving his bed.

Rob had not had the grace to wait to hand her into her

carriage for the journey so she could treat him to a display of frigid disdain. Indeed, he was already mounted at the head of the cavalcade on a fidgeting black gelding draped with the saddlecloth of his regiment, while behind him another groom, riding a raw-boned grey, led a spare horse. Her husband doffed his shako and gave her a long unsmiling look. She met it with a challenge in her golden eyes and he nodded, as if he understood perfectly well that battle was being offered and accepted, then he turned to Webb.

'Take good care of my wife,' he ordered brusquely, before leading his entourage out of the gates, easily leaving their coach behind as he blithely rode away.

'His wife,' Caro echoed faintly, as the carriage took the turn.

The significance of her new role hit her at last, now she was away from Rob's chilly scrutiny and could reassemble Mrs Besford in peace.

'That's just what I said when I got here yesterday, ma'am.'

'What? Oh, yes, I forgot that you did not know, Emily.'

'Then it's the truth, ma'am?'

'Yes, for whatever that's worth.'

'A good deal, if you don't mind me saying so.'

'Perhaps, if things had been different.'

'Begging your pardon, but it strikes me that's just what they are now,' Emily said shrewdly and Caro blushed like a schoolgirl.

'And you think my husband is an easy man to cross, do you? If you do, then I can only congratulate you upon your optimism.'

'He seems to have took it pretty well to me.'

Caro shuddered as she remembered that scene in the library. Last night she had thrown her bonnet right over the windmill, and he had merely added her to a string of conquests stretching from Spain to Mayfair. However often he called her wife in that hateful, mocking tone, that was the truth of the matter.

'You do not know him,' she murmured, more to herself than her maid.

'Colonel Besford don't behave like a man who wants rid of you.'

'He has a use for me, Emily, otherwise you can be very sure that we would be on our way back to London at this very moment.'

Emily shrugged. 'The trouble with the quality is you think too much. That Colonel of yours is a fine man, madam. Why worry over how you got him back?'

Why, indeed? She had what she had desired so badly once upon a time, a small corner of her husband's life. Yet might it not be better to really be Cleo Tournier, lightskirt to the nobility? At least he had liked Cleo. Could a man really counterfeit such passion, restrain his rampant desire in the face of her inexperience so tenderly and still despise her in his heart? How would she know, she decided bleakly, and furtively brushed away a tear. She refused to turn into a watering pot, especially after wasting so many tears on the wretch in the past.

Instead she would show Colonel, the not so Honourable, Robert Besford how superbly a cit could play the lady, and if she broke her heart doing it he would never know. As if practising for the role, she looked so regally unapproachable that even Emily sat silent until they reached the first stop, and Webb handed her down as ceremoniously as if neither of them had ever even heard of the muslin company.

'Why, thank you, Webb, how very deferential we are being

today,' she said, with a slight smile that told him she knew very well there was irony in his low bow.

'How else should I treat my master's wife, madam?'

'How else indeed,' she said with a bland smile, and swept into the inn with such magnificent disregard for the usual spectators that they immediately concluded she had been born into the purple.

Chapter Fifteen

Half an hour after they resumed their journey, Emily plucked up the courage to intrude on her mistress's brooding thoughts.

'Will you be employing a real ladies' maid now, madam?' she asked anxiously.

'Why on earth should I do that when I do so already?'

'I ain't what a proper lady like yourself ought to be calling such,' Emily persisted earnestly.

'And I am not a proper lady, in any sense of the word.'

'That you are. You always was, if you ask me, whatever the world chose to think.'

'And we all know what that was. I believe the risks are on your side if you choose to stay with me, Emily. Only think of *your* reputation if I am ever found out.'

'Seems to me that you already have been,' her maid said shrewdly.

'True enough, and most ladies' maids would not deign to work for such a charlatan.'

'But I ain't most ladies' maids.'

'As we have already established that I am not most ladies,

we should suit each other very well, then,' Caro replied and considered the subject closed.

At last the coach slowed, and she tugged down the window to peer out at Dover harbour and the sea, but the sight of more uniformed men getting ready to embark checked her initial sense of wonder. Once again, the reason for this journey was inescapable and contemplating the future made her shudder.

If only Rob had sold out like Will had after the Battle of Toulouse, surely then he would not risk battle when he too had a new wife? The difference between the way the two friends felt about their respective ladies probably explained why her husband was prepared to embrace danger. It was a notion she dare not dwell upon, in case her chilly composure broke down irreparably and she turned into a hysterical female after all.

This time Rob was there to hand her down, and she tried to ignore a current of fiery shock that insisted on streaking through her, even at the impersonal touch of his gloved hand on hers.

'I had intended that we should rack up for the night, but the captain insists that a storm will come tomorrow and we must sail on the tide to avoid it. If you would rather follow on later, you had better say so before Webb ships everything aboard.'

'No, I will come now, if you please,' she replied—after all, if she insisted on staying, he might infer all sorts of wrong-headed reasons from her reluctance.

'Oh, I do, wife, indeed I do,' he told her, sinking his voice to a confidential murmur so that to a spectator they must look like the most loving of couples.

'Then we had best make haste, had we not?' she managed, and felt rather proud of herself when her voice came out clear and a little cool.

She was so preoccupied with presenting an indifferent façade to the world, and especially to her husband, that it didn't occur to her to get in a fret over anything as trivial as crossing the Channel in the teeth of an impending gale. Soon after the packet left harbour, laden down with their coach and string of horses as well as a full complement of passengers, it occurred to her that this had been a sizeable omission from her calculations.

'Do you always travel in such grand style?' she asked, hoping to distract herself from the ominous churning in the pit of her stomach as the boat began to pitch on the white-tipped waves, as much as to establish an awkward sort of truce between them.

'No, and I would forgo the carriage if I could, but, since half the *ton* seem intent on scrambling to Brussels this spring, there's no saying whether I could hire one for you once we get there.'

'I dare say I could manage without.'

'Not if you wish to go about in society.'

'Well, I do not, I have no more liking for society than society has for me,' she told him, her mouth set in a stubborn line.

'All the same, you will pretend one, madam. I have no intention of facing down any more gossip on your behalf.'

'So I am to perform for your acquaintance, I suppose, like a curiosity at the fair?'

He sighed and flicked her an impatient glance, as if he had better things to think about, and she was foolishly preventing him from concentrating on them.

'You have already done that, have you not? All I ask now is that you play newlyweds with me, and outface those who have been having so much fun at our expense.'

His terse condemnation stung, but he was right in one way.

To hide away and pretend the social world did not exist would be sheer cowardice on her part.

'I suppose if I could act the drab, I might find it in me to play the lady.'

He seized her arms and swung her about, his feral eyes blazing down into hers.

'No pretence will be required, Caroline. You are a lady through and through,' he said, as if she insulted him by demeaning herself. 'I knew that, even when you had me dancing to your tune like the devious little devil you undoubtedly are.'

She defied him, forcing herself to glare into his eyes unflinchingly.

'That is not what you said either before or after our wedding.'

He didn't even have the grace to blush in the face of this truth.

'I was drunk,' he told her baldly, as if that fact alone explained and excused everything.

'In vino veritas?'

'No, I spoke like the damn fool I was then. I had yet to be refined by the divine Cleo's particular form of torture.'

'So now it is all my fault?'

At least he had the grace to look a little conscious this time.

'Not all of it, but I would have come round eventually— if you had only waited for me to come to my senses, instead of running off like a thief in the night.'

'How was I supposed to know that you would suddenly find that you needed a wife after all, when you avoided me as if I carried the plague for nigh on two months? I am neither a seer, nor entirely a fool, sir. You despised me then, and from what I have seen of it today, you still do. Perhaps you want me back so you may hold me up to ridicule again?'

'You think so?' His grip tightened and now he looked wild,

as if the demons that drove her were close acquaintances of his.

She flinched, feeling the warm pressure of his hand through the fine cloth of her sleeve, and on fire at every point of contact, even if his passion was born of anger, not love. He saw her involuntary movement and swiftly released her, and her knees sagged weakly so she was forced to grip the rail.

'I am a brute, and I beg your pardon,' he said stiffly. 'You seem to have a habit of bringing out the worst in me, Mrs Besford.'

'And the best,' she murmured softly, then could have kicked herself for wanting to comfort him, when he had tried so hard to trample her new-found confidence into the dust.

He turned to face her once again, and this time there was a tithe of last night's warmth and laughter in his eyes, as well as a hint of triumph and complicity.

'Last night was rather spectacular, was it not, my torment?'

'Yes, I am hardly likely to forget it.'

'And how I wish I was not sometimes forced to act the civilised gentleman, for I should like to take you below and do it all again this very minute.'

On that limited, wrathful declaration the vessel gave an almighty lurch as it rode the heaving sea, and Caro turned sharply aside to christen the troubled waters with her offering to Neptune, instead of his scarlet uniform jacket. For a while he let her retch, then gently pulled her into his arms. He took out an immaculate handkerchief and wiped her humiliated tears away with a tenderness she had not dared dream of only a few moments ago, then he gave her a rueful smile.

'You have very effective methods of discouraging a gentleman's amorous advances, have you not, Madam Wife? Perhaps I could be persuaded to wait until we reach dry land to continue our most intimate acquaintance after all,' he whispered and swung her into his arms to carry her below, despite her protests that she was best out in the fresh air.

She was amazed when he stayed to comfort her, even leaving his precious horses to Webb and his henchmen as the storm worsened, and the captain's weather forecasting abilities became ever more questionable.

It proved to be a very long night, and Caro eventually succumbed to exhaustion, helped by the potent spirit Rob insisted on pouring down her throat and his steadfast presence.

Waking to a grey dawn and a headache, she found her husband lying asleep beside her. He was fully clothed and chastely on the other side of the blanket, but she allowed herself to savour the novelty of waking with her lover's head lying next to hers on the pillow for the first time in her life.

She must have made some involuntary movement, for he stirred all too soon and she wondered if some of her feelings were displayed in her sleepy eyes as his leapt with green fire. Then he came fully awake and was so coolly composed that she felt like the goose girl, outside the castle gates once more where she belonged.

'Do you feel better?' he asked, with every appearance of concern, but she knew he only asked for form's sake.

He had remembered her sins, and they were still unforgiven, as they probably always would be.

'Yes, but you had a most uncomfortable night of it, I am afraid,' she replied stiffly.

'I have experienced worse.'

How was she to take that? Philosophically, she supposed.

'I dare say you have, but if we are safely in Belgium I suppose that must be some consolation.'

'Unless that rascally captain has lost his way and landed us in France, we should be at Ostend.'

Caro shuddered, then tried not to look as wistful as she felt when Rob rose and risked cracking his head on the deck timbers above them. She only had to be alone with him for the most immodest desires to spring to life, she decided despairingly, as she furtively watched his careful, catlike stretch with hungry fascination. She began to fuss over her dishevelled appearance to distract herself.

'I will send your maid down to you, if you feel ready to face the day, that is?' he said as he was on his way out of the cabin.

She knew that she was already half-forgotten as Colonel Besford went about the true business of the day, so she agreed and tried to look as if she would not miss him. Between the aftermath of seasickness and the disclosures and hurts of the day before, she would have been glad to find a comfortable bed and curl up in it for a week. She told herself that soldier's wives did not indulge in such weakness, and compared notes on their maiden voyage as she and Emily repaired the damage caused by their trials.

They both agreed that it was good to be out in the fresh air with steady ground under their feet, but Caro was heartily relieved when they left Ostend at last. She had disliked the strongly fortified city on sight for no logical reason at all. Well, no reason beside bitter disappointment that Rob's gentleness of last night had not borne up in the cold light of day. He was as distant as the white cliffs of Dover as he asked if she was ready to go on.

Because of the coach they went by road instead of travelling by canal, although the water would probably have been easier on their nerves and their derrières. If Rob had chosen to share it with her, no doubt the carriage would have been well-sprung and comfortable. As it was, Caro would have much preferred to sit on the box, enjoying the air and an occasional glimpse of her reluctant husband in the distance rather than be bounced about inside it like so much baggage.

It was only pride that made him endure her company, she soon decided. Despite what he had said at Westmeade, he made sure they slept in separate rooms that night and it was very obvious to Caro that he would far rather have been alone on this interminable journey. The same chilly pride that had made him marry her in the first place rather than see his mother's debts become a public scandal was forcing him to take her to Brussels and outface the gossips.

There, she was to present herself to the world as his convenient wife, even if whispers about a certain prime article of virtue circulated like wildfire and the *ton* laughed at her, yet again. All in all, she was glad when the carriage eventually rumbled into Brussels and diverted her gloomy thoughts, even if it brought the moment closer when she must face the merciless scrutiny of polite society once more.

'Good afternoon, madam, the Colonel sends his apologies as he is engaged to dine with his Highness the Prince of Orange, and instructed me to show you to your rooms as soon as you arrived,' a regally impassive butler greeted Caro as she entered a splendid house in the best part of Brussels.

Madam followed obediently through the beautifully appointed hallway, and up a broad staircase that would have done credit to an embassy.

'It's very grand, ain't it?' Emily whispered as they examined the white-and-gold splendour of Caro's echoing bedchamber.

'Yes, very fine indeed,' she agreed flatly.

It would be like sleeping in a beautifully appointed barn, she thought privately. One that was as grand, chilly and empty as Mrs Besford's arranged marriage to a man unable to pass up any opportunity to escape his wife's tedious company. She would be wise to expect no more out of their marriage than her husband's duty.

Such a removal of hope would once have sent her scurrying for a secure corner in which to lick her wounds. Luckily her sojourn with Alice had reminded her of the lively and hopeful girl she had been at school, before her father managed to browbeat her into believing she was worth nothing, and she had no intention of forgetting herself a second time. She had successfully hoodwinked Rob Besford and his raffish friends, until her luck ran out, so she could certainly act the part of elegantly detached society wife now.

'Mr Webb says this place is bang up to the knocker,' Emily remarked sternly as they both gazed about the lofty chamber.

'And who are we to argue with Mr Webb?' Caro replied wryly.

Her maid seemed rather enamoured of 'Mr Webb', but she doubted he would look kindly upon Cleo Tournier's handmaiden.

Thoroughly dispirited, Caro slept alone in her splendid bed and wondered if her husband would have forgotten a kept woman quite so easily. If a man thought his mistress exotic and fascinating, then Rob Besford's wife was proving to be neither. If he came home at all, she heard nothing of him.

He was certainly gone the next morning—and this time had left no hint as to his whereabouts, or what he wanted of his under-employed wife.

Emily presented a very proper morning gown of delicately embroidered white cambric for Caro's unenthusiastic inspection.

'There's more come from London, so you can pick another if this one doesn't suit, ma'am.'

'It will do very well, I suppose,' she replied indifferently.

At least her husband's taste was better than her father's, yet how she wished the highly respectable garment possessed a tithe of the style that had distinguished Cleo's dashing toilettes. Dressed in these subdued pieces of superiority, she felt like an elegant item of furniture, or a well-chosen *objet d'art* designed to fit the prevailing style. Somehow she had to keep a small part of her scandalous alter ego alive, if only to confidently conceal this ridiculous love she could never seem to kill, try as she might.

'We had best wash your hair again with that lemon-juice rinse before you gets dressed, then,' Emily prompted. 'If that dye is to come out as that rascal in London told us it would, then it needs some more encouragement.'

When Caro's hair was almost dry at last, Emily fitted an elegant cap over curls that were already more golden brown than auburn, and a little more of Cleo faded with it. Resigned to becoming dull again, Caro set about exploring her new domain. She surveyed the double-cube drawing room with trepidation, and dreaded the sophisticated gatherings she would be expected to hostess for her husband's friends within its chilly splendours. When the sound of an altercation in the hall interrupted her gloomy thoughts she was almost glad, until she heard a harsh female voice top the smooth tones of the butler and barely suppressed a groan.

'There you are, my girl! Knew the man was stalling,' barked Lady Samphire, once she had flung the door open and turned on the vanquished butler with a look of triumph. 'Can't imagine what Besford was about landing you with such a slow-top, Caroline, my dear, and you ought to know better than to try and fob off an old lady who has been travelling for days, my man.'

Caro wondered why it had not occurred to her to question the presence of such a superbly trained English butler and his staff in a Belgian household, and despaired of understanding the strange new world Rob expected her to face without his assistance. Slightly puzzled as to why Lady Samphire was addressing her as if she had known her all her life, she still managed to welcome her unwanted guest with composure. Once the butler had brought the Madeira her ladyship demanded as a restorative, he shut the doors behind him with a decided snap, and Caro turned to meet her ladyship's acute dark eyes with as much poise as she could muster.

'I dare say you wish me at the devil, but you need help, my girl, and you're getting it whether you want it or no,' Lady Samphire pronounced, after surveying her victim with a thoroughness that made Caro wonder if she had a smut on her nose.

'I am not sure I take your meaning, your ladyship,' she replied coolly.

'Stop trying to freeze me out, child. For one thing I've got a dashed thick skin and you'll be the one who ends up catching cold, and for another we ain't got time for any more playacting. Worked out who you were the second time I set eyes on you, and I can't think why I was such a noddy as to miss it before. Suppose that rubbishing nonsense on the stage distracted me, but if you don't want everyone else to realise what you've been up to, we need to act fast.'

'I have no idea what you mean, ma'am. Perhaps you have mistaken me for someone else, for I rarely attend the theatre. I lived very retired at Foxwell House when I was first married; since then I have been my father-in-law's guest at Reynards while recovering from a slight fever. So I have had little opportunity for such junketing,' Caro improvised shamelessly. 'Indeed, I cannot recall having made your acquaintance, ma'am, so I pray you will excuse my clumsiness if I inquire exactly who you are?'

'Hmm, thin…but I suppose the tale might head off the gossips if we only manage to tell it convincingly enough. The fact is that Tom Foxwell and young James asked me to help when they heard I was coming here, so you might as well stop trying to convince me black's white. Mind, I only agreed because I admire your spirit, girl. Wish I'd been more like you. I'm a bored and lonely old woman with a fancy to annoy the tabbies by bringing you into fashion.'

Caro marvelled at the efficiency of the Lords Foxwell and Littleworth. Lady Samphire must have set out only hours after she had left England herself, but a chilled part of her heart warmed as she realised they had known of her lies and still sent help. If James and the Earl had not yet cast her off, maybe there was still hope for her after all.

'We are not related, my lady. The *ton* would certainly question it if you took me up,' she protested, not yet sure that she preferred Lady Samphire's help to her hindrance.

'Let 'em. First lesson you need to learn is to take less notice of a pack of bored ninnyhammers, my girl.'

Caro nearly succumbed to a fit of the giggles; at least her ladyship bore no resemblance to the superior and scornful widow who had reluctantly launched Henry Warden's daughter into society for a huge fee. A few weeks in Lady

Samphire's brusque company should prove more entertaining than the dull months she had spent in London society, and Caro began to warm to the idea after all.

'Yet why would you help me, my lady? I am not considered good *ton*.'

'You will be by the time I've finished with you, and I already told you—I like you. You went after what you wanted with style, and, if you will only keep at it, you'll soon have that boy exactly where you want him.'

Somehow Caro doubted that, but drifting about this grand mausoleum mourning lost dreams would get her nowhere, so what did she have to lose?

'Since you appear to know more than enough about me already, I suppose it would be better to have you ranged on my side, Lady Samphire, instead of in the enemy camp plotting against me.'

Her ladyship barked her harsh laugh. 'Gracious of you,' she said and that was the end of that.

Once her vast quantities of luggage had been unloaded under the eagle eye of a formidable ladies' maid, her ladyship scornfully refused the offer of a rest.

'Far too much to be done for either of us to idle about on the sofa,' she said brusquely, and spirited her new protégée off to the salon of the finest *modiste* in Brussels.

Once there, Caro asserted her own taste at last and, as she considered it surprisingly good, Lady Samphire sat in her elegantly uncomfortable gilt chair with a knowing smile curving her thin lips and let her have her head. For a moment Caro almost felt guilty about the huge bill her husband would shortly receive, then decided Cleo would have cost him far more, and added a delicious peach silk to the heap of cloth and fashion-plates already awaiting the seamstresses.

After a satisfying couple of hours spending even more money on frivolous bonnets, exquisite underwear and shoes nobody in their right mind would ever consider sensible, Caro had the beginnings of a stylish new wardrobe and felt rather better about her latest incarnation. With Lady Samphire's influence, her appearance in society must be more successful than the last, and this time she would know much that the haughty *ton* did not, which should add spice to the dullest of *ton* parties.

'Just as well that rascally grandson of mine has put to sea again,' Lady Samphire interrupted her thoughts abruptly, as they rode back to the house Caro would never bring herself to call home. 'I am glad that your Miss Watson had the good sense to keep the rest of the Bond Street beaux at a distance. You have a good friend there, even if she is a minx.'

'Alice is the best of women,' Caro replied with a challenge in her eyes.

'I doubt many of the chaperons would agree with you.' Her ladyship held up her hand to stop the impulsive defence that flew to Caro's lips. 'I dare say she is as good as she is misunderstood, but you can't take her cause in hand when your own position is still shaky. If you leave well alone for long enough, the world might forget Miss Watson and remember that Will Wrovillton married the granddaughter of a duke— even if he was only Gronforde.'

Caro couldn't help but smile at such a crushing dismissal of that late man of power and her new friend's omnipotence.

'Do you know everything, ma'am?'

'I try to, and most of it is gathered by watching and using the brains no female is supposed to have. Your friend has the

Stoneleigh colouring as well as their unfortunate nose, for all she is clever enough to distract attention from it as often as possible. 'Tis to be hoped her children follow their father in that respect at least.'

'I dare say they will cope as best they can with what nature sends them, just as the rest of us have to. Yet I suppose you are right about championing her, and Alice said as much in the letter I found waiting for me here.'

'Then you had better listen to her—not that you can do otherwise with the English Channel between you.'

'You would be amazed what we Cyprians can achieve,' Caro said grandly and the old lady chuckled delightedly.

'No, I wouldn't—never thought I should see Rob Besford in such a spin.'

'Never, your ladyship?'

'If you think about it, the lad betrays a sad want of logic to have made such a fuss about an arranged marriage, when he always swore he would never marry for love.'

'Why ever not?'

'Because his father loved Clarissa Norton to distraction, before she finally managed to kill off his affection with her extravagance and infidelities. I admit theirs was a poor example to grow up with, but it's my belief that when a Besford falls in love, he falls headlong.'

'Then what shall I do if he does so now?'

'Lie back and enjoy it, I should think,' Lady Samphire said with a quizzical smile.

'Unlikely. He swore on our wedding day that he would never feel anything for me but revulsion.'

'I expect he also promised never to bed you?'

Caro nodded and wished for Cleo's protective maquillage to hide her blushes.

'There you are, then, got him so he hardly knows what day it is already. After doing that, I dare say gaining his affection will not prove beyond your ingenuity.'

Chapter Sixteen

Caro doubted it would be as easy to capture Rob's affections as her mentor declared, but hope stiffened her resolve not to become a wallflower again, just in case somebody associated Mrs Besford with a courtesan her husband had shown too much interest in. From now on, nobody would be able to accuse her of hiding her light under a bushel. In pursuit of this new resolution, both Emily and Lady Samphire's dresser spent the day reshaping one of the suffocatingly respectable evening gowns Rob had ordered, until even its creator would have been hard-pressed to recognise it.

Under her ladyship's supervision the sternly plain gown was transformed into a gloriously simple column of white satin and finest gauze. Dressed very much to her own taste for once, and with the henna rinse finally washed out of her golden-brown curls, Caro gave her reflection a satisfied nod. Although the fashion was for more decoration and display, nobody could deny that the elegant simplicity of the high-waisted and low-cut gown showed off her figure to perfection.

'Now that's much more like it. No point gilding the lily

when you have a shape like that,' her mentor said with a nod when she was finally ready.

Despite this encouragement, Caro was glad of Alice's strict lessons in deportment when she entered her first ballroom as Mrs Robert Besford. Newly elegant as she undoubtedly was, many would have ignored her, or openly marvelled at her cheek in turning up uninvited—if she had done so in the company of a lesser female. Even Lady Augusta Norbridge could not turn her away in such venerable company, however much she would have liked to from the distant expression with which she greeted her unwanted guest.

'You can take that look off your face, Gussie, for it don't become you in the least,' her ladyship briskly informed her goddaughter and namesake. 'Jane Littleworth ain't up to rattling about the Continent at the moment, so I'm staying with Mrs Besford for the season in her stead. If you don't like it, then I might just as well come and bide with you.'

Lady Augusta went almost as white as her unsuitably girlish evening gown, and promptly made her ladyship's protégée so welcome that Caro's success was assured, unless somebody discovered her scandalous past.

'You are a ruthless and devious old lady, ma'am,' Caro told her patroness once they were in the carriage on their way to another exclusive evening party.

'Maybe, but I get results. Gussie Norbridge is an elegant ninny, but she has influence and she'll use it in your cause from now on. If she don't, I might descend on her next, and I can be a damned uncomfortable guest if I choose.'

In the half-light her dark eyes met Caro's challengingly.

'I am quite sure that you can be, your ladyship,' she said meekly.

'Impudence,' the old lady said with a snort and waved Caro in front of her as the coach halted and a flare of lights announced their next port of call. 'Laxton's m'nephew,' she explained as they ascended the steps of another fine looking townhouse, and Caro only just managed to keep a suitably straight face as Lady Laxton proved even more eager to promote Mrs Besford's success in polite society than Lady Augusta Norbridge had been.

Thus Rob returned home after a weary day of fruitless endeavour at midnight to find his wife absent.

'Mrs Besford is attending an evening party with her guest, I believe, sir,' the butler informed him mournfully.

'Guest?' he managed to ask carelessly, as if the identity of the interloper who had spirited Caroline away was a matter of trifling importance to her husband.

'Mrs Besford has invited the Dowager Countess of Samphire to stay, sir.'

'The devil she has,' Rob muttered savagely, and went to change out of his dress uniform at long last.

Despite the lateness of the hour, sleep had never felt more distant. He had made such a complete mull of the whole business, he was surprised to find Caroline had not turned tail and bolted back to England in his absence. How right James had been about his wretched temper. Hurt pride and jealousy had cost him the respect of his wife, even if he had never actually had her love to whistle blithely down the wind after it.

Over and over again he had gone over that scene in the library at Westmeade and wanted to kick himself for letting fear rule him for the first time in his life. He had been so afraid of waking up to find she was laughing at his gullibility that he had destroyed all hope of gaining her affection. After that breathtaking, never-to-be-forgotten consummation, he should have been thanking God on his knees for granting him such a wife, and all he could do was lash out at her just in case she had only been intent on revenge. With hindsight he could see that little about that glorious night had smacked of vengeance, but now it was probably too late to put things right between them.

Taking refuge in drink would be the height of folly after their disastrous wedding day, so he retired to his echoing bedchamber and tossed and turned his way through a weary night. Dawn was lightening the eastern sky when she finally returned and he hadn't the heart to disturb her, even if he had been sure of his welcome.

Later that morning Caro was still half-asleep when he entered her room. Luckily for him, she smiled a sleep-misted welcome at her errant husband, before turning her face up to be kissed.

'You are already dressed,' she murmured reproachfully, at least some of his sins quite forgotten as her dreams merged happily with reality for once.

'Something that can very soon be remedied,' he replied huskily, with a caress that set her sleepy senses spinning further and further away from reality, and they promptly set about the task with a will.

In a matter of seconds, Caro went from comfortably sleepy to acutely conscious of every pore and sinew in her body. A passion that transcended all they had said and done rapidly scorched away everything but need. Love was something she dare not acknowledge, even in her mind, when they were so close there was nowhere left to hide. Refusing to think at all, she gave herself up to the delicious sensation of his hands and mouth urgent on her eager body, urging him on with inarticulate little moans that he seemed to find perfectly readable as he paid homage to her neck, her breasts, her belly and then lower, where she writhed and shuddered under his wickedly experienced tongue.

'No, I want *you*,' she protested with a brief return to coherence.

'Then you shall have me,' he grated, 'all of me.'

His voice was husky with passion and he thrust into her in a completion that left her gasping and wanting even more, as the reality of him filled her to the point where self-control and holding back became a poor jest. Riding wave upon wave of arousal, she moved frantically beneath him, striving for the rhythm that would drive them both beyond their everyday selves, and make a mockery of convenience and restraint.

Gentling her to stillness, he looked down at her impassioned face, the flush of colour on her cheekbones, her opened mouth, lips full and dewy and reddened with his kisses, and above all her golden, dilated eyes that met his with a mix of passion, plea, and demand in them.

'You will unman me, Cleo—trust me to set the pace?'

'Hurry, then, I do not think I can wait much longer,' she gasped as his green eyes blazed anew and he surged into her, dark and deep and satisfying.

This time he did not have to consider her inexperience, and her golden-brown eyes were unseeing with arousal as he met them with green fire in his own. She fought the overwhelming need for a moment as their eyes met, then saw the same helpless passion reflected in his that was driving her beyond all thoughts of modesty and self-denial.

Exhilarated by his driven desire, she leaned up to give him a quick, teasing kiss then imitated his seduction of her by exploring his firm chin with her questing lips. She felt the deep rumble of his laughter against her aroused breasts and wondered if she might melt away from sheer pleasure as he watched passion rule her. At least she could let that show naked in her gaze if nothing else. Suddenly it seemed part of the wonder of it all that they were truly making love, even if he did not know it. Luckily, he captured her teasing lips before she could let wistful ideas about the gap between love and desire spoil their idyll.

'This time you have really asked for trouble, my Cleo.'

He gently wrestled her slender arms from about his waist, shuffling them both a little further up the bed and urging her fingers to wrap themselves about the fanciful curls of the bed frame above her snowy pillows. His eyes held hers as he arranged her outstretched arms to his taste, then he met her bewildered amber gaze with a piratical smile.

'I thought you might like something to hold on to,' he promised darkly, and raised himself further on to his own arms so he could thrust even more satisfyingly into her welcoming depths.

'Ooh! Don't stop!' she cried as something half-forbidden and half-promised lured her to grasp her handholds with whitened knuckles and flex her delightfully stretched torso like a cat sensually stretching in the sun.

'I couldn't if you begged me to,' he admitted hoarsely as he saluted her lush mouth with quick, tantalising kisses in time with his deeper, harder thrusts. His eyes were still steadfastly on hers as he finally lost all vestige of control and surged into her, just as her world contracted to him and the golden ecstasy and oneness that felt even more wonderful than she remembered.

She gloried in his every spasm of release, her body sang with each convulsion that racked her as his weight sank momentarily on to her still-outstretched torso, and her fingers released themselves to caress his wildly dishevelled chestnut hair. Breathless and satiated, she still felt that wistfulness that must come to all lovers, that even such extraordinary oneness, such exquisite pleasuring one of the other, must end, and separateness intrude again. Rather to her regret, he shifted and rolled over, clasping her to him as he went, as if he too dreaded the cold light of day intruding between them as well.

'And a very good morning to you, too, Colonel,' she managed some time later when she had got her breath back, propping herself up on one elbow and surveying her husband's muscular person with frank appreciation.

'Good morrow, wife—would that all my duties were so agreeable.'

He gently ran one long finger over her silky skinned cheek, as if seeking to learn her likeness by feel as well as sight.

'Are the others so very tedious, Rob?' she asked softly.

'Beyond measure,' he told her, as his questing hand crept lower and began a more thorough exploration of his wife's exquisite body.

'Poor Colonel Besford,' she murmured, and wriggled down the bed to encourage such laudable attention to detail.

'Poor, indeed, when I got back last night and found you gone, my torment.'

'Oh, dear, it is quite dreadful to be all alone in a strange city, is it not?'

'You have no idea how heartily I cursed Slender Billy for hauling me off to meet a pack of princelings I would have happily consigned somewhere very warm indeed, Caro, rather than leave you alone.'

'I hope that you were polite to them?' she managed to ask, determined not to be rendered witless by the storm of passion he was intent on stirring up all over again.

'As correct as a curate at a soirée, but what of you, my Caroline-Cleo? What duties kept you from home last night?'

'The devil fly away with my duties,' she gasped and pulled his head down so she could stop his mouth with a brief, teasing kisses. 'This is neither the time nor the place to make polite conversation, husband,' she admonished.

'Then show me just what it is time for, Mrs Besford,' he murmured huskily, and she did so in such a brazen fashion that even Cleo Tournier might have been proud of her.

She was lying dreamily content in his strong arms, reluctant to finally descend from the clouds and face the day, when a hesitant tap at the door heralded the arrival of her maid. Emily tactfully informed the far corner of the room that an attaché from the embassy had arrived to speak to the master, before hastily departing.

'Dammit, how can it be eleven o'clock already?' Rob exclaimed, and sprang out of bed, cursing, and hastily began resuming his discarded uniform before Caro had properly registered Emily's announcement.

When she jumped out of bed to help, even allowing herself the luxury of combing her fingers through his disordered curls, he firmly pushed her away.

'I shall not get out of here before eleven tonight if you don't put something on, my Cleo,' he informed her brusquely, and completed the task with her delicate silver hairbrushes as she got back into bed and pulled the disordered sheets up to her chin.

He paused before going to meet his visitor, and her heart missed a beat at the barely banked fire still hot in his gaze when he surveyed her flushed face and tumbled curls, then met honey-gold eyes full of impossible dreams.

'We must talk soon, but I must go now,' he added with a quick kiss on her mouth, 'before I jump back into bed with you, woman, and be damned to duty and everything else.'

Then the door closed smoothly behind him and he disappeared as if he had been a figment of her overheated imagination.

Four days later Caro was not quite sure whether to be frantic over his continued absence, or deeply offended that he could forget her so completely he had not even sent her a note to tell her where he was going. At least he had come to her before he left, but even that seemed a mixed blessing with hindsight. If he thought he was going into danger, might he not have bedded her to try to ensure the heir his family needed so badly before he went?

Remembering his driven desire and his concern for her pleasure, she fervently hoped not. Yet doubts nagged as his warmth faded and those harsh words he had thrown at her in the library at Westmeade burned in her memory.

There was more between them than he had claimed, but less than there might have been between Colonel Besford and his improbable courtesan. She sighed for the effortless intimacy of his wooing of a lightskirt, and weathered the occasional pitying look and sarcastic comment about eager young husbands not being what they were with a careless shrug. She was a very different creature from the Caroline Warden who used to hide in corners, and at least nobody dared make such remarks in her fearsome chaperon's hearing.

'Done it before, ma'am,' Webb told her succinctly when she finally taxed him with her husband's disappearance, no longer caring what the man thought of her ignorance.

'So he might have done, but he was not married then,' she told him acerbically. 'We wives have an irritating habit of wanting to know where our husbands are every now and again, I am afraid.'

Webb looked uncomfortable, as if he was all too aware of the fact and found it very inconvenient indeed.

'I couldn't rightly say where the Colonel has gone this time.'

'Will not, more like.'

'Orders, ma'am.'

'Oh, and we could never go against those, could we?'

'No, ma'am,' he told her, shifting his feet under her sceptical gaze as if he wished they could take him somewhere else without being accused of insubordination. 'The Duke used to send him to find out what the enemy was up to,' he finally managed, looking as if just parting with that much information was physically painful.

'The Duke of Wellington is still in Vienna,' she returned implacably.

'Old Nosey ain't here, that's true, but his orders still get through one way and another.'

'I see, thank you for that much, be sure that I shall not broadcast it.'

'Shouldn't have said anything if I thought you would,' he replied with a conspiratorial wink.

Caro finally understood that her husband undertook to spy for his commander-in-chief on occasions, and the graceful self-possession Alice had taught her had never been more necessary.

'I could go and look for the master if you want, missus,' Webb offered hopefully.

'Can you speak French?'

'Enough to get by.'

Caro thought for a moment—the temptation to find out where Rob was almost too strong to resist.

'I doubt he would be very pleased to see you.'

'Sticks and stones.'

'No, it might endanger him,' she finally said reluctantly.

'Aye, happen you're right,' the man admitted on a sigh.

'I think my ears must be deceiving me.'

He grinned at her, and even made her a quick bow before returning to his immaculate domain in the mews.

After two more days had ticked painfully by with no word from Rob, Lady Samphire finally lost patience with her brooding companion.

'If ever I met a young man with as many lives as a cat it's the one you are married to,' she told Caro sternly as she sat picking listlessly at her luncheon. 'The things he got up to with Charles when they were children almost made *my* hair curl, and I gave birth to five boys, so it don't kink easily.'

Caro smiled, but her failure to find comfort in her ladyship's brusque words must have been plain to see.

'Don't be an idiot, girl, he would hardly have obtained his rank by demonstrating a rash disregard for his own safety and that of his men.'

Telling herself sternly that she was an army wife now and could not sit about moping every time her husband was in action, Caro braced her shoulders.

'If I promise to be stoic as a Spartan, will you tell me more, ma'am? I would rather hear of their past misdeeds than wonder what Rob is doing now.'

'We're supposed to be paying calls this afternoon, so there's no time to discuss those two resty devils now. Just ask him about the time they got on the London stage and disappeared for a sennight the next time you see him. I never did get the full story out of them.'

'Good Heavens! Their mothers must have been beside themselves.'

'Charles lost his very young, but Clarissa never even knew.'

'How could she not?'

'Once she bore Foxwell a second son, I doubt she set foot in Westmeade or Reynards more than four or five times during the boys' childhood.'

'Then they were as good as motherless?'

'Better than living in a bear pit, which is what it would have been if Foxwell had forced her to stay.'

'Then I'm glad she elected to stay in London. I don't think I could bring myself to be civil to her after hearing that, and she is my mama-in-law after all.'

'As Clarissa insists on hanging on the poor Prince like a ball and chain, she certainly won't be turning up here to bother us. Now, I want to look over those gowns that came this morning before we go out. I'm not at all sure about that orangey thing.'

'It is peach, not orange.'

'Whatever it is, I doubt there's one woman in ten who could get away with it. I ain't waiting beside you in a receiving line if you look like a milkmaid.'

'Then I promise to look like an anaemic cit instead,' Caro said with a toss of her head.

That night Mrs Besford was besieged by so many would-be cavaliers that she gave her peppery sponsor a triumphant look.

'Knew that orangey thing would brighten you up,' her ladyship said, looking unforgivably smug.

'Did anyone ever tell you that you are a ruthless old schemer?'

'Yes, you—but it worked didn't it?' she said, grandly gesturing at the eager group of beaux waiting to put their initials on Mrs Besford's dance-card.

'I almost wish I was a wallflower again if I could only have a rest,' she said, refusing to admit her satisfaction at her sudden success.

'Nonsense, you'd be bored senseless.'

'True, but my feet would not be so sore.'

'You can rest them when you're my age—for now, you owe *them* some forgetfulness,' her wise counsellor told her gruffly, waving a hand at the young men holding off in the face of the formidable Lady Samphire's adamantine gaze.

It was true; the young officers who sought out Colonel Besford's newly fashionable wife would shortly be risking everything in the coming battle, just as he would. It was to be hoped Rob knew that all she or her court sought was amusement. Not, she thought crossly, that he was in any position to object, having once more abandoned her to the less-than-tender mercies of the *ton*.

Then the young men were melting away in the face of more formidable opposition, and Caro's heart leapt at the sight of her errant husband strolling towards her as if nothing untoward had occurred. She was torn between wanting to box his ears or throwing herself into his arms, so settled for a compromise that pleased neither of them. Laying her gloved hand in his outstretched one, she smiled up at him as if they were meeting after a couple of hours and curtsied.

Even as they exchanged polite nothings, her eyes ran eagerly over his muscular frame, searching for any sign of hurt. His shoulders seemed broad as ever, his step as certain and his grip as strong, but there was a weariness about his eyes, a certain tautness to his mouth that spoke of prolonged tension as much as tiredness.

'I know I didn't order that,' he finally said, with a hard look for the peach satin and gauze confection Lady Samphire had cast such aspersions on earlier in the day.

She checked that the beautifully draped crossover bodice only exposed a respectable décolletage for a young married woman and gave him a demure smile.

'No, I did,' she admitted smugly.

'Why?'

'Because I am heartily tired of dressing to please everyone but myself, and I looked like an expensive governess in the gowns you ordered.'

'At least I had the good sense to keep you covered up,' he growled.

Caro was tempted to scream at him like a fishwife, at the same time as she longed to reach out and smooth the frown from between his brows. She might love him, but his possessive attitude argued little more than physical desire and that might prove as temporary as his sweet wooing of Cleo.

'You could have the "good sense" to trust me instead,' she replied coolly.

'You're right, I could and I will,' he admitted with a wry smile.

'I am? I mean, you will?' she stuttered, then reminded herself she was no longer a shrinking schoolgirl.

She gave him a queenly nod in reward for such husbandly discernment, not quite sure what to make of such a rapid volte-face.

'Given that I admit to being a dog in a manger, will you come home with me now, Caro?' he asked, and she met his rueful green eyes with a question in her own.

One moment she was greeting the harsh man she had married, the next her lover of that shining week among the half world of London's courtesans was back. Unable to trust herself not to blurt out her feelings if she stayed with him in such an odd mood, she fought a successful battle with her wanton self for once.

'I promised to attend your Aunt Tenby's dancing party later, so I must go, even if you do not wish to.'

'I see only that you have no wish to spend an evening with your naggy husband,' he replied with a smile that lacked sincerity, 'but you might change your mind when you are faced with an inquisition from my meddlesome aunt.'

'No doubt Lady Samphire has her measure, but I thought you wished me to go into society? Have you changed your mind now we are actually here?' she asked stiffly, wondering if he feared embarrassment, now even his most top-lofty relatives were keen to meet her after all.

'Of course not, I would be proud to take you anywhere,' he responded quickly enough, but Caro had already retreated and nothing he said seemed to bring the warm laughing creature he sought out of her protective shell.

They danced a waltz and prepared to depart one noisy party for another, still locked in misunderstanding. Rob sat opposite his perfectly turned-out society wife as the carriage bore them to his least favourite relative's lodging, and brooded on his past mistakes. What Caro really thought of her dilatory husband was beyond him, and after that scene he had enacted her at Westmeade she would almost certainly refuse to believe he had thought about her every other minute since he left her so reluctantly.

The stark fact was that his father lacked an heir in the next generation, and Caro would see that truth behind any attempt he made to create a better understanding between them. James had been right to say his so-called intelligence had flown out of the window the day he first laid eyes on Miss Caroline Warden, and it showed no sign of returning any time soon.

If only he had not let his imagination linger on that scene on their wedding day and the furious threats they had thrown at one another. He had lost his wretched temper and now she distrusted every single word he said. Still, he remembered Cleo and could not despair of winning something warmer from his wife than the very correct greeting he had endured tonight. But if she insisted on dancing all night long, what chance would he have to do that?

'So what have you been up to, young man?' the fearsome Dowager Lady Samphire quizzed her host from across the carriage.

'I have been visiting, your ladyship,' he told her succinctly.

'And how is the upstart Emperor?'

'A little too well for my taste.'

'Is he readying for battle yet?' Caro asked in alarm.

'He has too many problems at home for the moment, but he knows very well that a victory will silence his critics better than all the speeches and arguments he can summon. I believe we still have a few weeks to prepare.'

'I hope Arthur Wellesley hurries up and takes command of this riff-raff army then,' her ladyship said brusquely. 'We don't stand much chance of success until he does.'

'Very true, your ladyship—now can we speak of other things? I have had enough of war for one day.'

'Then perhaps you would like to know what a success your wife is proving with the gentlemen?'

'I suspect you know very well that I should not. Content yourself with the plaudits of those young fools, your ladyship.'

'So only fools seek my company now, sir?' Caro asked rather heatedly and was only a little pacified by his groan of protest.

'You know very well that is not what I meant.'

'I know no such thing. You were too ashamed of me to have me presented upon our marriage, now you expect me to be a success, but not with the gentlemen! I told you that you could trust me, but it seems that you cannot bring yourself to believe me.'

'I trust you, madam. I am not quite sure that I trust myself,' he said wearily, but as they drew up at the brightly lit house his aunt had hired at that moment, Caro could not examine that statement further.

'How fortunate that I do not have to rely upon you two for rational conversation,' her ladyship announced and swept up the steps ahead of them.

'If I promise that I value you above rubies, will you save your waltzes for me, Caro?' Rob asked as they followed in the redoubtable old lady's footsteps.

'Do you consider me a virtuous woman, then?' she asked with a challenge in her eyes.

'I think you a jewel among wives—now will you promise me?'

'That's not what you said at Westmeade.'

'I was a damned fool at Westmeade. I lost my temper again and said a great many things I did not mean. I have bitterly regretted them since, Caro.'

'You said you wanted me,' she said defensively.

'And so I do, but I believe I forgot to admit I need you too. So will you dance your waltzes with me, then let me take you home? Or must I go mad with frustration and jealousy, watching you dance so closely with another man?'

Why not? He was only asking for what she desired herself,

and that driven declaration lit a stubborn flame of hope she could not quite bring herself to douse. Maybe need was not love, but it was so much better than indifference.

'Very well, Colonel,' she said lightly and handed him her card as soon as she received it, only to hastily seize it back and cross out the cotillion and the country dance he had also initialled. 'Even a parvenu like me knows more than two dances are improper, husband.'

'Don't, Caro, you know exactly how to behave and I won't hear you traduce yourself in such a fashion.'

'No, Colonel, you would rather do that yourself, would you not?'

'Unless you wish to be set upon by your own husband and carried off to his lair in the midst of this very proper and very boring ball, I suggest you stop throwing my past follies back at me and remember our waltzes,' he told her gruffly.

Resisting the temptation to encourage such a scandalous idea, she greeted one of her eager swains with a polite smile and went off to dance a rather energetic country dance with him. She doubted if her husband would agree she had a duty to cheer the young officers who were now descending on the Belgian capital, but they had cheered her while he was away, so now the obligation was personal. Telling Rob so when they met for the first waltz seemed a step too far and she had to endure a thunderous silence until she challenged him.

'What would you have me do, Colonel? You wanted me to establish myself in society as your wife and I have done so.'

'I never said you should become the toast of every callow puppy barely old enough to salute you in his cups.'

'It seems to me that you have no idea what you really want,' she told him severely, and heard the governess she had renounced in her own voice.

'Oh, but I have, Cleo, and it isn't to look on from afar and not touch you,' he murmured and she cast a surreptitious glance at the chaperons' benches even as her knees wobbled at the fiery promises in his eyes.

'Someone will hear you,' she whispered, none the less awed by his very public claiming of her.

Even her detractors could hardly murmur about abandoned brides and marriages of convenience, when her Colonel was making it clear that this particular rake had only one target in mind. It was heady, and she might have let herself be carried away by this new model husband, if she had never seen the old one disclaim her with such disgust.

'And if you don't stop teasing me I will forget my steps,' she told him severely.

'Which would never do, would it, Mrs Besford?' he said with a hardness in his eyes now that told her without words just how exasperating he found her newly discovered social talents.

'No, it would not, Colonel,' she replied with her head held high as she pondered the inconsistency of husbands. 'What would I do with myself whenever you disappear without a word if I had not got all these social obligations to fulfil?'

'There's the rub, is it not? You are angry because I had to go away and could not tell you where I went.'

'Oh, no, only clinging wives with overindulgent husbands turn into watering pots every time they are deserted without so much as a word or a letter of farewell,' she assured him brightly.

'So you are punishing me for it by denying us the reunion we have both been longing for?'

'Isn't it odd how everything always turns out to be my fault?' she said politely, then sank into a graceful curtsy as the dance finally ended.

'I would have let you know I was going, if only those fools at the embassy had given me the chance,' he told her, bowing with the assured elegance of one born to the task.

'Why, thank you, Colonel, then I take it that next time you depart without warning I can expect a note?'

In reply to which sally he gave her a furious look and retired to the card room and only emerged to march her through the waltz before supper and glower at her throughout that memorable meal. The Colonel and his lady left the ball very shortly afterwards, and Caro was swept into such a tempest of passionate lovemaking that she was beyond protesting their precipitate departure. Indeed, she was beyond speech when they finally reached her bedchamber and her inventive husband managed to cram all the lovemaking they had missed in the last few days into just one night.

Yet the next morning she awoke alone once more, and it almost seemed more painful than it would have been if he had not come home at all. Refusing to give in to despondency, she rose and faced the day with a determinedly cheerful face that worried her mentor rather more than if she had presented a picture of misery for all to gawp at.

The Duke of Wellington arrived from Vienna at long last, just as if he had been listening to Lady Samphire's strictures on his tardiness. Caroline wasn't sure whether to be glad or sorry when Rob rejoined the Duke's aides, since he then spent his days rushing about the countryside with orders, and his evenings caught up in a social whirl on the Duke's coattails that would have made the most energetic débutante weary. Caro watched the great general take command with a certain awe, and fretted that the prospect of war somehow seemed more real now the commander-in-chief had arrived to wrest order out of chaos.

His Grace seemed determined to encourage the relentless sociability that had descended on the Belgian capital this spring, and while Rob admired his commander's hardheaded common sense, he rued its effect upon his marriage. Wellington had a polyglot army to push and persuade into some sort of coherence, and a large civilian population to keep from panic. His calm presence at the centre of it all reassured them all was well.

Somehow Rob managed to find time out of his busy schedule to brood over Caro's undoubted success in society, and the number of times he came home to an empty bed over the following weeks did little to improve his temper. Lady Samphire gleefully noted his fearsome frown as her protégée floated elegantly past at the latest ball, with no less than three gentlemen eagerly vying for her attention. Indeed, she was tempted to applaud when his wife gave an artistic start and deigned to notice that her husband was propping up the wall of her hostess's ballroom so he could watch her every move at last.

'La, husband, I did not think to see you tonight,' she informed him with a nice parody of submission, as Rob took her hand and tucked it possessively into the crook of his arm.

'That much is quite obvious, madam.'

'Then if you expect me to sit at home embroidering seat covers, you had best know that I am possibly the poorest needlewoman in Belgium.'

'Not seat covers, perhaps,' he said, with a suddenly fervent desire to have her at home at Westmeade with him, attempting the worst set of baby clothes ever born of optimism.

If she understood him, nothing showed on her face. Maybe

she shared his yearning for a pack of gold and green-eyed
brats in assorted sizes, and maybe she did not. He could
hardly wait to begin the project anew himself, but this was
neither the time nor the place to dwell on such incendiary
ideas and he found it impossible to fathom his wife's feelings
towards such an undertaking. She knew that the earldom
might die out if one of Lord Foxwell's sons did not provide
him with an heir, but Rob's longing to see their children
running wild at Westmeade, as he and Jas had done, stemmed
from far warmer impulses than his lukewarm interest in the
succession.

To confound any good intentions he might have of letting
her rest when she eventually came home, tonight his wife
was looking irresistible in an exquisitely cut gown of apricot
silk that highlighted the honey-gold lights in her hair and ac-
centuated her lioness's eyes. Her inherent good taste never
took her too close to the line that separated sophisticated
from outrageous and he should have trusted her, of all
people, to know where that barrier stood and to stay on the
right side of it.

He was distracted from his musings by the approach of his
commander, and had to reluctantly present Caro to the great
man. He regretted drawing her to the Duke's attention as
soon as he noted the familiar gleam of admiration in Wellington's dark eyes when in the company of lovely young women.
Luckily, Caro's mentor loomed on the horizon at just the
right moment for a change and the Duke hastily excused
himself. This time Rob was so sincerely grateful to see his
wife's fearsome champion that he gave her a welcoming
smile he had no doubt she understood perfectly.

'Flibberty-gibbet,' Lady Samphire pronounced roundly,
as the great Duke neatly eluded her.

'Hardly that, ma'am,' Rob protested, against his better judgement.

'Hah! You would know one if you saw one and that's a certainty. Only need to look in your mirror, young man.'

'That is simply not true, my lady!' Caro protested, stung out of her resolution to be as cool as a sorbet in Rob's presence. 'Both the Duke and my husband are intent on protecting us from another twenty-odd years of warfare, and I am grateful to them for that, even if you are not.'

'Here's a heat! Ripping up at an old lady in such a hoydenish fashion, not at all what I expect from a gal I took up out of the kindness of m'heart.'

'Yes, it is, ma'am,' Caro retorted with a smile. 'Otherwise you would never have done it.'

'True, but you're still a minx, and he don't deserve such a spirited defence from you, my girl. Supposed to be wearing a hair shirt.'

'Pray hush, my lady. You know perfectly well that I am not meant to know of my husband's past misdeeds.'

Actually she quite enjoyed playing the blindly innocent young wife, who had never even heard of Cleo Tournier and her ilk. Picturing the faces of ladies too high in the instep to welcome the daughter of a cit into their midst if she turned up in Cleo's scandalous glory, helped her ignore any lingering reserve. Luckily her partner for the first waltz came to claim her, before she could blurt out to her erring husband just how much she missed his dishonourable attentions.

As she exchanged polite nothings with her partner, she surreptitiously watched her husband bend his head to drink in everything his own very pretty blonde partner had to say, and just managed to hide her jealousy behind a social smile. Respectable young wives should not envision themselves closeted with rakish officers who believed they had no virtue left to compromise. Yet how she missed their shared laughter, and the teasing flirtation that had sharpened every encounter with the keen edge of unfulfilled desire.

While Caro and her Colonel shared polite respect in public, their passions were reserved for their bedchamber—each sphere so separate that the distance between watchful Colonel Besford and her passionate lover confused her. If not for his warmth in her bed, she might have thought her lover the fevered dream and her husband stern reality.

In the end she decided that Rob still craved her body, but her thoughts were less intriguing to him than Cleo's lightest word had been. Innocent as she still was in so many ways, she had no idea that, after spending all day trying not to neglect his duty or kill one of her many admirers, when he got his wife alone her much-tried husband was in no state to engage in witty repartee.

Meanwhile April slipped away and rumours of the formidable army Bonaparte was gathering dogged them as he began to reassert control over his self-declared empire. Sometimes Caro caught the same bewilderment she felt in the eyes of other officers' wives as they watched the unrelenting gaiety, and their gazes would occasionally meet in silent acknowledgement that this was mere froth. Outside, in the barracks and the encampments, was real life. The army being shaped by the Duke of Wellington was all that stood between Brussels and the martial genius who had once commanded Europe, and sooner or later they must fight.

Now and then there was a whisper of troop movements, or a discussion of strategy as wise heads were shaken in apprehension. Then society would dance on, while Caro was caught on a relentless seesaw of hope and fear for her husband's safety and left feeling more of an outsider than ever. Only the venue of the season seemed to have changed, as society span heedlessly on while the rest of Europe waited for the fate of nations to be decided on the battlefield.

One night in May, as war inched inexorably nearer with every tick of the gilded clock she had come to hate, Caro lay sleepless by Rob's side after yet another night of passionate lovemaking. How she wished sleepy contentment could follow on such a dazzling satisfaction of desire and give her some respite from her fears. Instead, holding back the words of love that trembled on her treacherous tongue became more of an effort every day and she was almost afraid to sleep, lest she gave herself away in her dreams.

The most ardent of lovers, Rob cherished and aroused every inch of her night after night, but frustratingly she still had little idea what went on in his private thoughts. Gazing at his beloved chestnut head as it became visible in the pre-dawn light, she held back from caressing the rebellious curls he normally kept so sternly in check, because sleep was precious and tenderness had never been a part of their bargain. He would not divorce her now, but bearing his child would bring her scant comfort if he were not there to share the experience, she decided, discovering she had managed to tumble even deeper in love with her Colonel than poor, silly Caroline Warden had done at first sight.

Now he certainly had plenty of enthusiasm for the begetting of an heir after all, so perhaps his family should get up a subscription for wayward Cleo, who had released such desire in a man who had once had no use for his common little wife. When they made love he always called her by that shady alias, and just what did that say about Robert the married man? That he would rather not be, she acknowledged sadly, and wondered what she could make of her life once he had got his heir and a spare and felt free of an irksome duty.

Eyes stinging at the very idea of him lavishing his passionate attention on another woman, she made herself turn over and tried to close her senses to the heady fact of his powerful body lying next to hers. She ordered herself to block the faint scent of lemon water and the intangible aura of dominant, satiated male from her too-sensitive nose. Even if there was no use trying to match her shallower breaths to his steady ones, when sleep brought dreams of him, it did her no good to lie here watching him sleep.

Mrs Besford had so much that Caroline Warden would have given her right arm for, yet not to be able to say 'I love you', or to hope for a murmured echo, was like dining off gold plate and being denied a simple drink of water. She could not turn to her husband for simple comfort, when her fear of the coming battle haunted her waking and sleeping, because she was his convenient wife and he needed rest.

It was no use, she decided at last, she could never truly ignore him. Instead she silently turned back over and let her hungry gaze linger on hawkish features softened by sleep. Then she dwelt too long on his face and powerful form, and need sprang to shameless life once again. She closed her eyes, tried to banish her baser self and opened them again to greedily drown her senses in her lover's presence, storing him up against the threatened drought, detail by beloved detail. At last he sighed, mumbled something and turned over, as if her very intensity made him restless.

'I love you,' she mouthed at the back of his unruly head.

'And how very much I wish I did not,' she whispered to herself, as the tears she furiously tried to halt slid heedlessly down her cheeks.

Afraid she might sob and wake him up, she settled a damp cheek into her own lawn-and-lace-covered pillow to muffle any noise, and courted an oblivion that seemed a very long time coming.

'Is anything amiss, Caroline?' Rob asked, making a rare appearance at the breakfast table, where she sat looking dubiously at a piece of toast and trying to summon up some enthusiasm for the day ahead.

'Not a thing,' she lied blithely, as her inner self silently listed what really ailed her. One: you don't love me; two: Bonaparte is probably massing his army ready to attack ours at this very moment; and three: when he does so, you will take part in the terrible battle that is coming and risk your life yet again. Apart from those trivial details, all is right with my world and I don't know why I am not dancing for joy, while false, social Mrs Besford brightly added, 'Why, do I look haggish?'

'Not in the least,' he denied gallantly, but his eyes lingered on her pale cheeks, and the blue shadows beneath her eyes and he frowned. 'Is all this too much for you?'

All what? He could not have penetrated her secret, and it must not be pity for her tumultuous feelings that made him not quite meet her eyes. She could not think of a reply that did not betray her tension. Meanwhile he watched her with such concern that weak tears threatened, and she had to berate herself soundly to keep them back.

'This incessant socialising,' he finally explained, and she just managed to suppress a sigh of relief as he continued. 'The hostesses are so intent on outdoing one another this spring that, if the French were to be defeated in the ballroom, I dare say we could rely on them being routed before a shot was fired.'

'True, but we women must keep our end of the bargain, I suppose.'

'Oh, yes, and you are very good at that, are you not?'

She thought she glimpsed a shadow in his eyes at that unanswerable question, then they were impassive again and his voice light, so she must have been mistaken.

'So tell me, where are we to dance today, Caroline?'

'Well, if you have forgotten that Lady Samphire has organised a Venetian Breakfast, I shall not be allowed to do so. Then, she informs me, she requires my attendance at a tea-drinking and a loo party before we even think about attending Lady Regis's ball, or consider going on to Mrs Treaven's supper party.'

'I am glad I joined the army instead of being designated Lady Samphire's aide-de-camp. Trying to train boys just out of the nursery to use a musket, and persuade men to fight an enemy they served with only months ago sounds like child's play compared with your punishing schedule. Don't let her tire you out.'

She could not help laughing at this brusque command. 'I can give her ladyship nearly fifty years. Will you be back tonight?'

'Perhaps. Will you care if I am not?'

'Yes,' she said, surprised into telling a stark truth for once.

'Then I will be back,' he replied with a rather satisfied smile. He left her carefully returning her fine china coffee cup to its saucer because she was so tempted to throw it after him for extracting that revealing admission from her and then blithely walking away.

Chapter Seventeen

Rob continued to attend so many balls in his Commander-in-Chief's train that he wore out his dancing shoes as May slid relentlessly into June. At most of them he had to grit his teeth and watch his wife smile and waltz with other men, and even flirt mildly with the Duke. He learnt new feats of self-control to stop himself dragging her home and locking her up somewhere no other man could see her, let alone trifle with her, and hoped self-denial was good for his soul.

One evening he stood brooding on the ironic fact that he had been given exactly what he had once desired most, Cleo as his true wife, when she was so much changed he sometimes wondered if he knew her at all. As she circled the room on the Duke's arm, he ordered himself not to watch her like a hungry cur, yet, try as he might, he could not stop himself doing just that—until a sharp tap from a ladies' fan distracted him effectively enough.

'I said, she's polished up nicely, that little wife of yours, ain't she?' Lady Samphire informed him sternly, testing her fan against her palm as if he was a schoolboy awaiting punishment.

'Yes, she is a remarkable female,' he told her shortly.

'And you would prefer her at home, barefoot, pregnant, and adoring I dare say,' she chortled in her gruff way and he thanked heaven she wasn't a shrill woman, or the whole room would have heard her.

'Lady Samphire, whatever my wishes might be, I prefer to keep my personal life just that,' he told her repressively.

'Then you should never have washed your dirty linen in public in the first place, m'boy.'

'Yet how assiduously everyone is stopping me airing it in private,' he told her acerbically, which amused her so much he thought she might have an apoplexy.

At last she recovered and he told himself to be glad, if only for Caro's sake, as she wielded her dread fan once more.

'Do you good to hunt rather than be hunted,' she said, getting in a sharp dig in his midriff no man would have even ventured for fear of his famous fists. 'Keeps you on your toes, and you must admit that you treated the poor girl appallingly in the first place.'

'I did, didn't I? And just what makes that your business, ma'am, I freely admit I have never quite managed to fathom.'

'Entitled to be a busybody at my age, especially as Charles has been sent off to the Americas on some wild goose chase. Don't see why I shouldn't look to his friends to amuse me in his absence, and I must say you're making a remarkably fine fist of it so far.'

'So glad to be of service, my lady,' he told her coolly, and bowed a graceful farewell as he went to claim his partner for the next dance with considerable relief.

This time it was Caro's turn to stand by her patroness's side and watch surreptitiously as her husband danced with Lady Samphire's great-niece, the lively and impeccably bred Miss Georgiana Laxton.

'Chin up, girl,' ordered Lady Samphire, brusque as a sergeant major.

'Miss Laxton is just the kind of female Rob ought to have married.'

'I admit she ain't a complete widgeon like her mama, but she's not his type at all. I could tell you were ideal for that scamp the instant I laid eyes on you. Seems obvious that he agrees with me now, at least if that unfashionable trick he has of watching your every move around a ballroom is anything to go by.'

'Does he really do so?'

'Lord above, I give up! The most handsome blade in the room is obviously mad for you, you are lucky enough to be wed to him and going home with him tonight, and still you insist on thinking he wishes you at Jericho? I should never have wasted a moment of my remaining time on you. You are a weak-kneed want-wit after all, my girl, and I was wrong about you all along.'

'That I am not,' Caro protested, stung by her mentor's surprise attack.

'Prove it then! Take him home and sort this whole sorry mess out once and for all.'

'Very well, then, I will,' Caro told her with a decided nod, and began to plan a rapid exit from this very trying ball in her husband's vigorous arms.

'So get on with it and stop shilly-shallying,' Lady Samphire told her with a much more benign smile. Caro realised how fond she had grown of the peppery old woman and impulsively kissed her withered cheek.

'Good Lord, whatever was that for?'

'Because I never had a grandmama, and to say thank you, I suppose.'

'You're welcome, and I always did like you for some odd

reason,' Lady Samphire said gruffly and patted Caro's hand, before she recollected her fearsome reputation. 'Now run along, do, child, and remember to take that man of yours home and talk to him for a change, instead of letting him run you up to bed before you can find breath to straighten things out between you.'

'How on earth did you know he did that?'

'Silly child, been a new wife m'self, ain't I? Aye, and an eager one.'

With this parting shot, Lady Samphire pushed her protégée in Rob's direction and melted away to leave the field clear.

Caro considerately waited until he offered to fetch his erstwhile partner some refreshment, then let out an artistic sigh and wilted as if her legs barely had the strength to hold her up.

'Mrs Besford! Oh, no, she is overcome! Pray give her some air everyone and do not crowd her so.'

Miss Laxton hurried to Caro's side and began to chafe her hands, fending off the efforts of those nearby to see what was toward. Seeming painfully at a stand for once, Rob went white and then hurried off to get the refreshments his partner had refused. It was Miss Laxton who helped the supposed invalid to a couch, ruthlessly evicting its occupants and ordering her patient to lie down quietly while they awaited his return.

'It is so easy to be overcome at these crushes, is it not, Mrs Besford?' she said, mischief sparkling in her fine eyes as she noted the slight colour in Caro's cheeks and drew her own conclusions.

'Indeed it is,' Caro agreed meekly.

'Ah! Colonel, a cool drink is just the thing to revive a fainting female,' Miss Laxton observed solemnly when Rob reappeared, and tried not to notice the tremors of suppressed laughter suddenly afflicting her new friend.

'Georgie,' he acknowledged absently, but to Caro's delight the raven-haired beauty might have been invisible for all the attention Rob paid her.

'Rob?' Caro whispered so softly that he was forced to bend close to hear her, 'I suspect I should be taken home,' she murmured softly.

Painful anxiety vanished from his green eyes and they became full of laughter, although he somehow managed to keep his expression solemn as befitted a concerned husband. The minx was no more faint than he was, probably less so given the bold message in her extraordinary golden eyes.

'So you should, my torment,' he observed and shot her a look he hoped made her knees as weak as his felt at the moment.

Then he knelt by her side and, pretending to chafe her hands, let his wicked tongue explore her sensitive ear on the pretext of whispering comfort, in front of all the dowagers, until she was shivering for real at last.

'Can you walk, wife, or have I completely lost my touch?' he finally murmured.

'You are still a rake, sir,' Caro replied softly, confident of her inability to take a single step without her knees turning to jelly.

It was no good, thought Caro distractedly, talking would have to wait whatever her mentor said. Luckily Rob seemed to agree with her, and was about to lift her into his arms and carry her triumphantly off to his lair when another military gentleman came strolling up to them as if he hadn't a care in the world.

'There you are, Besford,' he announced unnecessarily. 'Most elusive cove I ever came across. His Grace urgently needs to find a certain gentleman, and discover exactly what he's been up to since you last met.'

From the significant look that went with this demand, there was a hidden meaning behind his words, and it did not need Rob's suppressed groan to warn Caro this was one task that would not wait.

'If only I had remained elusive for five more minutes,' he whispered and gave her a raw, rueful look and a tender kiss, before departing to find the Duke as ordered.

'I shall call in the morning to see how you do,' Miss Laxton told her, as Caro was tenderly shepherded from the room by their hostess for the night under Lady Samphire's cynical eye.

Caro smiled back at her new ally, reflecting that letting something of Cleo emerge from correct Mrs Besford's shadow had not made the sky fall in on her head just yet.

Three days later there was still no word from Rob. By now everyone in Brussels knew Bonaparte was in Belgium, and her husband was out there somewhere, trying to get intelligence to his commander, or racing in front of the advancing French army. All that she had dreaded was happening and she had no control over any of it.

She told herself sternly that she had a duty not to give in to the dark fear stalking her and she stood quietly under Emily's skilled fingers, as martial sounds of all kinds echoed through the city. Her husband was already engaged in the struggle to circumvent Bonaparte's relentless ambition, but some of his fellows had yet to go, and long faces or tears from the ladies left behind would do them little good.

'We have to attend, child,' Lady Samphire had said brusquely when she pointed out the triviality of dancing while the troops were gathering for war. 'Arthur Wellesley has told the Duchess of Richmond to go ahead with her ball, so we are obliged to go. I believe young Arthur is trying to avoid the mêlée that would ensue if panic breaks out. I shall certainly go, even if you cannot find it in you to pretend a little cheerfulness tonight for the public good.'

Caro had reluctantly conceded it was not much to ask when so many of their acquaintance were about to risk their lives.

'Although I don't feel much like dancing.'

'Maybe not, but neither of us would get a wink of sleep tonight with the soldiers marching about like a herd of elephants anyway.'

Caro privately thought she would not sleep if Brussels was silent as the tomb, but she put on her peach silk gown as a flag of defiance and set out for her Grace's impromptu ballroom—a converted coach-house on the Rue de la Blanchisserie.

It was a strange affair, one that she was to remember for the rest of her life with a feeling of surprise—firstly, that it had taken place, and, secondly, that she had been there to witness it when it had. As more and more officers left the ball, Lady Samphire managed to garner the news that Bonaparte had advanced by the Charleroi road rather than toward Mons, and the Duke of Wellington was busy ordering his army into place for a battle somewhere along that road. With the noise of the troops marshalling, then marching away often audible over the music, Caro doubted anyone else present forget the Duchess of Richmond's ball, however long they lived.

The brutal fact was that the war she had grown up with was back, but distant horrors, fought out in far-off lands, had become a deeply personal terror taking place mere miles away. Her fear of losing Rob was so acute tonight that she almost felt like fainting for real at this particular ball. She felt a sheen of perspiration on her brow that had nothing to do with being overheated from dancing. For a moment she teetered precariously on the verge of hysteria, but she was a soldier's wife and told herself sternly that she could not collapse at the first whisper of trouble.

Still feeling as if the bottom would drop out of this unreal world any second, she danced with one or two of Rob's friends on his Grace's staff, as their commander held an impromptu council of war in the Duke of Richmond's study. Then they were gone too, and at last she could go home and take up a vigil so many women would share tonight.

'The Colonel said I was to get you safely back to England soon as the first shot was fired,' Webb told when they got back from the ball.

'Not even if you bind me hand and foot, then try to drag me there,' she told him, echoing her mentor's grandest manner.

'And you'll tell himself you refused to obey orders, will you, missus?'

'That I will, and with compound interest,' she replied, and refused to even consider the idea that she might never get the chance.

'Right you are, then,' he said cheerfully enough.

No doubt he would far rather be out there with his master than closeted with a house full of anxious women, but for now at least Brussels was closer to the action than England.

'If you can find the Colonel, then you have my leave to join him,' she offered.

'And abandon my post? He would have my hide if I did, an' quite right too.'

'Then I shall be glad of your help and advice.'

'And you shall surely have it, ma'am,' he replied very correctly and, for the first time since they met, bowed with due respect.

Reports of the brutality endured by conquered cities in the late war haunted Caro briefly, but she calmed her household as best she could and gave them leave to go if they wished to. To her surprise, only a few took advantage of her offer and even the top-lofty butler elected to stay, while Emily stoutly declared that wild horses would not drag her back to her native land.

The next morning the whole household occupied themselves by getting dressings ready and arranging makeshift camp beds to accommodate the inevitable wounded. As Lady Samphire said sourly, someone had to, since the army would do precious little for them.

By late afternoon, rumour was rife that the French Emperor had fallen on the allies unexpectedly and beaten them soundly.

'Stuff and nonsense,' Lady Samphire told Caro roundly. 'Bonaparte will not roll us up that easily.'

Next morning one of Rob's friends from the embassy called with what news he had managed to garner. The Allied army had held off Marshall Ney after some vicious skirmishing and now the Duke of Wellington was falling back to stay in touch with the Prussians, who had fought a desperate battle with Bonaparte at Ligny. The whisperers would put the worst gloss on their retreat, but the equerry was reassuring.

'Blücher promised to back the Duke to the hilt and, from what I have seen of the man, he would march through hell itself to keep his word. More than that I could not tell you, ladies, even if I knew it.'

'Of course not, sir, and thank you. You are very kind to think of us at such a time.'

'Colonel Besford asked me to keep you informed, ma'am,' the man said, leaving as hastily as he had arrived.

So her husband had guessed she would not go, had he? For a moment Caro was indignant that he presumed to know her so well, then the voice of common sense told her that he had been quite right, and she should be grateful for his forethought. She caught back a sob and wondered if she would ever be in a position to quarrel with her infuriatingly omnipotent husband again.

'We shall attend church,' Lady Samphire informed her gruffly, 'even if it is Roman—I dare say God will listen to our prayers just the same.'

'It is to be hoped the service is in French, then, because I doubt I could understand a word of Flemish.'

'It will be in Latin, of course, child, wherever have your wits got off to?'

'Goodness knows, and I can't say that will be much improvement.'

'Whatever do they teach in those expensive schools for young ladies?'

'To be young ladies, ma'am, so, needless to say, we learnt not to be too clever.'

Her ladyship laughed and took Caro's cold hands in her bony ones. 'Not noticeably, my girl, but come anyway. The words will comfort you even if you don't understand 'em, and I can't sit through another sermon at the Embassy.'

As it turned out, her ladyship was right. The singing and the rhythmic chanting of the liturgy soothed her, and the obvious fervour of the prayers made her feel a common bond with the Dutch Belgians waiting on events they had no control over either.

'Now all we can do is trust in God and young Arthur Wellesley,' her ladyship said brusquely.

It soon became apparent that many among the English community did not share her faith, for wherever busy rumour flourished, panic broke out in its wake. Suddenly the city was full of carts and carriages, the roads blocked with fleeing English families heading for the coast. His Grace's orders that all horses must be requisitioned for the army had obviously not counteracted the lure of so many English guineas, and Webb told his ladies not to go out. As Caro pointed out, that was all very well, until wagonloads of wounded began to roll into the city in dire need of help.

She was tempted to disobey her protector and go out to meet them, but soon there was so much to do on their own doorstep that she could not even spare time to fret about Rob more than once every five minutes. Yet whatever they did seemed too little, as the army had indeed made little provision for their own.

'Yon Lady Samphire says you're to stop now, ma'am,' Webb told her late that day, the stern light in his eye informing her that he would pick her up and carry her to her bedchamber if she disobeyed orders.

'But there are so many still out there,' she protested.

'Always the way,' he told her with a shrug, and watched sternly as she clambered wearily to her feet. 'Colonel Bob would flay my hide if he could see you now,' he told her gruffly.

He gave Caro no room for argument by placing a surprisingly gentle arm about her waist and towing her towards the small sitting room her ladyship had decreed would be kept free of wounded.

'I *can* still walk, you know,' she informed him, 'but anyone seeing you towing me off into custody would think I was either a prisoner under guard or an inveterate drunkard bound for the sponging house.'

'I'll be one or the other if I don't do as I was told and look after you, ma'am, seeing as how the Colonel will have my hide.'

'That's a piece of underhand strategy if ever I heard one, and I prefer to be busy. Webb, you are as big a rogue as my husband.'

'Perhaps, but I learnt not to take no for an answer from a master,' he replied with an unrepentant grin.

This sally won her first laugh of the day out of her, and, hearing it, her self-appointed protector decided she was unlikely to go into a decline just yet, so went off to make sure his stable lads knew a war was no excuse for so much as a blade of straw being out of place.

As soon as she was forced into idleness, Caro's fears came flooding back. Somewhere out there Rob might be dead or dying. At best he was hungry, weary and perhaps afraid, and at worst…

The worst for her now was the not knowing, she told herself, but a small part of her knew that she lied. If he was dead, and every instinct she possessed rebelled at the very idea, she knew the blow would cripple her just as surely as if one of Bonaparte's soldiers had put a bullet into her instead.

Then it started to rain, 'What about the men still outdoors, Webb?' Caro asked, emerging from the sitting room to find her protector back in the hall, glowering at the fastidious butler.

'The natives is seein' to them, missus.'

Sure enough, when he reluctantly got out of the way so she could see for herself from under the shelter of the porte-cochère, the good citizens of Brussels were gathering up any soldiers left without shelter and opening their doors to them. This time she allowed herself to cry in the face of such disinterested kindness, and looked a very sorry spectacle indeed when Lady Samphire finally ordered her to bed.

Chapter Eighteen

Late the following morning the crack of cannonfire several miles outside the city announced the start of a great battle and Caro's heart beat heavily in panic as she heard the ominous boom grow into a thunderous cannonade. There was no point in thinking the worst. Still, the helpless horror and frustration that mothers and wives, sisters and daughters all across the city must be feeling with her was never far away as she acted as Lady Samphire's lieutenant in ordering their makeshift hospital to her satisfaction.

An hour or so later a troop of gorgeously dressed Dutch Belgians careered through the city, shouting that all was lost and the French hot on their heels. For a moment Caro's heart pattered a fast march in time with their hoofbeats, but as she listened to the forthright comments of some of the Duke's veterans, gradually it slowed to something like normal.

'It's all right, ma'am,' one explained earnestly. 'Them's their version of Hyde Park soldiers. We ain't got no need to panic 'til old Nosey hisself comes gallopin' arter 'em and 'e wunt do that, even if the devil himself gets on 'is tail,' the injured trooper informed her from his makeshift bed.

'No need to worry about herself neither. Throw her heart over anything my lady can,' Webb informed the man smartly, before marching off to fetch more bandages.

His lady straightened her shoulders and tried to feel worthy of this unlooked-for accolade, but she wasn't feeling quite so gallant when afternoon turned to evening and still the pounding of artillery fire boomed in the distance. Suddenly she felt older than Lady Samphire as her legs shook so badly when she stood up that she had to sit again before she fell down. From the distant thunder of arms a huge battle was being fought out just a few miles away, and only time would reveal Europe's fate as well as her own. If Rob was dead, she knew all too certainly that she would only ever be half-alive.

Somehow the butler had kept enough water for her to bathe in and she lay in her tub at the end of the day, brooding unhappily as the warmth soothed away her physical aches. If Rob was only alive she could endure anything, she told herself. He could set up a troop of mistresses from here all the way to Paris and on to London if the fancy took him, and she would have to learn to bear it.

'It's bed for you straight off, and no argument, ma'am,' Emily ordered and, for once, Caro let herself be gently bullied into her night rail.

Her tired mind reacted to too many sleepless nights and painful anxiety at last and shut down on her, so she had no choice but to succumb to exhaustion.

When she awoke the next day, her heart slammed in her chest as she jumped out of bed, hating to think she had been lying abed sleeping when Rob might need her. Today, God willing, she would find out what had happened to him. If he was dead, she did not know how to go on living, but she dared not linger over that thought.

'They say it's a great victory, ma'am,' Emily told her excitedly, bringing with her warm rolls and chocolate that Caro could no more face than a bank of London chaperons just then.

'What about the wounded?' she asked painfully.

'Terrible many of them there are,' her maid told her quietly, all joy in the victory fading from her animated face. 'I dare say the rumours are just as daft as usual though,' she said in an effort to offer some comfort. Caro knew she could not find any until and unless she knew that Rob was alive.

She dressed hastily and soon found that Webb had not trusted anyone else to discover his master's fate on the battlefield, once he was sure the city was safe. With a suspiciously heightened colour, Emily admitted the head groom had set out at dawn to search for the Colonel, and Caro spared a moment to speculate on how Emily knew so much about Webb's movements.

'He's a good man, Emily,' she observed gently.

'Aye, he'll do,' the maid replied with a serene smile and Caro knew she had no need to worry about her maid's future after all.

The hideous cost of victory forbade wild relief and this morning Brussels felt breathless and exhausted, rather than wildly exultant. Maybe that would come later, after the wounded had been counted and the dead buried, but all anyone seemed to be able to manage now was a numb relief that there would be no more battles.

Every movement in the square made Caro look up with

hideous anxiety from whatever task Lady Samphire had found her. There was plenty to occupy her, with every available room turned into a makeshift ward, and even Rob's staff and the redoubtable Lady Samphire hard pressed to cope with all the injured men they had taken in. At last Caro went to the window, for about the hundredth time, to look impatiently for her husband and her heart leapt almost into her mouth. Webb and the groom Rob had taken with him had just ridden into the square, with long poles rigged between their horses to provide a makeshift litter.

'Oh, Rob, my darling!' she cried desperately, and ran for the stairs with tears running unheeded down her cheeks.

He was alive, at least if their intent faces were anything to go by, but what state was he in to come home thus? So long as he was alive, she told herself, she would not care. She squared her shoulders, ready for a battle of her own, for if he thought she would turn tail and run at the sight of a badly injured man, especially one she loved beyond reason, then he had best prepare to be thoroughly wrong.

Every step seemed to take minutes instead of seconds, but she finally arrived on the pavement, breathless and pale as milk and trying hard to control her shivering apprehension. Webb was watchfully supervising the butler and two stalwart footmen as they attempted to get his master down without hurting him more than could be helped. Webb managed to spare her a grim smile of encouragement, but he too was pale beneath his tan.

'Damn me if I've ever seen such sights, ma'am, savin' your presence. Worse than anything we went through in Spain, but at least the Colonel will be good as new in a few weeks.'

She nodded her profound thanks, unable to speak just yet and beyond noticing anything much besides the fact that Rob was still alive, even if he was battered and bloody and weary half to death. His poor face was scratched and filthy, but his smile was all his, and he seemed determined to enter his house on his own feet.

'Devil take it, I'll not have the neighbourhood saying I'm on my deathbed,' he told his helpers. 'Webb, lend me a shoulder and I'll come about.'

'No point argufyin' with the Colonel, missus, it only makes him worse. So, right you are, sir. Now, missus, you tip one of them rascals off the sofa in the parlour, and we'll soon have him as good as new again.'

Coming out of her daze, Caro ran indoors, to find that Lady Samphire had ruthlessly cleared the well-scrubbed scullery she was using to assess the wounded and was calmly unearthing a cache of bandages, salves and hideous-looking instruments hoarded especially for this occasion.

'Good God, ma'am, I didn't know you had taken up leech-craft,' Rob said faintly, as Webb and the groom half-supported and half-carried him in.

'Birthed nothing but boys, and the village quack was an idiot. What else was there for me to do when Samphire always turned queasy at the sight of blood?'

Over the last few days Caro thought she had learnt to handle the wounded with calm efficiency, but she now realised how wrong she was. Too involved to be much use, she hovered at Rob's side and anxiously watched his officer's sash being gently unwound from the makeshift sling that supported his arm, and the grime washed from his face and the oozing bump on his forehead. He said nothing, but reached his uninjured hand for hers, and her heart raced with joy at the warm contact of his flesh against hers.

Now she could feel his living touch against her skin, nothing else mattered. If an earthquake had levelled the rest of Brussels, she would have stepped over the ruins to reach him. She carried his hand to her cheek and cradled it there, looking down at him with her heart in her eyes, and a warmth she had only allowed herself to dream of shone back at her from his dear eyes. He looked up at her, all concern for her pale face and overbright eyes, as if he wanted to banish her doubts and fears for his safety and her lips wobbled perilously as she fought back tears.

'Arm's broken,' Lady Samphire told them brusquely, then ignored Rob's sensibilities as she ordered Webb to undress his master so she could inspect his leg more closely.

'Not here, surely, my lady,' Rob protested half-heartedly.

'Feel equal to climbing upstairs to your bed, do you, young man?'

'Not exactly,' he admitted at last.

'Then lie still and do as you're bid.'

'Yes, ma'am!'

'So I should think.'

For all Webb's careful handling, as they cut the bloody uniform breeches off him, Rob was in danger of fainting. They gently eased him free and her ladyship carefully searched his wounds for loose fibres that could cause infection.

'Caro should not be here,' he protested, sweat beading his brow as he made a supreme effort to hang on to consciousness.

'I'm no fine lady to faint at the sight of a little blood, so I'm staying here and wild horses won't move me,' she told him firmly and snapped out of her trance at last to do whatever she was ordered to help him.

'D'you know that at times you sound remarkably like your mentor, my love?' he whispered and she did not know whether to laugh or cry at his determination to hang on to consciousness.

'Keep still, then, and let us get on,' she chided, but smiled radiantly as he fixed his gaze on her face, rather than view the injuries their efforts had uncovered.

Caro was tempted to follow suit and stare into his beloved, pain-haunted green eyes. Instead she forced herself to tear her gaze from his for a moment, and saw a great sabre gash down the side of his leg that made her draw in her breath at the agony it must have cost him.

'Luckily it was a downward thrust, and it don't appear to have severed any arteries, so hold up, my girl,' her ladyship ordered brusquely, 'looks worse than it is.'

'Then it must appear quite dreadful,' Rob joked weakly.

He tightened his hold on Caro's hand, before releasing her to ball his into a fist as his nurse cleaned the wound with warm water, then poured on a measure of his finest cognac. As soon as the agony subsided to a bearable level he sought Caro's touch again and she snuggled her small hand in his large one, holding on to him as if she never intended letting go.

'Common humanity should have made you give me that stuff to drink, rather than wasting it making my damn leg sting sharper than ever, my lady,' he finally grated out through pallid lips.

'Distilled alcohol is sovereign against infection,' Lady Samphire told him.

'Aye, it is sovereign against most things if swallowed in large enough doses. You have been reading the wrong book of spells, my lady.'

'I'll thank you for a little more respect. It will be me or nobody for you today, my lad. Surgeons are rare as hen's teeth now they have so much butchery to carry out that they don't know who to maim first, and at least I never yet chopped a man's leg off because I didn't know what else to do with it.'

'I cannot tell you how pleased I am to hear that, your ladyship.'

'Although, of course, there's a first time for everything,' his chief attendant muttered darkly.

'I always thought novelty was highly overrated.'

'And why Caroline wanted you back so badly, I'm damned if I know.'

'Did you, my darling?' He looked a question at his wife, who was trying hard not to be sick as she felt an echo of every painful movement while the wound was sewn and the needle punctured his suffering flesh again and again.

'More than life.'

'No, love, for what would mine be without you?' he told her and promptly fainted at last.

'Well, thank the Lord for that,' exclaimed Lady Samphire and went doggedly on with her stitchery while Caro was thoroughly unwell in an empty hot-water can.

'The youth of today have no stamina,' her ladyship informed Webb, who grinned his agreement and held Rob's leg rigid so she could work more easily.

Finally it was done and a couple of stitches put in the gash on his forehead as well. Then Webb set his master's broken arm and splinted it under his principal's stern instructions, and Caro managed to gain enough control over her heaving stomach at last to supervise the delicate task of carrying Rob upstairs.

'Should he not be awake by now, ma'am?' she asked anxiously as they finally got his nightshirt on over his bandages and gently pulled the covers over his inert, beloved body.

'I gave him a little laudanum, child, as you would know if you had not been otherwise engaged while I tipped it down his throat. He needs to sleep and this is the best way to ensure he does so without tossing and turning and breaking those stitches open, and leaving us with it all to do again.'

'Yes, I suppose it is.'

'And you, miss, will get into bed and rest before I have two invalids on my hands.'

'No, I shall stay with my husband, and I am most certainly *not* a miss.'

'Just as well, given that you are quite obviously *enceinte*. All the same, you owe it to both your babe and your husband to look after yourself better than you have been doing.'

'I'm not breeding,' Caro told her confidently and did some quick mental arithmetic to prove it.

She stood wide-eyed at her own stupidity as she added two and two, and finally reached the inevitable conclusion. She gasped as singing joy momentarily wiped out her anxieties. If only Rob could have shared the moment with her, it would have been perfect.

'How did you know?' she whispered, overcome with awe that she was to become a mother.

'I've been in the family way often enough myself to know it just from the look of you. Been off your feed in the mornings as well, and your performance just now only confirmed my suspicions that you are with child.'

'I thought that was because I was anxious about the battle.'

'You were wrong then, weren't you, girl? Now, there's no need to fret over this young rascal, because he'll be right as ninepence and driving us all distracted with his orders in a few days. So you get into bed and look after the next generation for him, even if you refuse to consider yourself. He'll not thank you for wearing yourself to a shadow, just so you can watch him sleep.'

Caro thought that was probably an overly optimistic view

of his recovery, given the nature of her husband's injuries, but finally consented to lie down on her bed with the door between them wide open, so she could hear if Rob made the slightest movement. She was comforted by the fact that her ladyship did not appear to think her husband needed constant nursing, and dared to hope at last. They had a future, and suddenly it looked so full of promise it even exceeded her wildest dreams, if only Rob was better.

Chapter Nineteen

Quite certain that she would not sleep a wink, Caro got into such an inextricable tangle trying to work out when she had last seen her courses, and when her baby might be due, that she was asleep before she even realised how exhausted she still was. After days of little sleep and great anxiety, she made up for lost time by sleeping the day and most of the night away.

Towards dawn Rob began to mumble in his sleep. At the first murmur she awoke and sprang out of bed to run to his side, ignoring an indignant complaint from her uneasy stomach in her hurry.

'It was hell itself, hard pounding, men dying everywhere. Can't begin to describe it, Cleo.'

'Then pray do not try, my love, just rest,' she murmured soothingly, stroking his hand and trying to change the course of his dreams by love alone.

'Rest? No, can't, Boney's yet to be beat.' Rob's head moved restlessly on the pillow and Caro longed to calm him somehow, before he wrenched his stitches.

'Bonaparte has been routed, so you can sleep now, my love.'

'No sleep yet, too much to do. All the other aides are dead or wounded.'

'You must sleep, Colonel. The Duke ordered it most particularly!' she told him sternly and her improvised command penetrated his confusion better than all her gentle reassurances had done.

At last he grew quiet, and she let out a long sigh of relief, then climbed on to the large bed to hold his good hand in hers with some degree of comfort. As he seemed determined not to let her go now he had captured it, she might as well stay where they both wanted her to be. After so many anxious, exhausting days of missing him, she let out a long sigh of contentment and promptly fell asleep once more.

Rob opened his eyes some hours later to find it was full morning and he was back in his comfortable bed in Brussels, instead of lying on the sodden battlefield outside the village of Waterloo with the injured and the dying groaning in agony around him after all. He felt weak as water and it was an effort to so much as turn his head on the pillow to look about him, but he was alive and the various agonies that had racked his battered body on the battlefield were now almost tolerable.

Finally he managed to shift far enough to let his wondering gaze rest on a familiar mass of golden-brown curls on the pillow next to him. Caroline, he thought contentedly—his Caroline, his Cleo and his beloved Mrs Besford all rolled into one. He moved to watch her more closely and, as even that slight movement woke her, unconditional love suddenly stared back at him out of sleepy amber eyes.

Caro saw strong emotion burning in his green gaze, and anxiously inspected his face for the signs of the fever Lady

Samphire had warned her to look out for. No, he was pale and drawn from pain and loss of blood, but there was no sign of the burning heat and confusion they had feared. Her husband obviously had the constitution of an ox, just as his chief nurse had sturdily declared in the face of her own anxiety. All the same, she should not have slept for so long and so deeply that someone had been able to come in and cover her without her even stirring.

'Are you in great pain, Rob?' she murmured, resisting the urge to yawn and stretch after her long sleep, in case she jarred his hurts.

'No more than I would be if a battalion had ridden over me, then retreated over the same ground,' he told her in a low voice, so she had to move even closer to hear what he said and her laugh was half a sob.

'Well, it's only a trifling sabre slash to your leg, a broken arm and a crack on the head fit to addle what few wits you had to begin with, husband. Nothing much to trouble ourselves over when you think about it.'

'As you say,' he agreed and grinned at her, then grimaced as a brief twist of agony racked him as he moved unwarily and his battered body protested. 'Not much of a hero, am I?' he said, his expression rueful.

'You're my hero,' she said sternly, 'and I won't let you disparage yourself in such a fashion.'

'Thank you, my darling, but you must look elsewhere for your perfect gentle knight I fear. When I finally caught up with the army after going on that wild goose chase for the Duke, I dare say I was more trouble than I was worth to him and he wishes I had stopped away. My poor horse was shot from under me when I was carrying orders, and as soon as the action got hot the grey panicked and threw me against a wall at Hougemont like a rank amateur. Then he promptly deserted the field at the double and is probably eating some farmer out of house and home as we speak.

'Then the Beau had to send another aide on my mission and, like the dove dispatched from the ark after the raven, he found me staggering about the battlefield getting in everyone's way. Once I was back in the saddle of my third and last mount and about Wellington's business again, a French cavalryman put a stop to my capers rather emphatically and I remained in the wilderness until Webb and Colley unearthed me. For all the use I have been, I might just as well have stayed at home,' he told her, an expression of self-disgust on his face that told her he was not entirely joking.

She refused to give in to tears, although how he could regard himself as a failure after braving such terrifying events with unflagging resolution was beyond her. He needed her to be strong, not the milk-and-water creature she might still be if Cleo had never been born. She stalwartly refused to turn into a watering pot now.

'You men must always be rushing about proving what heroes you are, must you not?' she finally managed to say lightly. 'Only consider how tame my life would have been if you had not come along. I could never have indulged in midnight escapades and scandalous masquerades, before trailing round Europe fretting myself into a fever, while all the time deceiving respectable society twice over with brass-faced impudence.'

He smiled weakly, and reached out his good hand to capture hers and kiss it lingeringly, before clasping it as if it was unthinkable to ever let her go.

'And only think how boring my life would be if I were not for ever wondering what scrape you will get me into next, my Caroline.'

'You called me Cleo in your dreams,' she observed wistfully.

'I have to admit that I liked Cleo extremely,' he told her with a wolfish grin.

'Did you, indeed? I shall make sure you have nothing to do with the likes of that scandalous baggage in future, you may be quite sure of that, husband. I have no intention of playing second fiddle to a lightskirt.'

'I shall never dare take my eyes off you long enough to chase females of questionable morals again, my darling. Heaven alone knows what you might get up to while I was doing it.'

'Indeed, I might even run off with a handsome infantry officer.'

'Just try it, madam, and you will soon discover how mistaken you are in believing you have netted yourself a complacent husband.'

'I never wanted a complacent husband, only you,' she whispered and reached up to gently kiss the scratches on his battered face, her heart worn firmly on her sleeve.

'Truly, love?' he asked and there was real anxiety in his eyes.

'Always, from the very first moment I laid eyes on you.'

'Pray don't remind me. I was so careless then, and so cruel afterwards.'

'And I was so ashamed, Rob, so appalled at what my father had forced on you, and my own cowardice in obeying him.'

'He did me the biggest favour one man could ever do another, and even my mother is guilty of doing good unawares for once,' he said with a rueful smile.

'I was always in such awe of your mama,' she told him, 'she is so stylish, so self-assured and impeccably bred.'

'As is my brother's best team of carriage horses, and I would rather spend five minutes in their company than hers.'

A dreadful thought struck her and she sat up all of a sudden.

'You don't suppose any child of ours will ever feel thus about either of us, do you?' she asked in hushed tones, one hand spread protectively over her still-flat stomach.

'Not unless they are changelings. Do you mean what I think you do, love?'

His tone was urgent as an ardent young lover, not a sober married man racked with pain and weary from battle, and Caro felt warmth flood over her. It had nothing to do with the fact that they were lying so close. No, this time it was the matchless sweetness of being loved after all, being blessed with a child so early in their re-match and, most wonderful of all, revelling in the fact that he was alive and here with her to enjoy such bounty.

'I do, although I did not realise it myself until Lady Samphire pointed out that I can't add up for toffee.'

He let out a great whoop of joy and she hushed him urgently, but footsteps sounded from all over the house and the door opened on half their household, plus any of the wounded who could walk, staring in at them with expectant and sometimes anxious faces.

Rob grinned sheepishly. 'Madam was just reassuring herself that my heart is strong enough to bear the strains of civilian life.'

'Well, that's the barber, then,' Webb said with a wide, knowing grin, and began shepherding the craning spectators out again, like a dog rounding up a flock of uncooperative sheep.

Once he had succeeded, he turned and added his parting shot, 'No capers now, sir and madam. Plenty of time for that when them wounds is all healed and we'm home for good at long last.'

'Who does he think we are, a pair of mountebanks in the circus?' Rob asked once the door was firmly shut on their household at last.

'He would not be so far off after some of the things we have done.'

'Speak for yourself, madam. I never tried to deceive my spouse by claiming to be something I am not,' he said virtuously.

'Yes, you did, you pretended to be my keeper when you knew perfectly well that you were my husband.'

'A small deceit compared with yours, madam.'

'Maybe, but I wish you would tell me how I gave myself away, or did Will betray me after all?'

'First, I burned for you more than I ever have for any other woman in my entire life, so I could not wait to court you as Caroline while I had that promise of Cleo's, now could I? Second, I was unaware that my so-called friend knew I was being royally deceived and, last, I do not quite know what finally made me realise what an idiot I was. Walking into that church and seeing you, just the same height as my wife and watching me with those lovely eyes of yours so full of mysteries? A gesture that suddenly recalled Caroline in Cleo and the spark that suddenly burned so hot between us on our own wedding day? I cannot even be sure myself, but that day I knew it as certainly as if it was written over the altar in letters a foot high.'

'I suppose that explains why you were so odd before—' Caro broke off, her cheeks bright scarlet under his ironic gaze.

'Before what? Now, why is it you always stop at the most interesting parts, wife?'

'Very well, then—before you seduced me.'

'Hardly,' he said, trying to look sheepish and not succeeding.

'You are a rake, though,' she reproached him.

'No, I *was* a rake, my darling. I'm told that reformed ones make the best husbands,' he said with such a conscious air of self-satisfied virtue she might well have thrown something at him, if it would not have hurt him.

'I love you so much,' she observed fatuously instead, and was touched by the vulnerability in his green gaze, suddenly as solemn on hers as an Old Testament prophet's.

'And I you, my darling. You are my one and only love, until death and beyond.'

'Speak only of life, my love. After the last few days I cannot even admit we are mortal yet,' she said shakily, fighting stupid tears all over again.

'Then, my life, for heaven's sake kiss me, since anything more seems impossible just now.'

'That is one order I find myself perfectly willing to obey, Colonel.'

'Good, I do like having a quiet and biddable wife, so come here and prove it.'

'Quiet?' she asked teasingly. 'Biddable?' she said after a considerable interval that left them both breathless and bright eyed.

'What a complete noddlecock I am to believe you could ever be either, my torment.'

'That you are, Colonel,' she told him, 'that you are.' And, returning to her wifely duties, carefully bent to kiss him even more thoroughly.

At last she drew away and gazed down into his beloved face. She was so lucky, so unbelievably, undeservingly lucky.

'You don't suppose the poor child will be anything like my father, do you?'

'Since you are not, I very much doubt it, and you may be very sure he will be allowed no say at all in our sons and daughters' upbringing after the way he treated you. Trust me on that, if nothing else, my Caroline.'

'He has no scruples at all,' she admitted uncomfortably. 'If he can find a way of thrusting himself into our lives, he will do so.'

'Well, he cannot. James had a rather shady friend of his investigate him when you went missing. You can take that indignant look off your face, as you were no more missing than the moon has escaped the heavens because we do not see her for a day or two.'

'True, but I'm not quite sure I shall like what the man found,' she replied ruefully, thinking of the unpalatable things her father had done over the years.

'Enough to keep him at arm's length for a lifetime, and if he were upright as an archbishop, I would still not give him house room after the miserable childhood you endured at his hands.'

'He never hit me,' she offered lamely in Henry Warden's defence.

'No, he just convinced you that you were less than nothing, a task your husband eagerly continued, until I am amazed you did not decide to put a bullet into both of us.'

'I have no wish to dance a Tyburn jig, Colonel, so your penance will be to live with me for the rest of our natural lives. That should be punishment enough.'

'Then a man never got such a magnificent reward for such a poor deed. If you were made provost, the men would queue up to receive judgement, love.'

'Promise me you really will sell out now, Rob?' she demanded, a sudden rush of anxiety turning her golden-brown eyes dark. 'Everyone says Bonaparte is well and truly beaten, and that this time the Allies will have the good sense to put him somewhere he can't do any more harm.'

He managed a weak chuckle, 'Wild horses would not stop me, Caro,' he confessed. 'If I was ever one of the death-or-glory boys, I got over it a very long time ago. Indeed, I have spent the last weeks cursing myself for not selling out after Toulouse. I longed to be at Westmeade with you and our children and now I find that you have already got that task well in hand, like the good and obedient little wife you have obviously become.'

She pretended to frown and shake her head at that accolade, but suddenly it did not seem such a bad idea after all.

'Would you like a good little wife then, Colonel?' she asked, with a bold look from under her curling eyelashes that was pure Cleo.

'I would like you, my love, and only you, for ever and a day. Only think what intrepid brats we shall have with a roaring girl like you for a mother.'

He ran his uninjured hand down the front of her demure night rail and settled it on her flat stomach with a gentleness that was almost reverent, and she felt such a leap of joy it was almost as if their child danced.

'And a rake and devil-may-care for a father,' she said shakily.

His voice was not quite steady either. 'I told you I am a rake no longer, and sooner or later you will just have to believe me. Nevertheless, our poor brats stand little chance of becoming pattern cards of all the virtues, with such a dubious pair for their parents, do they?'

'Never mind, I expect we shall be foolish enough to love them despite all their faults. Just as we have somehow managed to fall in love with one another.'

'It is not despite your faults I love you, Caro, but because of them.'

'How dreadfully ungallant, Colonel.'

'Isn't it? I confess I'm not quite sure if I first fell in love with Cleo's gorgeous body or her uninhibited tongue, yet I think on one level I knew you as yourself all along.'

'You despised me, and you could not even remember what your wife looked like,' she told him coolly.

Suddenly he was gravely serious, 'There is no way to undo the past, my love, although I would give anything if I could go back to do so. Forgive me, Caro?'

She decided to let all the pain and misery of unrequited love go, and savour the glorious promise of the future instead. If she had to go through that to get to where they were now, she would do it twice over, however much pain it took to reach the wonderful destination at the end of it all.

'Very well, but it will be a sentence for life for you, Colonel.'

'Then, my Caroline-Cleo, take the prisoner into custody.'

'Willingly,' she murmured and snuggled down by his side again, with a sigh of such smug contentment he chuckled and jarred his hurts.

'Lord, what a fine pair we are, Mrs Besford,' he murmured when the pain had subsided to a bearable level. 'Here I am, with the love of my life warm and willing in my bed, and there is damn all I can do about it.'

'Hmm, what a dilemma,' she replied, pressing a butter-fly kiss on his cheek.

'Baggage.'

'I have turned respectable, I will have you know.'

He looked unconvinced, then smiled at her with some of the old wicked sparkle back in his eyes.

'If only I had the strength to prove just how wrong you are.'

'Never mind, love, there is always tomorrow.'

'Indeed there is, and all the other tomorrows after that, my darling,' he told her with such tenderness and promise in his deep voice that it was in the nature of a vow.

Medieval
LORDS & LADIES
COLLECTION

VOLUME ONE
CONQUEST BRIDES
*Two tales of love and chivalry
in a time of war*

Gentle Conqueror by **Julia Byrne**

Lisette knew there was little she could do to resist
her Norman overlord – but she was determined to try.
Her delicate beauty belied her strength of character,
and her refusal to yield won Alain of Raverre's respect.
Now the courageous Norman knight would have
to battle for Lisette's heart!

Madselin's Choice by **Elizabeth Henshall**

Travelling through war-torn England, she needed a
protector. To her horror, the haughty Lady Madselin
was escorted by an arrogant, rebellious Saxon!
Edwin Elwardson's bravery and strength soon
captivated her. Yet could Madselin defy her
Norman upbringing and follow her true desire?

Available 6th July 2007

www.millsandboon.co.uk

M&B

Medieval
LORDS & LADIES
COLLECTION

When courageous knights risked all
to win the hand of their lady!

Volume 1: Conquest Brides – July 2007
Gentle Conqueror by Julia Byrne
Madselin's Choice by Elizabeth Henshall

Volume 2: Blackmail & Betrayal – August 2007
A Knight in Waiting by Juliet Landon
Betrayed Hearts by Elizabeth Henshall

Volume 3: War of the Roses – September 2007
Loyal Hearts by Sarah Westleigh
The Traitor's Daughter by Joanna Makepeace

6 volumes in all to collect!

UNA HORNE
Child of Sorrow

A compelling
North-East

*A compelling
North-East saga*

**A compelling
North-East
saga in the
bestselling
tradition of
Catherine Cookson**

Born the day of the great mining disaster at
Jane Pit, Merry Trent is brought up by her only
surviving relative, her feisty grandmother Peggy,
and lives in stricken poverty. Times are hard, and
when an unwelcome visit from the ruthless mining
agent, Miles Gallagher, leaves her pregnant, she tells
no-one.

When Merry begins training as an apprentice
nurse she attracts the attention of dashing young
doctor Tom Gallagher, Miles' son, and Merry
falls pregnant again. She loses her job and
accommodation at the hospital, and her future looks
bleak as she faces a tough choice: a marriage of
convenience, or destitution and the workhouse…

Available 18th May 2007

M&B

FREE!

2 Books
and a surprise gift!

We would like to take this opportunity to thank you for reading this Mills & Boon® book by offering you the chance to take TWO more specially selected titles from the Historical series absolutely FREE! We're also making this offer to introduce you to the benefits of the Mills & Boon® Reader Service™—

- ★ FREE home delivery
- ★ FREE gifts and competitions
- ★ FREE monthly Newsletter
- ★ Exclusive Reader Service offers
- ★ Books available before they're in the shops

Accepting these FREE books and gift places you under no obligation to buy, you may cancel at any time, even after receiving your free shipment. Simply complete your details below and return the entire page to the address below. You don't even need a stamp!

YES! Please send me 2 free Historical books and a surprise gift. I understand that unless you hear from me, I will receive 4 superb new titles every month for just £3.69 each, postage and packing free. I am under no obligation to purchase any books and may cancel my subscription at any time. The free books and gift will be mine to keep in any case.

H7ZEF

Ms/Mrs/Miss/Mr ....Initials ....

Surname ....

BLOCK CAPITALS PLEASE

Address ....

....

....Postcode ....

Send this whole page to:
UK: FREEPOST CN81, Croydon, CR9 3WZ